Joan Aiken

A Bundle of Nerves
Stories of horror, suspense and fantasy

Penguin Books

PENGUIN BOOKS

Published by the Penguin Group
Penguin Books Ltd, 27 Wrights Lane, London w8 5tz, England
Viking Penguin, a division of Penguin Book USA Inc.
375 Hudson Street, New York, New York 10014, USA
Penguin Books Australia Ltd, Ringwood, Victoria, Australia
Penguin Books Canada Ltd, 2801 John Street, Markham, Ontario, Canada l3r 1b4
Penguin Books (NZ) Ltd, 182 190 Wairau Road, Auckland 10, New Zealand

Penguin Books Ltd, Registered Offices: Harmondsworth, Middlesex, England

First published by Victor Gollancz 1976
Published in Peacock Book 1978
Reprinted in Puffin Books 1986
Reprinted in Penguin Books 1989
10 9 8 7 6 5 4 3

Acknowledgements
Cricket, Do you Dig Grieg?, Belle of the Ball, Five Green Moons, Furry Night,
As Gay as Cheese, Sultan's Splash, A Set for Every Sheep, Lodging for the Night,
Sonata for Harp and Bicycle, Searching for Summer were in *Argosy*;
Our Feathered Friends, Postman's Knock were in *Women's Journal*;
The Cold Flame was in *The Fifth Ghost Book*; Marmalade Wine was in *Suspense*
and *Pan Book of Horror*; Dead Language Master was in *Fontana Horror Book*,
Cricket, Belle of the Ball, Smell, As Gay as Cheese, Marmalade Wine,
Searching for Summer, Dead Language Master were in *The Windscreen
Weepers* (Gollancz, 1969).

Printed in England by Clays Ltd, St Ives plc
Set in Linotype Granjon

Contents

Cricket

There had been a persistent knocking from within the septic tank for several days, and by degrees it could not but become plain that someone must be trapped inside it.

The Beauclerks were too cautious, nay, parsimonious, to use anything for its rightful purpose; consequently the tank was employed as a storehouse for kilner jars, sugar soap, trunks, manuscripts of Christmas carols and other things used only once a year. A distant portion of the orchard, known as the Belvedere, was allotted for the usual purpose of the w.c., which housed live bait.

Mrs Beauclerk was sowing late peas in the hot afternoon sun when the Reverend Henry Dottel came weaving on his bicycle across the lawn.

'So like the powdered tomato soup, isn't it?' she said, straightening up and scratching her back with the dibber in a manner as dignified and archaic as that of a priest in a formal ritual. Mr Dottel peered anxiously at the mixture of red lead and paraffin which she had in her saucepan. It did resemble tomato soup with a few dried peas rolling about in it, and he felt that Mrs Beauclerk would be quite capable of serving it up at table.

'When you bury my husband you had better be sure to ask for an autopsy first.'

The deep voice over his head made him jump. She had read his thought with disconcerting accuracy, and it was unfair that she should be so much taller than he; towering over his head she was like some primitive African goddess.

'You want to speak to Fred, no doubt,' she said, and indeed the Admiral was swinging himself across the garden in his chair, which was something between a flying fox and an overhead cash-conveyor, slung from tree to tree.

'Do you want to discuss the match against Sleeve?' he asked eagerly, as the chair came to rest under the Florence Court Yew. 'You had better put Beeswick in to bat first. I've been thinking about it all night.'

'No, I hadn't come about that.' The Admiral's face fell. 'My errand was of a more serious nature. I wanted to remind you once more that it is time little Daffodil was christened.'

He had evidently screwed up all his courage to speak, but met with a blank reception; the Admiral was bored and disappointed, while his wife assumed a withdrawn, dispassionate air, and dropped a few more peas into her drill.

'That's really Jasper's affair,' she remarked. 'After all, he's her father.'

'My son will see to it,' the Admiral agreed. 'Here he is.'

The Hon. Jasper Beauclerk was as tall as his mother, but looked wild where she was patrician. He came prowling towards them, glancing from right to left as if only visible palisades kept him from escaping.

'Mr Dottel wishes to christen little Daffodil,' his mother observed. She glanced in the direction of the converted pig-trough where her grandchild lay kicking and cooing.

'No!' Jasper almost shouted.

'But my dear boy! supposing she were to contract polio or measles – unlikely eventualities, thank Providence, but such misfortunes do occur – how would you feel if she were to die without having been christened?'

'At least she'd be in the same place as her mother, wherever *that* is,' snapped Jasper furiously and miserably.

'My son still feels his wife's loss very deeply,' the Admiral apologized, as Mrs Beauclerk led Jasper aside and appeared to soothe and restrain him. 'In a way it's a mistake, you know, marrying these Melanesian women. Marvellous cooks, of course, I've never for one moment regretted marrying Lobelia, but some of them are too delicate for the English climate. And what's worse, they none of them take any interest in sport. I can't even get Lobelia to follow the Test Match, and Jasper takes after her, though I've done my best with the boy. There's precious little hope for Daffodil, having the strain from both parents.'

Jasper and his mother had finished their colloquy and returned to the other two.

'Let's stroll down to the millrace, Mr Dottel,' said Mrs Beauclerk. 'It's cooler down there, we can discuss the matter more comfortably.'

Jasper let out an inarticulate protest, but she hushed him with a gesture of calm authority.

The Admiral eyed them with suspicion as they crossed the sunbaked lawn.

'You must understand,' Mrs Beauclerk went on, 'that my daughter-in-law's last wish was that the baby should *not* be christened. She belonged, as I do, to the Kiya religion, which, of course, is a form of sun worship.'

'Rank heathenism,' said Mr Dottel, shuddering. 'Some of them are cannibals, too, aren't they? Of course I don't mean to cast any aspersions at *you*, dear lady, though indeed, living in the Manor House as you do, it would be greatly appreciated if you were to attend morning service some time to time.'

Mrs Beauclerk gazed at him abstractedly. She might have been measuring him for a shroud.

'*Now*, I think,' she said to Jasper, as they crossed the narrow catwalk above the millrace, and seizing Mr Dottel by his shoulders she tipped him in. He went round in the swirl two or three times while Jasper, with a long pole, adroitly kept him from climbing out. After the fourth revolution he sank, and did not reappear.

'We still have a barrel of vinegar,' observed Mrs Beau-clerk with satisfaction. 'If you pour it in he should keep nicely till Sunday.'

At this moment a clanging and tingling of wires announced the furious advent of the Admiral, bearing down on them like an avenging angel.

'You've done it!' he said. 'I thought you were up to something of the kind. Play these tricks on strangers, if you must, but now what the devil are we to do for a wicket-keeper?'

'Oh really, Fred, he was getting to be a terrible nuisance,' remonstrated Mrs Beauclerk. 'You'll find somebody else to keep your wicket easily enough.'

'Find someone, indeed! Just tell me who, in this blasted countryside!'

'How about the person in the septic tank?'

'That's an extremely good idea,' said the Admiral, brightening. 'Of course it may be a woman,' he added, relapsing into gloom. 'Still, it's worth trying.'

He swung his chair round and propelled himself feverishly in the direction of the manhole-cover. The baby's improvised cot was on it, and it took a moment to move her aside, during which time the banging from beneath grew more excited and obstreperous.

The Admiral raised the thick metal cover and peered through the crack.

'Do you play cricket?' he bawled.

A faint reply came back. The Admiral let slip the lid, which fell into place with a clang.

'Hockey!' he said, with an expression of disgust, and climbed heavily into his chair.

The Man Who Had Seen the Rope Trick

'Miss Drake,' said Mrs Minser, 'when ye've finished with the salt and pepper will ye please put them *together*?'

'Sorry, I'm sorry,' mumbled Miss Drake. 'I can't see very well as you know, I can't see very well.' Her tremulous hands worked out like tendrils across the table and succeeded in knocking the mustard on to its side. An ochre blob defiled the snowy stiffness of the tablecloth. Mrs Minser let a slight hiss escape her.

'That's the *third* tablecloth ye've dirtied in a week, Miss Drake. Do ye know I had to get up at four o'clock this morning to do all the washing? I shan't be able to keep ye if ye go on like this, ye know.'

Without waiting for the whispered apologies she turned towards the dining-room door, pushing the trolley with the meat plates before her. Her straw-grey hair was swept to a knot on the top of her head, her grey eyes were as opaque as bottle-tops, her mouth was screwed tight shut against the culpabilities of other people.

'Stoopid business, gettin' up at four in the mornin',' muttered old Mr Hill, but he muttered it quietly to himself. 'Who cares about a blob of mustard on the tablecloth, anyway? Who cares about a tablecloth, or a separate table, if the food's good? If she's got to get up at four, why don't she make us some decent porridge instead of the slime she gives us?'

He bowed his head prayerfully over his bread plate as Mrs Minser returned, weaving her way with the neatness of long practice between the white-covered tables, each with its silent, elderly, ruminating diner.

The food was *not* good. 'Rice shape or banana, Mr Hill?'
Mrs Minser asked, pausing beside him.

'Banana, thank'ee.' He repressed a shudder as he looked
at the colourless, glutinous pudding. The bananas were unripe, and bad for his indigestion, but at least they were
palatable.

'Mr Wakefield! Ye've spotted yer shirt with gravy! That
means more washing, and I've got a new guest coming tomorrow. I cann't think how you old people can be so inconsiderate.'

'I'll wash it, I'll wash it myself, Mrs Minser.' The old
man put an anxious, protective hand over the spot.

'Ye'll do no such thing!'

'Who is the new guest then, Mrs Minser?' Mr Hill asked,
more to distract her attention from his neighbour's misfortune than because he wanted to know.

'A Mr Ollendod. Retired from India. I only hope,' said
Mrs Minser, forebodingly, 'that he won't have a great
deal of luggage, else where we shall put it all I cann't
imagine.'

'India,' murmured Mr Hill to himself. 'From India, eh?
He'll certainly find it different here.' And he looked round
the dining-room of the Balmoral Guest House. The name
Balmoral, and Mrs Minser's lowland accent, constituted the
only Scottish elements in the guest house, which was otherwise pure Westcliff. The sea, half a mile away, invisible
from the house, was implicit in the bracingness of the air
and the presence of so many elderly residents pottering out
twice a day to listen to the municipal orchestra. Nobody
actually swam in the sea, or even looked at it much, but there
it was anyway, a guarantee of ozone and fresh fish on the
tables of the residential hotels.

Mr Ollendod arrived punctually next day, and he did
have a lot of luggage.

Mrs Minser's expression became more and more ominous

as trunks and cases – some of them very foreign-looking and made of straw – boxes and rolls and bundles were unloaded.

'Where does he think all that is going?' she said, incautiously loudly, to her husband who was helping to carry in the cases.

Mr Ollendod was an elderly, very brown, shrivelled little man, but he evidently had all his faculties intact, for he looked up from paying the cab-driver to say, 'In my room, I trust, naturally. It is a double room, is it not? Did I not stipulate for a double room?'

Mrs Minser's idea of a double room was one into which a double bed could be squeezed. She eyed Mr Ollendod measuringly, her lips pursed together. Was he going to be the sort who gave trouble? If so, she'd soon find a reason for giving him his notice. Summer was coming, when prices and the demand for rooms went up; one could afford to be choosy. Still, ten guineas a week was ten guineas; it would do no harm to wait and see.

The Minser children, Martin and Jenny, came home from school and halted, fascinated, amongst Mr Ollendod's possessions.

'Look, a screen, all covered with pictures!'

'He's got spears!'

'A tigerskin!'

'An elephant's foot!'

'What's this, a shield?'

'No, it's a fan, made of peacocks' feathers.' Mr Ollendod smiled at them benevolently. Jenny thought that his face looked like the skin on top of cocoa, wrinkling when you stir it.

'Is he an Indian, Mother?' she asked when they were in the kitchen.

'No, of course he's not. He's just brown because he's lived in a hot climate,' Mrs Minser said sharply. 'Run and do yer homework and stay out from under my feet.'

The residents, also, were discussing Mr Ollendod.

'Do you think he can be – *foreign*?' whispered Mrs Pursey. 'He is such an odd-looking man. His eyes are so bright – just like diamonds. What do you think, Miss Drake?'

'How should I know?' snapped Miss Drake. 'You seem to forget I haven't been able to see across the room for the last five years.'

The children soon found their way to Mr Ollendod's room. They were strictly forbidden to speak to or mix with the guests in any way, but there was an irresistible attraction about the little bright-eyed man and his belongings.

'Tell us about India,' Jenny said, stroking the snarling tiger's head with its great yellow glass eyes.

'India? The hills are blue and wooded, they look as innocent as Essex but they're full of tigers and snakes and swinging, chattering monkeys. In the villages you can smell dust and dung-smoke and incense; there are no brown or grey clothes, but flashing pinks and blood-reds, turquoises and saffrons; the cows have horns three yards wide.'

'Shall you ever go back there?' Martin asked, wondering how anybody could bear to exchange such a place for the worn grey, black and fawn carpeting, the veneer wardrobe and plate-glass, the limp yellow sateen coverlid of a Balmoral bedroom.

'No,' said Mr Ollendod, sighing. 'I fell ill. And no one wants me there now. Still,' he added more cheerfully, 'I have brought back plenty of reminders with me; enough to keep India alive in my mind. Look at this – and this – and this.'

Everything was wonderful – the curved leather slippers, the richly patterned silk of Mr Ollendod's dressing-gown and scarves, the screen with its exotic pictures ('I'm not letting *that* stay there long,' said Mrs Minser), the huge pink shells with a sheen of pearl, the gnarled and grinning images, the hard, scented sweets covered with coloured sugar.

'You are *not* to go up there. And if he offers you anything to eat you are to throw it straight away,' Mrs Minser said, but she might as well have spoken to the wind. The instant the children had done their homework they were up in Mr Ollendod's room, demanding stories of snakes and were-wolves, of crocodiles who lived for a hundred years, of mysterious ceremonies in temples, ghosts who walked with their feet swivelled backwards on their ankles, and women with the evil eye who could turn milk sour and rot the unripe fruit on a neighbour's vine.

'You've really seen it? You've seen them? You've seen a snake-charmer and a snake standing on its tail? And a lizard break in half and each half run away separately? And an eagle fly away with a live sheep?'

'All those things,' he said. 'I'll play you a snake-charmer's tune if you like.'

He fished a little bamboo flageolet out of a cedarwood box and began to play a tune that consisted of no more than a few trickling, monotonous notes, repeated over and over again. Tuffy, the aged, moth-eaten black cat who followed the children everywhere when they were at home and dozed in Mr Ollendod's armchair when they were at school, woke up, and pricked up his ears; downstairs Jip, the bad-tempered Airedale, growled gently in his throat; and Mrs Minser, sprinkling water on her starched ironing, paused and angrily rubbed her ear as if a mosquito had tickled it.

'And I've seen another thing: a rope that stands on its tail when the man says a secret word to it, stands straight up on end! And a boy climbs up it, right up! Higher and higher, till he finally disappears out of sight.'

'Where does he go to?' the children asked, huge-eyed.

'A country where the grass grows soft and patterned like a carpet, where the deer wear gold necklets and come to your hand for pieces of bread, where the plums are red and sweet and as big as oranges, and the girls have voices like singing birds.'

'Does he never come back?'

'Sometimes he jumps down out of the sky with his hands full of wonderful grass and fruits. But sometimes he never comes back.'

'Do *you* know the word they say to the rope?'

'I've heard it, yes.'

'If I were the boy I wouldn't come back,' said Jenny. 'Tell us some more. About the witch woman who fans herself.'

'She fans herself with a peacock-feather fan,' Mr Ollendod said. 'And when she does that she becomes a snake and slips away into the forest. And when she is tired of being a snake and wants to turn into a woman again she taps her husband's foot with her cold head till he waves the fan over her.'

'Is the fan just like yours on the wall?'

'Just like it.'

'Oh, may we fan ourselves with it, may we?'

'And turn yourselves into little snakes? What would your mother say?' asked Mr Ollendod, laughing heartily.

Mrs Minser had plenty to say as it was. When the children told her a garbled mixture of the snakes and the deer and the live rope and girls with birds' voices and plums as big as oranges she pursed her lips together tight.

'A pack of moonshine and rubbish! I've a good mind to forbid him to speak to them.'

'Oh, come, Hannah,' her husband said mildly. 'He keeps them out of mischief for hours on end. You know you can't stand it if they come into the kitchen or make a noise in the garden. And he's only telling them Indian fairy tales.'

'Well anyway ye're not to believe a word he says,' Mrs Minser ordered the children. 'Not a *single* word.'

She might as well have spoken to the wind . . .

Tuffy the cat fell ill and lay with faintly heaving sides in the middle of the hallway. Mrs Minser exclaimed angrily when she found Mr Ollendod bending over him.

'That dirty old cat! It's high time he was put away.'

'It is a cold he has, nothing more,' Mr Ollendod said mildly. 'If you will allow me, I shall take him to my room and treat him. I have some Indian gum which is very good for inhaling.'

But Mrs Minser refused to consider the idea. She rang up the vet, and when the children came home from school, Tuffy was gone.

They found their way up to Mr Ollendod's room, speechless with grief.

He looked at them thoughtfully for a while and then said, 'Shall I tell you a secret?'

'Yes, what? What?' Martin said, and Jenny cried, 'You've got Tuffy hidden here, is that it?'

'Not exactly,' said Mr Ollendod, 'but you see that mirror on the wall?'

'The big one covered with a fringy shawl, yes?'

'Once upon a time that mirror belonged to a queen, in India. She was very beautiful, so beautiful that it was said sick people could be cured of their illnesses just by looking at her. In course of time she grew old, and lost her beauty. But the mirror remembered how beautiful she had been and showed her still the lovely face she had lost. And one day she walked right into the mirror and was never seen again. So if you look into it you do not see things as they are now, but beautiful as they were in their youth.'

'May we look?'

'Just for a short time you may. Climb on that chair,' Mr Ollendod said, smiling, and they climbed up and peered into the mirror, while he steadied them with a hand on each of their necks.

'Oh!' cried Jenny, 'I can see him! I can see Tuffy! He's a kitten again, chasing grasshoppers.'

'I can see him too!' shouted Martin, jumping up and down. The chair overbalanced and tipped them on to the floor.

'Let us look again, please let us!'

'Not today,' said Mr Ollendod. 'If you look too long into that mirror you, like the queen, might vanish into it for good. That is why I keep it covered with a shawl.'

The children went away comforted, thinking of Tuffy young and frolicsome once more, chasing butterflies in the sun. Mr Ollendod gave them a little ivory chess set, to distract them from missing their cat, but Mrs Minser, saying it was too good for the children and that they would only spoil it, sold it and put the money in the Post Office 'for later on'.

It was July now. The weather grew daily warmer and closer. Mrs Minser told Mr Ollendod that she was obliged to raise his rent by three guineas 'for the summer prices'. She rather hoped this would make him leave, but he paid up.

'I'm old and tired,' he said. 'I don't want to move again, for I may not be here very long. One of these days my heart will carry me off.'

And in fact one oppressive, thundery day he had a bad heart attack and had to stay in bed for a week.

'I certainly don't want him if he's going to be ill all the time,' Mrs Minser said to her husband. 'I shall tell him that we want his room as soon as he's better.' In the meantime she put away as many as possible of the Indian things, saying that they were a dust-collecting nuisance in the sickroom. She left the swords and the fan and the mirror, because they hung on the wall, out of harm's way.

As she had promised, the minute Mr Ollendod was up and walking around again, she told him his room was wanted and he must go.

'But where?' he said, standing so still, leaning on his stick, that Mrs Minser had the uneasy notion for a moment that the clock on the wall had stopped ticking to listen for her answer.

'That's no concern of mine,' she said coldly. 'Go where you please, wherever anyone can be found who will take you with all this rubbish.'

'I must think it over,' said Mr Ollendod. He put on his panama hat and walked slowly down to the beach. The tide was out, revealing a mile of flat, pallid mud studded with baked-bean tins. Jenny and Martin were there, listlessly trying to fly a home-made kite. Not a breath of wind stirred and the kite kept flopping down in the mud, but they knew that if they went home before six their mother would send them out again.

'There's Mr Ollendod,' said Jenny.

'Perhaps he could fly the kite,' said Martin.

They ran to him, leaving two black parallel trails in the shining goo.

'Mr Ollendod, can you fly our kite?'

'It needs someone to run with it *very* fast.'

He smiled at them kindly. Even the slowest stroll now made his heart begin to race and stumble.

'Let's see,' he said. He held the string for a moment in his hands and was silent; then he said, 'I can't run with it, but perhaps I can persuade it to go up of its own accord.'

The children watched, silent and attentive, while he murmured something to the rope in a low voice that they could not quite catch.

'Look, it's moving,' whispered Martin.

The kite, which had been hanging limp, suddenly twitched and jerked like a fish at the end of a line, then, by slow degrees, drew itself up and, as if invisibly pulled from above, began to climb higher and higher into the warm grey sky. Mr Ollendod kept his eyes fixed on it; Jenny noticed that his hands were clenched and the sweat was rolling off his forehead.

'It's like the story!' exclaimed Martin. 'The man with the rope and the magic word and the boy who climbs it – may we climb it? We've learnt how to at school.'

Mr Ollendod couldn't speak, but they took his silence as consent. They flung themselves at the rope and swarmed up it. Mr Ollendod, still holding on to the end of the rope, gradually lowered himself to the ground and sat with his head bowed over his knees; then with a slow subsiding motion fell over on to his side. His hands relaxed on the rope which swung softly upwards and disappeared; after a while the tide came in and washed away three sets of footprints.

'Those children are very late,' said Mrs Minser at six o'clock. 'Are they up in Mr Ollendod's room?'

She went up to see. The room was empty.

'I shall let it to a couple, next time,' reflected Mrs Minser, picking up the peacock-feather fan and fanning herself, for the heat was oppressive. 'A couple will pay twice the rent and they are most likely to eat meals out. I wonder where those children can have got to . . .?'

An hour later old Mr Hill, on his way down to supper, looked through Mr Ollendod's open door and saw a snake wriggling about on the carpet. He called out excitedly. By the time Mr Minser had come up, the snake had slid under the bed and Mrs Pursey was screaming vigorously. Mr Minser rattled a stick and the snake shot out towards his foot, but he was ready with a sharp scimitar snatched from the wall, and cut off its head. The old people, clustered in a dithering group outside the door, applauded his quickness.

'Fancy Mr Ollendod's keeping a pet snake all this time and we never knew!' shuddered Mrs Pursey. 'I hope he hasn't anything else of the kind in here.' Inquisitively she ventured in. 'Why, what a beautiful mirror!' she cried. The others followed, pushing and chattering, looking about greedily.

Mr Minser brushed through the group, irritably, and went downstairs with the decapitated snake. 'I shall sound the gong for supper in five minutes,' he called. 'Hannah, Hannah! Where are you? Nothing's going as it should in this house today.'

But Hannah, needless to say, did not reply, and when he banged the gong in five minutes, nobody came down but blind old Miss Drake who said, rather peevishly, that all the others had slipped away and left her behind in Mr Ollendod's room.

'Slipped away! And left me! Among all his horrid things! Without saying a word, so inconsiderate! Anything might have happened to me.'

And she started quickly eating up Mrs Pursey's buttered toast.

Do You Dig Grieg?

Have you ever been haunted by the ghost of a bear? No, neither had Arnold Key, but it happened to his brother Simon, with whose story we are not at present concerned. This is just to give you Arnold's background, and to help account for the troubles that overtook him.

His father was a coalminer, his mother the seventh daughter of a seventh daughter, and Arnold himself was one of those tall, copper-haired, rather gangling but engaging Scots who are often first violins in orchestras. His eyes were blue, his long nose turned up, and he looked altogether as inoffensive as a bunch of daffodils. He did in fact play first violin in the City of London Studio Orchestra, but his main interest was the composition of non-associative music. That and listening.

Stop reading now and listen. What can you hear? A clock ticking, a kettle boiling. Footsteps in the room above. Traffic, gulls, a tap dripping. Your own ears whispering, your own heart beating. But beyond *that*?

Arnold's compositions were at the other end of the scale from programme music. They were carefully constructed to remind the listener of nothing he had ever heard in his life before.

Arnold's wife Erzebet was a sultry, smouldering beauty, sooty-haired, sloe-eyed, and rather the shape of an alto clef. She came of mixed Czech and Hungarian extraction, and had married Arnold in order to get out of a passport predicament. She was fond of him, in a mild way, but he left her feeling slightly baffled, as if she were scored for more parts than he could provide. He, on his side, occasionally wondered whether the phosphorescent glow which seemed to envelop her at times could be accounted for by tea parties with the second violas or gossip with the flautist's wife.

Also, she irritated him. She was fond of the music of Haydn, whose compositions were so far from being non-associative that they had been nicknamed after common objects and animals..

'Good God,' Arnold muttered sometimes. '*The Hen! The Bear! The Clock!* Preserve me from such nursery banalities!'

Very well. It was spring. Arnold was walking home through the City of London from the Chiropodists' Hall, where rehearsals were held, sniffing the fresh scents of violets on barrows, part of his mind fidgeting at a concerto for two trombones and a triangle.

Suddenly he stopped walking. His attention had been caught by one of those builders' observation platforms, now so common about the city, overhanging a deep construction pit filled with machinery and ant-like workmen, which would in due course contain the five basement storeys of a massive new office building.

Arnold stepped up on to the platform. What had chiefly taken his fancy was the row of shocking-pink telephones along the platform rail, and the notice:

LOOK AND LISTEN
BY COURTESY OF WAPSHOTT CO., LTD.

Arnold picked up a telephone and, gazing down into the pit, listened.

'... site foreman Mr Percy Jones,' said the voice. 'On your right you will see a stack of hollow pillars which will be sunk to a depth of forty feet and filled with liquid concrete. Superintending this part of the work is Mr Mick Smith. The architect in charge of the whole operation is Mr Bernard Mauleverer. The completed building will house twenty thousand office workers, a restaurant, a basement car-park, two shopping arcades, and a cinema. We shall be bringing you a different progress report every two days. Thank you for listening.'

Arnold was disappointed. He had hoped for the sounds of construction, for some quintessence of clangs, rumbles, tintinnabulation, grinding, whizzes, and thuds which might have stimulated him to new ideas.

The other men on the observation platform replaced their phones and moved off. Arnold kept his receiver to his ear, in the faint hope that something besides a repetition of the commentary would come through.

He was rewarded.

First there came a drift of silence – silence so clear, so pure, so bell-like that in comparison with it any sound seemed a mere smirch on the eardrum. Then a faint faraway voice whispered.

'Key? Arnold Key? I'm waiting for you.'

Echoes carried the words in canon to his ear. 'Key, I'm waiting, Key I'm waiting, waiting for you, waiting for you, for you, for you, for you, you, you . . .'

And then the silence again.

He replaced the receiver. Stared at it. Picked up his violin and wandered home like a man in a trance. What did this message mean? Was it the buried voice of some musical offering inside himself, asking to be let out?

'Hon-nee!' Erzebet greeted him with a rich fragrance of soup and a voluptuous eye. She rubbed her biscuit-coloured cheek on his and cradled his ear on her collarbone.

Tick! tick! he could hear her heart beating and, beneath it, faraway, the tiny voice: 'Key! Arnold Key! I'm waiting for you!'

If only it were possible to go somewhere deep and quiet, where he could really listen, really pay attention . . .

'I must do some digging,' Arnold said abruptly.

'Deeging?' Erzebet stared at him as if he had gone crazy. 'You weesh to deeg? Why?'

He crossed restlessly to the window and stared at a small bird's-eye view of windblown Thames. 'I don't know. I just feel I want to get down – deep – to the roots of things. Where there isn't any noise.'

'You need a peell, my leetle one,' said Erzebet, following and curling herself round him like a continental quilt, with one cool hand on his brow. 'Where you deeg here? Ees no garden, no earth at all.'

They lived on the ninth floor.

'No, I know there isn't,' said Arnold angrily, glowering at the pavements. 'You can't even *see* the earth in London. We'll go to Horseley for the week-end.'

Erzebet loathed Horseley, where his brother's untenanted bungalow was always available for Arnold. Like a city cat, she hated out-of-doors in any form. The wind ruffled her fur.

Once there she stayed by the bungalow fire, wrapped in eiderdowns and eating marzipan, while Arnold rushed fretfully out into the nettle-grown garden with a rusty spade. But after half an hour he came indoors again.

'They're driving me mad!' he exclaimed in a rage.

'You weesh some marzeepan?'

'No, thanks,' he said shuddering.

'Who drive you mad?'

'Those damn birds! And the wind! How can I get on with my concerto in all that confounded natural racket? It's like a – a tonal picture-postcard!'

'We go back to town, yes?' Erzebet said agreeably, uncoiling herself and finishing the last bit of marzipan. Her husband nodded glumly.

Erzebet was a bit disconcerted, though, to observe, as they retreated through the garden, that Arnold's digging had not produced a useful plot, where asparagus might be raised, or strawberries, but a ten-foot-hole of no conceivable use to anyone except an undertaker.

'What you deeg thees beeg peet for?'

'I tell you, I want to get down, deep down, where there's no noise.'

'You try Peecadeely tube, no?'

'Oh, be your age, Erzebet,' he said crossly. 'You can't hear yourself *think*, down there.'

Erzebet's brow was furrowed. 'I theenk you should visit psychiatrist, yes?'

'*No!*' he shouted. 'What's odd about wanting a bit of peace and quiet?'

However, Erzebet was not one to let the grass grow under her feet, and the next day saw her visiting Dr Killgruel, a Harley Street mental therapist, for a confidential consultation. She had waited until Arnold was safely at a rehearsal because she could see that he was going to be difficult about the whole business.

Dr Killgruel was a susceptible man. Erzebet's smouldering beauty acted on him like a cigarette-end on a corner of dry newspaper.

'Tell me your trouble, my dear,' he said invitingly.

'Ees not mee,' Erzebet told him, arranging herself with devastating effect on his couch. 'Not a theeng wrong weeth mee.'

'No; no, of course I can see that, but then –?'

'Ees my husband, he oll time weesh to do notheeng but deeg!'

'He must be crazy,' said Dr Killgruel, using in the excitement of the moment, a word customarily eschewed by members of his profession.

'Crazee? You theenk so? What shall I do? Ees not good business to be marreed to a crazee man.'

'You must get him to come and see me.'

'He never do that, nevair,' declared Erzebet with conviction. She gazed consideringly at Dr Killgruel. 'I haf idea. I come to see you, you tell me proper treatment to geeve to Arnold, no?'

The suggestion had its points. Dr Killgruel saw that at once.

'A kind of remote control? It might do some good.'

'We try, yes?' Erzebet gave him a dazzling smile. The smile finished him.

'We'll try. First, you must make sure that as often as possible he is completely calm. Make him relax, stroke his brow –'

'Like thees?'

'*I* do the stroking. I'm showing *you* how. Give him a soothing drink.'

'Such as cocoa?'

'Cocoa? Heaven forbid. Such as brandy. Of course it must be *good* brandy,' said Dr Killgruel, fetching a bottle and two glasses from a cupboard. 'See that when he rests he is completely limp, even his fingers and toes – feel them to make sure.'

'Docteur, you are teeckle me,' sighed Erzebet, 'but just the same, I theenk thees treatment do Arnold good.'

The treatment, carried on in daily doses, did Erzebet a great deal of good, but Arnold continued to grow more and more fine-drawn, haggard, and inattentive. Since he never told Erzebet of the little deep faraway subterranean voice which interrupted his work and sleep with the reminder, 'I'm waiting for you, Arnold Key!' it is not surprising that the remote-control cure was not a hundred per cent successful.

'I am lose oll my patience,' snapped Erzebet, coming into Dr Killgruel's office one day with a large bunch of roses. 'He steel want to deeg! And keep ollways the cotton wool in his ears, he nevair hear a word I speak. Hees conducteur deesmees heem because he nevair leesten to other playeurs. I am leave heem, I theenk.'

'Leave him? Oh, I shouldn't do that,' said Dr Killgruel hastily, foreseeing complications. 'No, no, I'll find him some congenial occupation. Therapeutic, you know. He wants to dig? I think I know the very thing . . .'

Erzebet put it across quite well.

'You weesh to see a beeg hole?' she said cunningly to Arnold that evening, after obliging him to unplug one of his ears.

'All right,' he said with grudging interest. 'Where?'

'Ees on the South Bank. Where they beeld that skyscraper of thirty storeys. He teelt sideways, I am read in evening paper. He lean even more than the Leaning Tower of Pisa.'

'They didn't shore up the base enough, I suppose. That's what comes of building on mud. What a waste if it all falls into the river.'

'Not so,' said the well-informed Erzebet. 'Now they deeg even deeper hole beneath, feell foundations with frozen concrete. We go see, yes? Ees eenteresting, no?'

'All right.'

All round the leaning skyscraper was a scene of frenzied activity. Giant rotary concrete-mixers were at work, with a noise like dinosaurs gnashing their teeth; trucks rolled up one behind the other with the great tanks of carbon-dioxide ice which would freeze the concrete to impregnable toughness; and in the cellars of the half-finished building the apparatus was being hastily installed which would keep the surrounding ground permanently at fifty below zero. A huge notice by the site entrance said, LABOURERS WANTED. ANY ABLE-BODIED MAN WITH A FEW HOURS TO SPARE IS INVITED TO APPLY TO THE SITE FOREMAN. GENEROUS PAY.

Erzebet led Arnold to an observation platform, and his wondering eyes dropped down and down into the fantastically deep shaft that was being sunk to take the concrete shoring. The jaws of the excavators snapped and flung up crumbling mouthfuls of clay and rock, containing who knows what, hippopotamus teeth, Viking shields, Mithraic emblems, even the head of Thor's hammer.

'I must get down there,' Arnold said, straining away from Erzebet like a caught fish held above its native stream.

A smile momentarily curved her pale, full cheek as he threw her a perfunctory wave and darted down to join the insect-hordes below. She remained a moment, gazing at the scene. It was really very fine, like one of Hieronymous Bosch's wilder masterpieces; far away the sunset sky, smoky red behind the Houses of Parliament; near to, the blue-white glare of arc-lights and the mad, intricate masses of toiling humans, pushing, pulling, digging, hurling; the grotesque machines, the crablike shadows, and over all the leaning threat of the skyscraper which resembled nothing in the world so much as the upper half of a great and gaping pair of jaws.

Perhaps it fall and flatten the lot of them, thought Erzebet comfortably. That solve my problem once and for all, no?

Then, losing interest, she turned, waved up a taxi – taxis swooped on Erzebet, no matter how pitch-dark the night or remote the street, like bats to torchlight – and told it to take her to 406D Harley Street.

The excavators could dig just so deep and no deeper. Below that, the final clearing at the bottom of the shaft had to be done by hand. There were not many volunteers for this part of the work, which was dangerous because of falling fragments, and Arnold's offer was accepted at once.

He was let down by cable, and as he descended the clang, rumble and clatter up above him died away in the distance and vanished, to be replaced by a thick, unnatural, earth silence.

His job was to dig, scoop, and load earth into a container

like a gigantic coal-scuttle which was lowered, raised, and lowered again as he tirelessly filled it.

After some hours a message came down, pencilled on a slip of paper, *Don't you want a rest?*

No thanks, wrote back Arnold with the next load of hippos' teeth and Vikings' bones.

He was enjoying himself as never before.

He had been instructed to make a star-shaped cavity with radiating tunnels, which were to be packed with ice. A dozen such grottoes were being dug out round the skyscraper's roots. Some tunnels were already packed with their frozen filling. Under the dangling light, frost shimmered on smooth surfaces of sweating clay. It was deathly, unearthly cold; only Arnold's constant activity kept him from turning blue.

Suddenly his pick, swung with double vigour because he was nearly at the end of a tunnel, bit clean through an expanse of soft rock and left a crumbling hole behind.

'A cave,' Arnold said to himself. 'That saves trouble.'

He swung his pick again and cleared the sides of the hole until it was big enough for him to step through.

It was like a glade in an underground forest – a long, pillared passage, wide as a motorway, silent as a crypt. And at the far end burnt a little light.

'Key, Key, Key,' said the whispering voice. 'Come this way. Come to me.'

When he reached the end of the gallery he saw a Being, sitting on a throne, waiting for him. Arnold's education was only mediocre, but he recognized the being from far-off fairytales – the blue skin, the three heads, the hair that stood on end, and the fact that the air all round the throne for a distance of about three feet vibrated like heat-waves over a tin roof on an August day.

Arnold stood shivering-still and his knees locked together.

'Wh-who are you?' he said, although he knew.

The creature turned its six glittering eyes on him and spoke with all its three mouths at once.

'I'm a Troll, oldy-woll,' it said, adding reflectively, 'and I'll eat you for supper.'

Its voice rolled through the vault, touching Arnold on some exquisitely sensitive part of his tympanum with the effect of an electric shock.

'*Eat* me?' he exclaimed. 'No, no, that would be ridiculous! Surely it wasn't for that you fetched me down here?'

'It was, it was,' said the Troll. 'Few people nowadays can hear my voice. I get hungry. I haven't had a decent supper for a thousand years, thousand years, thousand years, years, years.'

It rose to its full nine-foot height and made for Arnold.

'No, but please don't eat me!' he screamed. 'Your voice has given me such a superb idea for a musical composition.'

The Troll stopped, baffled. 'Well, I'll let you off *this* time,' it said reluctantly, 'but you must give me the first live thing you set eyes on when you get home.'

'All right.' The chances were, Arnold knew, that this would be the porter's revolting little dog, which lurked inside his cubicle, ready to nip the ankles of passers-by.

'I must go now,' he said in a hurry, before the Troll could change its mind. He ran back along the gallery, and the Troll settled down calmly on its throne to wait, glowing blue in anticipation.

A load of frozen concrete was waiting in the shaft, and Arnold hastily scooped it up and packed it into the cave doorway, though aware that this would make little difference to the Troll if it intended to come out.

Then he jerked the cable, signifying that he needed a rest spell.

It was four a.m. when Arnold got home. He had walked through the grey, silent reaches of Southwark, Lambeth, and Battersea, with music twirling in his head like a corkscrew.

He forgot the Troll, his promise, everything, in his anxiety to get the new composition on to paper.

The caretaker's little dog was fast asleep, dreaming of juicy, tempting ankles. Arnold let himself quietly into the flat.

'Pencil,' he said to himself. 'Put coffee on to heat up, find paper. Where the devil did I put that new stack of manuscript paper? Bedroom, was it?' He went in, switching on the light, very much disconcerting Erzebet and Dr Killgruel who had not expected him home that night.

'Ah, here's the paper,' Arnold said, 'I knew I must have left it somewhere,' and he was about to return to the livingroom when the Troll, prompt to collect its debts, spun into the room like a nine-foot top giving off incandescent sparks. The whole room whirled round it, much as a potful of vegetable soup whirls round the stirring spoon, and then the Troll was gone again, taking with it Erzebet and the protesting psychiatrist. The whole thing happened between two ticks of the clock.

Arnold hardly noticed. He flung himself down at the table and set to work on the piece of music in which disgusted critics would later find so much resemblance to *The Hall of the Mountain King*.

He never dug another hole.

Belle of the Ball

Easter came late that year. The first summer race-meeting was on Easter Monday and I came over from Brighton for it, idling along in the train. Trains didn't go fast in those days and you could hear cuckoos seesawing in and out of the woods as we made our leisurely way, and twice as loud when we stopped.

It was one of those bright blowy days with bits of toffee paper everywhere, kids with their candy ribbons whipped out of their hands, feathers blowing and swooping on the big oyster-shaped hats that all the women were wearing that year. Down on the front it must have been a regular gale but, of course, up at the race track it was a bit more sheltered by the downs.

You hardly noticed the downs at first, with all the running and shouting and carrying-on, and the laughing and whistles and rattles, old fellows wagging their sausage-balloons, girls trying to hold down their skirts and squealing when the paper streamers tangled round their legs – and then you'd look up and see a greenish-grey shoulder of hill sloping away, as if someone had his back turned on the whole affair.

It's a pretty part. I love it. Still do.

I was over for the day, thinking I'd pick up a bit of money, which was always short with me at that time. I was young and my blood was quick-circulating and kept me restless; nothing seemed to last with me very long, and cash no time at all.

I suppose on an everyday Monday the High Street would be quiet as a river-bed, but that afternoon it was like bedlam with traffic – some cars, but mostly carts and traps – jammed from the bridge right up to the castle. They used to keep a thundering great white cockatoo at the hotel in those days, tame, and it was out and flying up and down the street like a zeppelin, rowing on those great brawny wings; every time it passed over there'd be an oo! from the crowd, and women would duck and scream. It flew so low you could see the mad orange glare of its eye; I daresay it thought we were all a bit cuckoo, too.

It was a big help to me, that bird. I'd fixed on the handkerchief game and I was working my way slowly up from the station to the racecourse, taking my time over it. I'd a gross of cheap machine-lace-edged wipes, nicely folded in tissue, and the trick was to tap some old girl's shoulder most politely, and say, 'Ma'am, your reticule's come open, did you know?'

'Gracious,' she'd cry, 'when did that happen?' and be all of a flutter saying, 'Thank you so much for telling me,' and 'I never noticed.'

Of course she hadn't noticed because I'd flipped it open as she craned up at the cockatoo.

'Better look and see if everything's there,' I'd say, looking around as if to expect to see two or three tiaras and a pearl necklace lying on the pavement.

'No,' she says, 'purse, comb, pins, peppermints – everything seems to be here. I am very much obliged to you, young man.'

While she's in this happy grateful mood I sell her one of my lace-edged hankies to add tone to her collection of frippery. People will buy anything in the street, specially when they feel obliged, for five times the price they'd ever consider laying out in a shop, and in a couple of hours I'd got rid of fifty fourpenny dusters for half a crown apiece.

I wasn't really in it for business, just for pin-money, and when I got up towards the racecourse I eased off. For one thing, the last old die-hard, after I'd sold her my story about Chantilly lace and she'd handed over her half-crown, disconcerted me by very deliberately flicking open the tiny handkerchief and blowing her nose on it, fixing me all the time over the top of it with a bright triangular blue eye like a flint arrowhead.

'Young man,' she said, 'you'll go far. Too far, if anything.'

There I stood, rooted, unable to move out of the presence of that eye until she dismissed me with a little nod, not unkindly.

So I strolled off and started paying attention to the runners. I made out with a couple of low-priced ones right away, so then I took a pull and relaxed. No sense in hurrying a good chance. Mother always used to say, 'Blow on your luck and give it a rub.'

Crowds were still whirling up from the station, with whistles and paper snakes going full blast. It was a good day. You could smell the salt from the sea, five miles off.

I went and had a glass of stout and a sandwich at The New Pin, a chilly, smelly little place but nearest to the course, and then I strolled back, looking about, as I say, taking my time. Then, in the three o'clock, I noticed an outsider at 100 to 1, Clever Cockatoo. That's for you, my boy, I thought, so I put a fiver on him. Silly thing to do I suppose, really, but I was feeling happy and relaxed and I knew it was my lucky day.

Clever Cockatoo strolled home by about five lengths.

In a way I was quite annoyed. I felt it had happened too early in the day. I knew if I had any sense I wouldn't bet any more though it seemed a waste of the rest of the afternoon. Anyway, I thought, I'll give it a rest for a race or two, so I collected the takings and wandered off to a corner of the track where they'd got a little bit of a carnival going.

There were coconut shies and hoop-las and the usual side shows, strong men, a snake-charmer, bearded lady, Astounding Peep Show, some performing dogs. I watched the snake-charmer which was not a bad shilling's worth, though she was a skinny girl and the snakes definitely were not cobras.

Then I moved on to the last tent. In front of it was a notice that made me rub my eyes and look again, for it said ADMISSION £5. Over that there was a picture of a naked girl standing still and staring straight ahead of her, crudely enough done, and, in larger letters: ELANA – THE GIRL IN THE BALL.

I stared at the chaps going in and, sure enough, they did seem to be handing over fivers or grubby batches of notes. Well, I thought, this is putting it over on the grand scale, and makes me look like an amateur. What persuades them to part with their money?

There was nothing so startling about the notice, and I wasn't going to be hurried into making a gull of myself just because I had all that money burning a hole in my pocket, so I hung about and watched. After five minutes or so a hand came out of the tent and reversed the notice so as to show the words, FULL UP. Then some vaguely eastern-sounding music began, plaintive and squeaky. Apart from that there was dead silence from inside the tent – not a grunt, not a murmur.

The silence lasted for about ten minutes, and then the music ended on a high, drawn-out quaver and, after a pause of a moment or so, the chaps began coming out again. I studied their faces. They certainly didn't look disappointed, or as if they thought they'd been tricked; far from it. They were discussing eagerly, excitedly, among themselves, sometimes glancing back; but as soon as the last of them was out the tent-flaps were firmly laced together again.

'Is it good?' I asked an old fellow, a military-looking man.

'Remarkable,' he said. 'Quite remarkable. How the devil did he get her in there? Go and see for yourself, young feller.'

That decided me and when the tent-flaps were opened once more I joined the stream of ingoing customers and handed over my fiver to a giant of a man in a turban. We went past him through a curtain, and you could hear a sort of sigh as each man stepped in.

The inside of the tent was quite bare, except for a roped-off square in the middle. Outside the rope was grass, trodden into chalky squidge by this time. The centre square was covered by one great piece of Indian carpet which was thin and worn, but you could still see the original colours and patterns glowing in that queer, green, luminous light that you get inside a tent in daytime.

Each man as he came in made straight for the rope and leaned out over it, the later arrivals peeling off and working farther and farther round the square till the rope was completely lined with silent, staring faces.

Occasionally a man would murmur to his neighbour.

'Is she real?'

'Looks like it.'

'Why don't she move then?'

'Dunno.'

In the middle of the carpet was a clear glass ball, like the ones fishermen weight their nets with; only this one was perhaps three foot six in diameter, perfectly clear glass that looked no thicker than a brandy balloon. There was no visible mark or join on it, and yet inside sat a naked girl, quite still, but, so far as we could see, alive.

She was holding a bunch of spring flowers – narcissi, grape hyacinths, and so forth – and there was a whole mass of flower heads tumbled into the ball with her.

'She must be a waxwork,' somebody said, and just after that the girl moved.

She had been looking down at the flowers she held, now she lifted up her eyes and gave us a clear, attentive look, unsmiling. She was dark-eyed, with a wide mouth and long blue-black hair that hung down her back to her waist. It had a ripple in it, and looked very soft, like dark feathers. The girl was slim and, so far as I could decide, not tall, perhaps five foot two or three. As she sat the top of the ball just cleared her head.

There was a lot of charm about that girl; she was the sort of girl you'd like to have come and sit herself down beside you on the top front seat of a double-decker bus on a fine spring day at the start of a twenty-mile journey. The only fault in her was that she never smiled, but then I daresay she couldn't be expected to feel much like smiling inside of a glass ball. Though if she was getting a half-share of the profits you'd think she might have felt inclined to smile at the thought of twenty five-pound notes standing round her and gazing at her so seriously.

In a moment the turbaned fellow came from his seat at the entrance, ducked under the rope, brisk and businesslike, and picked up the ball. He did it quite effortlessly, but you could see the muscles in his arms ripple. Holding it before him like a beach-ball he made the tour of the ring.

'You see, gentlemen,' he said, 'there is no deception about this. The girl is alive, the flowers are alive, and the ball is pure glass, unflawed. If I were to drop it, it would break. Tap it if you like.'

Most of us did tap it, and it rang like glass all right.

'Now,' said the man, 'I shall show you some juggling.'

There was a little portable phonograph in one corner of the ring, and he wound this up. It had a record already on it and in a moment the doleful squeaky music began and he started his act.

It was really dancing more than juggling. He postured about with the ball for a minute or two and then tossed it in the air. When he did that the flowers whirled up inside like those snow-storm paper-weights, and then settled again as he caught it, some of them lying on the girl who was now curled up in a new position.

You could have heard twenty sighs as we all let out the

breath we had been holding, and then he shifted the ball in his hands and tossed it up once more. That girl must have been made of rubber; you'd have expected her to be black and blue but I couldn't see a bruise on her. I daresay most of the audience had stiff necks next day, though, from following the ball in its flight.

Once or twice the man launched the ball towards the audience, and then dived after and caught it like a rugger player, just as they were ducking, or reaching up to finger it down. Inside the ball was like a kaleidoscope with the girl's white arms and legs at all angles and the flowers bursting upwards like bees, and her black hair sprayed across it all.

Ten minutes lasted no time at all. The record came to an end, the man stopped his weaving around and put the ball carefully down in the midde of the carpet once more.

'You like it?' he said cheerfully, and there was a murmur of 'Not half' from the chaps beginning reluctantly to file out into the daylight. The girl began calmly combing her hair with her fingers, shaking the flower heads down to the bottom of the ball, and straightening her bouquet.

I filed out with the rest and stood stupidly in the raw daylight, not knowing where to go or what to do. In the end I went down into the High Street and sold off the rest of my handkerchiefs, but it was really just to give my mind time to settle; I felt as if I had the girl and the flowers whirling about inside my head.

Then I went back and watched another performance. It was dark by now, the races were over, but the carnival was going full swing, and people were dancing in the street and up on the racecourse. There was a bonfire and some men had those torches they use for Guy Fawkes – metal holders with paraffin-soaked rags flaring in them – and were running about letting out whoops and scaring the women.

The tent was lit up by greenish flickering hurricane lamps and the light reflected in the ball and in the girl's eyes was uncanny, inhuman – more like the light you see in a cat's eyes, caught in the headlights at night. The audience was tense, on edge – and very unwilling to go at the end of the performance. But the man in the turban shepherded them all out, shouting 'Closing down, closing down now. No more tonight.'

He caught hold of my arm as I edged between the flaps and said, 'Wait.' So I waited till the last man had gone grumbling out into the dark and said, 'What is it?'

'You like this little show? It's a good little show, no?'

'Not bad,' I said.

'You like to buy?'

'Why? You want to sell?'

'I must sell. I shoot a man in Chatham – see? Police after me. I am leaving tonight for France.'

'How much?' I said.

'A thousand.'

'Make it five hundred.'

'O.K.,' he said, 'I have no time to argue.'

All the time we were talking he had been changing out of his white rig and turban. I gave him the five hundred in notes and he left, blowing a kiss to the girl in the ball, and slipping out quickly between the tent-flaps.

I stood holding on to the rope staring at her, and I must confess I felt a bit scared, didn't know what was going to happen next. This certainly was shaping out into a queer day, like a page torn out of a dream. I wondered what I ought to do with the girl – did I throw a rug over her for the night, like a canary? Or what?

Then I noticed that she was making signs to me, pointing over to one corner of the tent. I looked where she was pointing and saw a hammer. When I held it up she nodded and began another pantomime. It took me a bit of time to get her drift, but at last I realized that she meant me to break the ball. That shook me a bit, because if the ball was broken where was my show? But then I supposed she couldn't spend her life in the ball; she had to eat. I reckoned there must be a supply of balls somewhere behind the scenes.

So I broke the ball with the hammer.

I was rather startled when I discovered that she was French, couldn't speak a word of English. Her name was Marie-Laine. While she was slipping on the navy-blue dress that lay in another corner of the tent and twisting her hair into a chignon, I pointed to the bits of broken glass ball and said, 'Où sont les autres?'

She flung out her hands, shrugged, and made a noise like Pfui.

'Alors, comment construire ...?' My French was pretty rusty and I laboured over the point I was trying to make: how the devil do we get you into another ball?

'Sais pas, moi,' she said.

I gave it up for the time and, as I was pretty hungry and I reckoned she must be too, tucked my arm into hers and took her down for a steak and chips at the Anchor Hotel.

It was a funny sort of meal. She certainly was hungry – she waded into that steak, chattering away nineteen-to-the-dozen all the time in French about her stamp album which she had brought with her tucked under her other arm. She was mad about stamps. The waiter who served us got all excited and before the end of the meal she had him swapping a Suid-Afrika for a Togoland. All the men in the room were watching her with absolute fascination, she was so pretty and so much alive. She had the sort of velvety darkness and lightness of a kitten as she sat waving her expressive hands about and showing me her *timbres*.

'Come on,' I said at last, 'marchons. Time to go.'

And we strolled back up the High Street which was empty by now, peaceful and starlit.

In the morning she was gone, with her stamp album and

the rest of my money, leaving me only the tent, which was hired anyway as I soon discovered, and the memory of the sweetest night that two people ever spent on a faded old Indian carpet.

Five Green Moons

This small town was of course full of people and, like all such places, so beautiful and so interesting that it would take a lifetime to describe it. But we will pick one particular morning in May when children were at school, and washing was blossoming out on lines, and delivery vans were edging their way from the narrow streets out into the countryside and, generally speaking, in all the town's not very numerous alleys and back yards and shops and houses, life, as vigorous and complex as grass roots, was being lived in the usual way.

Mr Makins, the bus conductor, was sitting in the small communal courtyard outside his back door smoking a pipe and reading the *Daily Mirror*, since he would not be on duty till twelve. He was soaking his feet, as a precaution against the sudden warm weather, in a polythene bowl of mustard and permanganate, and his solid bulk was comfortably accommodated in an upright canvas deckchair. Sam, the large black Labrador from the Kings', next door, lay alongside him, chin on paws, extending a blissful stomach along the warm concrete.

Mrs Bowling, Rita, from next door on the other side, was doing a little weeding in the centre flowerbed; old blind Mr Thatcher, next door but one, in panama and dark glasses, was methodically shaking out his doormat before taking his white stick and tip-tapping through the peaceful town to do some shopping for himself and his grand-daughter Lucy, a nurse at the cottage hospital.

That takes care of the externals. And as for what was going on below the surface – Mr Makins was wondering should he or shouldn't he put on a kettle and make a cup of tea for his wife Lily who would soon be back from washing-up at The Crown; Sam the Labrador was waiting in warm suspended animation for eleven-year-old Michael to come home from school; Rita Bowling, wan, washed-out and pretty, was making up her mind to leave her husband Fred; Mrs King, who, since the recent death of her husband, had, from unhappiness, been more or less actively unkind to her son Michael, was reading the day's horoscope in her curtained, fusty, north-facing front room before going to call on the vet; and old Mr Thatcher was wondering whether Lucy would fancy a nice bit of haddock for supper.

Father Fogarty came up the alley to visit Fred Bowling.

'Morning, Harry. Lovely show of grape hyacinths you've got there,' he said, looking admiringly round the little court which, between walls and concrete paving, was cosy with flowers as a chintz chaircover. 'You can smell them half-way down the alley. Morning, Mrs Bowling. Is Fred about?'

'Ah, what's the use of speaking to him then, Father?' Rita straightened herself dispiritedly. 'You might as well save your bre —'

It was at this moment that an unusual event occurred.

With a brilliant, silent flash — so brilliant, so silent, that it was as if all the light in the world had been sucked in one direction and then blown back again — something came to rest in the middle of the courtyard, crushing to slime, regrettably, a lot of Mr Makins' grape hyacinths and Mrs Bowling's narcissi. Three of the four people in the court jumped back instinctively and now stood goggle-eyed, gazing at this strange object which rested in their yard as neatly as a cabbage in a colander.

It was like nothing in the world so much as a duck-egg — only, of course, a great deal larger. Higher than Father Fogarty's head, shining, spherical, and slightly translucent, there it stuck among the narcissi and it was slightly cracked.

'Gor blimey,' said Mr Makins, removing his pipe from his mouth. 'Someone's laid an egg. Whatever blessed chick's going to come out of that there?'

'It's a missile!' shrilled Rita. 'I bet you anything you like it's got Russians inside it!'

'This is most uncommon,' remarked Father Fogarty. He approached the thing gingerly and laid a hand on it. It tipped slightly. 'Why, it's quite light. Do you suppose –?'

'Hold on,' Harry warned him. 'There's someone inside it. You're right, Rita, it's a blooming spaceship.'

Sure enough they could see through the semi-transparent skin of the egg that someone was bumping about inside.

'Shall I fetch a hammer?' suggested Harry.

'What's going on, what's going on?' cried old Mr Thatcher impatiently.

Lil Makins arrived with her shopping-bag and let out a little scream. 'Oh, Harry! Whatever is it?'

'Wait a minute,' said Father Fogarty. 'He's coming out.'

A tiny biting blade, a kind of circular saw, was cutting a neat division along the line of the crack. As they watched, a section of the egg-surface swung back. The knuckles of a hand appeared on the side of the hole. A foot came through, and then a leg. The other leg emerged, followed, with a wriggle, by the torso and head of a young man. He stood up and stared somewhat dazedly at the people confronting him. They stared back.

He was a very thin individual with a shock of light brown hair, an indeterminate nose, and a good-tempered mouth. His eyes, set wide apart, were grey and dispassionate. He had a pair of wings, white, and rather untidy as to the feathers.

'Do you speak English, young man?' said Father Fogarty, obviously feeling that it behoved him to make the first move.

'He must be an angel!' audibly whispered Mrs Makins to Mrs Bowling.

'What's going on? What's happened?' asked old Mr Thatcher irritably.

'Is this the Isle of Albion, sir?' the young man said, addressing himself to Father Fogarty.

'Why, yes – yes, I suppose it is. May one ask where you come from?' The priest achieved a masterly blend of respect, cordiality, and judgement in suspense with these words: if you are an angel, he might have been saying, I am naturally prepared to extend professional consideration and trade rates, as it were, but although I have a kind heart I am not to be imposed on.

'Mars is my home planet,' the young man said diffidently. 'But –'

'Mars!' shrieked Mrs Makins. 'He's a Martian!'

'Are there any more of you on the way?' asked Harry, casting a weather eye up to see if other cream-coloured eggs were drifting out of the blue sky.

'It's a Martian invasion! We're doomed!'

'Belt up, Lil,' said Mr Makins goodnaturedly. 'They'd send a reconnaissance first, wouldn't they? Well then, we've just got to discourage this one.'

'You are not an angel, young man?'

'You just fly back to Mars and tell them to invade somewhere else. We like our own ways.'

'What is it? What *is* it?' snapped Mr Thatcher.

'It's a Martian invasion,' Rita Bowling explained patiently to the irascible old man.

Fred Bowling, roused by the tumult, put his bleary head out of the window and said, 'Gawd!'

His wife called up to him, 'It's a Martian invasion, Fred!'

The young man from Mars pressed his hands to his forehead. 'No, no. You are making a mistake, I assure you,' he said earnestly. 'I am not invading you and I am not an angel.'

'What are you then?'

'My name is Onil. I'm a refugee.'

At this moment Police Constable Vyall appeared, taking a short cut through to the station-house. 'What's all the ruckus about?' he said. 'Strewth! Where did that come from? This is a right of way, I'd have you know. You can't park it here.'

'I regret,' said the young man faintly, 'I am rather exhausted. If you will tell me —'

He looked helplessly round at the ring of simple, wondering, not unfriendly faces watching him, said again, 'I'm a refugee,' took a staggering step, and fell among what was left of the narcissi.

'Passed out,' said Harry. 'Better get him to hospital.'

'My car's at the end of the alley,' said Father Fogarty, 'I'll take him. Have you a jacket, Harry, just to cover up the – the wings? We don't want a lot of talk.'

11.09 a.m., Constable Vyall wrote in his notebook. *Martian and spaceship landed in Viner's Court. Martian removed to hospital.*

It was surprising how quickly the townspeople settled to the fact that they had their very own Martian in a side ward at the cottage hospital. (His trouble turned out to be simply a slowness in adjusting to the atmosphere; so long as he had an oxygen mask handy, he was all right.) Naturally there was a stream of visitors both to the hospital and to see the ship, which had to be left in the yard since it was too large to go through the alley, but it was tacitly and universally agreed that the news should not be allowed to spread outside the town.

'We don't want half the country traipsing here to see him,' said Father Fogarty.

'That we don't,' agreed Harry Makins.

As Onil had no kinsfolk of his own to visit him, the neighbours took it in turns bringing him grapes and confiding their troubles. He listened with kindly, dispassionate attention and told them things they hardly knew about themselves.

'Shall I leave Fred or not?' said Rita Bowling.

'You don't really want to. Why not teach him to play chess?'

'What does Lil want for her birthday?' said Harry Makins.

'A pudding basin. One of those red glass ones.'

'What shall I get for Lucy's supper?' said old Mr Thatcher.

'A nice bit of cod and chips from The Red Lion.'

'You're putting me out of business,' said Father Fogarty.

'I am so happy to be here.' The young man Onil looked with love out of his bedroom window at a bit of hedge, all bursting with May-buds, and some fat, brown, contented hens.

'Tell me, why did you leave Mars to come to this rather backward little planet?'

'Mars has developed too far,' Onil explained. 'Nothing remains unknown there. Oh, it is terrible! All we can do is organize each other.'

'I can sympathize. That wouldn't do for us down here,' said Father Fogarty, and he rose to go as Nurse Thatcher came in with Onil's lunch on a tray. Young Michael King appeared with a bunch of radishes and his dog Sam. Boy and dog sat down in a puddle of sunshine on the polished floor.

'Go on telling about your trip,' said Michael, and Lucy lingered, dusting the windowsill with a teacloth as she listened.

'Well, space is like a jungle, you know, and each star or planet is a potential Something that might eat you up . . . I went drifting through the forest keeping a sharp lookout for a place where people still had time to knit and gossip with their neighbours and read books and sew on buttons and listen to music . . .'

'No buttons on Mars?'

'Nothing but zips.'

'Go on.'

'And I saw one or two possibles – yes, there was one nice little planet that I noticed, a long way off, with five green moons and four blue oceans and three extinct volcanoes –'

'And a partridge in a pear tree?' suggested Lucy, sitting on the windowsill so that the sun made a Saturn's ring round her fair hair.

'– but it had no inhabitants, so I thought I'd be too lonely there. And then I saw this one and heard the cuckoos – they don't have any cuckoos on Mars – and I thought, That's the world for me.'

'Tell more about the little planet. What was its name?'

'Sirun. It had birds and apple trees, but no people.'

'I'll go there when I'm old enough to be a space-pilot,' said Michael. 'Won't we, Sam?' Sam thumped his tail on the floor.

'Time I tidied you up for the doctor,' said Lucy, and she took away Onil's tray and straightened up his wings.

Dr Bentinck was kind, busy, and preoccupied as always. 'I think you can soon leave off the oxygen for good. But no violent exercise at first, mind. Thinking of taking a job in the town? Well, be sure it's not too active – librarian, bank clerk, something like that, eh? Nurse Thatcher, can you see where I put my glasses? Ah, thank you, thank you. Good day, young man.'

In the evening Fred Bowling came in to play chess. 'That Rita,' he said. 'Honest to God, sometimes I think she'll drive me clean crackers. I swear I don't know, sometimes, what goes on inside that head of hers.'

'Think yourself lucky,' said Onil, moving out his queen.

'Eh?'

'Think how much worse it would be if you did know. Why not buy her a record-player with your pools winnings?'

'Eh – oh, yes. Forgot I'd told you about that. Yes, come to think, that's not a bad idea, she'd like a player. I've always wanted one too. Then we could listen to records instead of arguing, I suppose. Young Michael's very upset,' he went on, hustling a bishop in front of his king.

'Oh yes?'

'His dog's lost. You know how much store he sets by Sam. That's why he's not come up to see you this evening – he's out on his bike, scouring the place.'

'Time you were off, Mr Bowling,' said Night Sister, putting her head round the door.

'Have a heart, Sister! I'm in check! Nurse Thatcher would let me stay.'

'Nurse Thatcher spoils this patient.'

But even Night Sister was not averse to sitting in the side ward for half an hour and listening to descriptions of washing-machines on Mars.

Three days later Onil was allowed out for a brief spell. He strolled through the town to inspect his spaceship, and stopped for a chat with Harry Makins, who was soaking his feet in the yard.

'Getting quite used to it,' said Harry, nodding at the bright translucent globe. 'Puts me in mind of the Festival of Britain.'

Lil brought them a cup of tea, and old Mr Thatcher pottered by on his way to the shops.

'Don't you have blind people on Mars?' asked Harry, noticing a troubled expression in Onil's eyes as he turned to look after the old man.

'No, we do not – but it is not that. Could I have warned him?' the young man said, half to himself.

'Warned him of what?'

'His grand-daughter Lucy is my friend, you see.'

'Course she is – and a nice girl too. What's the matter, Onil?'

The young man shook his head and asked after Michael.

'Still hasn't found that dog of his. You'd better go in and see him.'

When the tea and biscuits were finished, Onil knocked at the door and was let in by narrow-nosed, bead-eyed Mrs King, who seemed genuinely pleased to see him. 'If you can do anything with that boy of mine – he's so upset about his blessed dog. I've told him and *told* him it was too big for this house anyway.'

Michael King was lying on the black wool hearthrug which had been Sam's bed for five years. 'He won't speak, he won't eat,' she whispered.

'The dog is still not found?'

'No. Michael, here's Onil and Mr Makins to see you. Come on, get up!' The boy slowly turned round at his friend's name. Onil was shocked at his appearance. He seemed to have lost pounds in weight.

'Sam must be dead, I know he must be. He'd have found his way home by now if he wasn't.'

'That's just not true, Michael,' Onil said.

'It is true. Mum says so too. And if he's dead, I don't want to live.'

Mrs King pressed her lips together and said, 'Don't talk in that wicked way, Michael.'

Onil looked troubled. 'Do you want me to help him, Mrs King?'

'Of course!' she snapped. 'If you can talk a bit of sense into him.'

'Well then, Michael, your mother is lying to you when she says she does not know where the dog is. She gave him to the vet, who found a home for him on a farm nine miles from here.'

'*What?*'

Michael, whitefaced, stared at his mother who cried in anger and guilt, 'It's a lie, it's not true! Who told *you*, anyway? Coming in here so smarmy! Anyway how did you know? No one in the street did, I made sure of that.'

'What's the name of the farm?' Michael asked, taking no notice of his mother.

'Pingold's, North Dean.'

Michael was out of the door in a flash. Onil and Mr Makins followed him, leaving Mrs King protesting uselessly in the empty room. 'I couldn't help it. The dog cost too much to feed –'

'Was that a kind thing to do?' said Harry. 'The boy will never trust his mother again. All the same,' he added, 'what a filthy mean trick to play on the kid. How did you find out?'

'Oh,' Onil passed a hand wearily over his eyes. 'I can hear people's thoughts.'

'*Can* you now?' Harry Makins put his feet reflectively back into the permanganate. 'So you know all that goes on inside me, eh?'

'Everything.'

'Gawd. That takes some thinking about, dunnit? Do you know,' pursued Harry with a fearful curiosity, 'do you know when I'm going to die?'

Onil looked at him with tortured eyes. At that moment Lil, haggard and dishevelled, hurried into the court, dropped into the chair beside her husband, and burst into a flood of tears.

'Oh, that poor old man! Oh, what an awful thing! It's shook me all to pieces.'

'What, Lil? What has?'

'Poor old Mr Thatcher. Run over by a motorbike as he was crossing the High Street. Oh, however are we going to tell his poor grand-daughter?'

Harry Makins turned his head slowly and stared at Onil. 'You said you – you said you could have warned him. Was *that* what you meant?'

'Warned him that it would happen – yes. To prevent it – no.'

'Oh, my goodness,' Harry said, mostly to himself. 'Oh, my goodness. You poor soul. Think of living with a thing like that.'

He pulled his feet out of the basin, thrust them dripping into his slippers, and walked heavily indoors.

That evening no one came to visit Onil at the hospital.

'They're afraid,' he said sadly to little Nurse Thatcher, who was back on nights – she had said she would prefer to go on working if no one objected. 'They're afraid I shall tell them when they are going to die.'

'*I'm* not scared,' she said, and gently tucked his wing under the sheet.

'They won't come to see me any more.'

But he was wrong. Father Fogarty turned up and, after some beating about the bush, came to the point.

'My boy,' he said, 'if that's how life is on Mars, I can quite see why you wanted to leave. It must be terrible. I'm used to God having access to my thoughts, but the neighbours too – no. Well, you can see how it is.'

'Yes,' Onil said sadly. 'You won't want me here. And I had hoped I was going to be so useful in the library –'

'You'll find somewhere else, my boy; somewhere just as good, with that grand little spaceship of yours. I've sealed up the crack with Polymix and if I were you I'd get going just as soon as you feel strong enough. The people in the town are very sorry – they don't bear any hard feelings – but they just don't like the thought of seeing you any more.

'Au revoir then, my dear fellow; send a picture postcard to let us know how you are getting on –'

The door shut behind him.

Wordlessly, Nurse Thatcher began moving Onil's one or two little oddments out of his locker.

'Oh well,' he said. 'It's a fine moonlit night for a flight. And that did look quite a nice little planet, the one with the five green moons –'

'And the partridge in the pear tree.'

'If only it weren't so uninhabited.'

'I'm coming too,' said Nurse Thatcher.

'Lucy! You mustn't think of such a thing.'

'You can't stop me! *I* don't mind,' said Lucy firmly. '*I* don't mind you knowing what I'm thinking.' And she gave him such a clear and beautiful look as she stood in the moonlight pressing six handkerchiefs and a cake of soap against her white starched bib that that was the end of the matter.

An hour later, as he bicycled dreamily homeward from North Dean with Sam loping beside him, Michael King saw the white ship burst upward like a giant pingpong ball from its nest in Viners' Court.

At first he grieved for the loss of his friend.

'But never mind, Sam,' he said consolingly, 'in eight years I'll be old enough to be a space-pilot, and then we'll go up to Sirun and see the five green moons and the four blue seas and the three extinct volcanoes . . .'

And two turtle doves and a partridge in a pear tree.

Smell

'Have you put that it's for a poor old lady who's very hard of hearing and nearly blind as well? Have you asked them to do it as quick as possible?' said Mrs Ruffle.

She was a massive old woman; her round, soup-plate hat encircled a heavy face, fixed in the expression of stony non-communication habitual to the deaf.

'Yes, I told you so twice, I put it,' her son said impatiently and then, remembering she could not hear him, gave several emphatic nods, stooping towards her over the post-office counter. But she continued to watch him with an intent, peering, distrustful stare as he folded the letter he had written, tucked it among the wadding in a small sturdy cardboard box, bound up the package with adhesive tape, addressed it in large capitals to HEARING-AID REPAIR DEPARTMENT, Stanbury Ear, Nose and Throat Hospital, Stanbury, and stuck on a stamp.

'How soon do you think they will send it back, George?'

'Three days, four maybe, *Four days*,' he shouted, mouthing the words.

'What do you say, dear?'

He tried to shake her hand, to demonstrate by counting on her knobbed, aged fingers, but, physical contact being a rarity with her nowadays, she started back nervously, like a wild animal in hostile surroundings, and by her movement dislodged a tall pyramid of biscuit tins which stood on the floor beside her. Marie, Nice, Oval Osborne, Petit Beurre, Sponge Fingers, all came cascading down on to the uneven brick floor of the little shop. Hardly noticing the chaos she left behind her, Mrs Ruffle tapped her way, with her heavy white-painted stick, towards the street entrance, through a group of other customers who made solicitous way for her. In the door she paused to sniff disapprovingly and say,

'There's something smells not all it should be round here. George! You've let some of the biscuits go pammagey! Not putting the lid on tight that's what does it. There's mice here, too, if you ask me. I never could fancy a Marie biscuit that's gone soft, that the mice have run over.'

George Ruffle, angrily shovelling biscuits, strips of corrugated paper, and shavings off the bricks, made to answer but shrugged in response to sympathetic grins as if to say 'What can you do?' He dumped the spoilt stock in an empty wooden barrel and went back to serving customers behind the counter.

His mother put her head through the door again.

'Your father wouldn't ever have let such a thing happen! Nothing but fresh goods there was in the shop when he was living. None of this frozen stuff then, that costs double the money and doesn't do you a bit of good.'

And she directed a short-sighted malignant glance at the deep-freeze, installed by George after his father's death in spite of her vehemently expressed objections.

'How often d'you clean that contraption out, anyway? Every other August Bank Holiday? Wouldn't hurt to get that lazy boy of yours to do it once in a blue moon.' She gave a grim chuckle and shook off the hand of a man who offered to help her down the two steps into the village street. 'Someone round here been fishing by the smell of him,' she muttered, and tapped her way out of sight.

'Independent old lady, your mother,' a farmer said, buying national insurance stamps at the post-office counter.

'Independent!' said George. 'You can't do a thing with her. The Health Visitor doesn't like her being out there in the cottage on her own, but she won't budge. Says she means to die among her own things, not in an old people's home that's only the workhouse by another name.'

'Still, she's good for a tidy few years yet by the look of her.'

'Oh, she's as healthy as they come,' agreed George, rapping down a pile of coppers and sliding them under the grille. 'It's just that, being so deaf, she's a bit of a risk on her own – wouldn't hear a pan boil over, or a tap left running. Specially without her aid, like now. Still, what can you do? You can't shift her. She's got enough to live on, she was born in that cottage, and she reckons to die there – Yes, Wally? Postal order for three and eleven? Frank,' he called to his son at the back of the shop, 'just leave loading up those orders into the van and give a hand at the counter a moment, will you?'

Frank, a handsome, sullen-looking boy in a white overall, dropped the carton of groceries he had just picked up and reluctantly obeyed.

Meanwhile old Mrs Ruffle slowly pursued her familiar course. Butcher: chopped shin and a bone for the dog. Rendell the chemist: digestive tablets. 'No hearing-aid batteries today?' he inquired, but receiving absolutely no response, abandoned the attempt to communicate and handed her the tablets and change, which she carefully counted, feeling the milled edges of the sixpences with her thumbnail.

Two pairs of woollen stockings at Miss Knox the draper's.

'She buys two pairs a month, regularly,' Miss Knox confided to her visiting cousin when the door closed behind Mrs Ruffle. 'Extravagant, but she says she can't see to mend, and she might as well spend her cash as let it lie.'

'She must be nicely off.'

'Oh, they say in the village that she's got quite a little nest-egg tucked away somewhere in that cottage of hers.'

Miss Knox glanced out at the solid old back, slowly retreating along the village street.

Old Mrs Ruffle tapped her way home by touch, sight within a four-foot radius, and smell. Whiff of scorching hair and cuticle from the blacksmith's. Steep grassy bank in front of the church. Dandelions on it. Church gate, newly painted, with a reek of warm creosote in the June sun. Stretch of yew hedge round the churchyard: a dark, dusty smell. She went through the lych-gate and checked on Bert's grave; yes, they had changed the flowers and the grass was clipped; no more than they ought to do, either, but she wouldn't ever be surprised if they left off doing it, George never having shown the proper respect for his father, Doris thinking herself a cut above her husband's family, and Frank a spoilt lazy young scamp, his mind on nothing but pools and motor-bikes.

After the ritual visit to the grave and ten minutes' rest on the churchyard bench (it bore a plaque In memory of Albert Edward Ruffle, donated by his widow) she went slowly on. Past the Ring of Bells: smell of sawdust and beer through the open door. Down the hill that led from the village on its knoll to the flat salt marshes below. Dark, first, between shady banks. Smell of damp earth and long grass. Then out into the sun again. Tang of ammonia borne along the breeze from the sheep pastured on the marshes beyond the dyke. When she had on her hearing-aid Mrs Ruffle could just catch their thin, incessant bleating but now the sound was lost to her, dispersed into the great bright vault of sky. She stumped on, sniffing the salt of the five-mile-distant sea, keeping carefully to the middle of the narrow little flat road between its neatly tended dykes. The only vehicles to pass that way were farm trucks and delivery vans; the drivers were familiar with the sight of her stocky figure ahead of them, and slowed carefully to skirt round her, two wheels on the verge.

Now she began to get the fragrance of her privet hedge, her broad beans in full flower; as she drew nearer home the accustomed smell of the cottage itself came out to greet her: old brickwork, reed thatch, the boiled potatoes of a thousand dinners. Rover the bull-terrier lumbered wagging from his kennel – so familiar was his greeting that she almost deceived herself she could hear the joyful rattle of his chain. She gave him the bone, and he settled down to worry it in a patch of dust and sun.

With unerring fingers she reached for the key, hidden on its nail under the thatch – and paused. It was hanging the wrong way round. Muttering distrustfully to herself she took it down, inserted it in the lock, and opened her front door.

The instant she stepped inside she knew that an intruder had been there – might, for all she could hear, be there still. She stood motionless, with dilated eyes and nostrils, desperately straining her blocked ears to listen, until fear and the vain concentration turned her giddy. Only after more than five minutes had gone by did she dare creep tremulously forward, turning her head from side to side like a tortoise, moving across her room from one piece of furniture to the next. Yes! That chair had been shifted, so had the table. The cupboard door was unlatched. She reached in, right to the back, and brought out a small pink lustre-ware teapot; with shaking fingers removed the lid.

The teapot was empty.

It took Mrs Ruffle a very long time to assimilate this fact. A dozen, two dozen times she replaced the teapot, took it out again, felt inside it. Then she took out other teapots – jugs, bowls, dishes – and feverishly, uselessly hunted inside each in turn. She ransacked the whole cupboard – the room – the house. She put everything back and then started again. By the third time round she could not be bothered to replace the articles she had moved. There was no strength left in her. She sat down weakly in the bony old armchair that had adapted itself to her shape through forty years of use, and went straight to sleep. In her sleep she twitched and shivered like a dog that dreams of hunting; her hands opened and shut in a ceaseless, obsessive search.

Next morning she woke early and began searching again; then broke off, remembering that Sid the milk boy would soon arrive, and went out to watch for him. As soon as his faded blue pony-trap stopped outside she ran out to the gate.

'Sid! I've been robbed! I've been robbed, Sid! You'll have to get the police.'

'Are you all right, missis?' Sid was alarmed by her haggard whiteness and vacant, unfixed look; he offered to take her along to George's in the trap but she ignored the offer, which indeed she had not heard, and finally he drove off, promising to send help right away.

When P.C. Trencher came to the cottage she was at first reassured by his imposing dark-blue uniform and bright buttons. He searched the place, from attic bedrooms to the back cellar under the garden that was never used because the septic tank tended to flood into it in wet weather. Everywhere the constable went, Mrs Ruffle followed.

'How are you going to get the money back?' she kept saying. 'How are you going to get back my five hundred pounds? You will get it back, won't you?'

When he tried to explain the obstacles to this outcome: the absence of fingerprints, the lack of clues or witnesses the fact that, although almost everybody in the village had suspected the existence of her hoard, in fact there was no proof at all that it had amounted to as much as she claimed, or even to a tenth of that figure; when he tried to lecture her on the folly of keeping five hundred pounds in a teapot, she gave no evidence of having heard him, but continued to repeat, 'You will get it back, won't you?'

He wondered if she was quite right in the head, if the shock had damaged her wits. At last he appealed for guidance to his superior, Superintendent Bray, who sensibly postponed talking to her until the hospital had sent back her repaired hearing-aid and communication, if only of a patchy kind, was once more re-established.

George, angry, embarrassed, touchy, and ashamed, escorted his mother to the police-station.

'You realize it was a very foolish act, to keep all that money at home, Mrs Ruffle?' the Superintendent addressed her loudly. 'We can't promise to get it back, you know.'

'Don't you lecture me, young man!' the old woman snapped. 'You just do get it back, that's all I want. He can't spend it yet awhile, can he, or the neighbours will get suspicious.'

'He?'

'The thief, the one who took it.'

'He may have used it to pay a debt outside the district. And we haven't any clue as to who took it at present.'

'Well, use your wits, you drumble-headed fool!' 'Mother!' said George, scandalized, but Mrs Ruffle went on undeterred, 'It must be someone who comes to the house regular, mustn't it, or Rover would have kicked up a shine. Who comes to the house regular? Well, there's Sid Curtis with the milk, young Tom Haynes the postman, my grandson Frank brings my groceries once a week, there's my son George here –' 'Mother! Really!' '– my daughter-in-law Doris, not that *she* comes more than once in a month of Sundays, there's Wally Turner reads the electric meter, Bernard Wiggan does a bit of digging for me when the pub's shut, Alf Dunning delivers the coal, and Luke Short and Jim Hamble from the council, they come and empty out my septic tank when it chocks up. So it must be one o' them, mustn't it?'

'That's all very well, missis,' the Superintendent pointed out, 'but that gives us quite a choice, doesn't it? Unless you have any idea which it might be?'

'Oh, I know who it is,' she said scornfully. The two men gaped at her.

'What do you mean, you know, Mother? How do you know?'

'I smelt him, didn't I?'

'You *smelt* him?'

'Folks smell different, don't they? *You*,' she said to the Superintendent, 'you smell of nice clean broadcloth. My son George mostly smells of cheese. Sid Curtis smells of pony. Tom Haynes smells of that flake tobacco he smokes; young Frank reeks of aftershave lotion, you can smell him halfway down the road; same with Wally Turner only with him it's those pigs he keeps; Doris uses white violets scent; Bernard always smells of the chips they fry in the public bar; Alf Dunning smells o' coal and sacking, very strong; Luke and Jim they smell of sewage, poor souls, how their wives can stand it I don't know, but we've all got to live I suppose.'

'But how can you possibly be sure?'

'If I'm not sure now,' said Mrs Ruffle, 'I'll be sure next time I smell him.'

'So which do you think it was?'

'Huh! I'm not telling you,' said Mrs Ruffle cunningly. 'Not unless you give me your promise you'll arrest him. Otherwise, what's to stop him cutting my throat first?'

'But, good heavens we can't arrest somebody just because you say you smelt him,' the Superintendent exclaimed, irritable with the effort of speaking loud enough to make her hear. 'A smell's not evidence.'

It took him a morning's arguing to persuade her that he really did not intend to proceed on her suggestion; when George finally took her home she had lost the temporary vigour induced by her belief that she could convince the Superintendent, and relapsed into her state of semi-shock. She sat listlessly in her armchair, paying no attention to George, who was telling her that now she must certainly leave her cottage and move in with him and Doris. 'You can't stay here alone any longer, Mother, do you understand? What'll you live on, for one thing?'

At that she roused up a little and said, 'I'll live on my old-age pension, like I always have. I just won't be able to buy any new stockings, that's all. Doris'll have to put up with mending me old ones, whether she likes it or not. Now get along with you George, *you* haven't been much use, have you? And don't you dare mention what I told that policeman unless you want me murdered in my bed.'

She locked up after the disgruntled George and then returned to sit muttering and twitching in her armchair, staring with a set, heavy face into the fire.

A month went by, during which time nobody in the village gave evidence of sudden and suspicious wealth. Various people were questioned by the police, without result; it became plain that the matter was going to be allowed to drop. The regular visitors paid their regular calls at Mrs Ruffle's cottage: Sid, Frank, Bernard came and went; Alf Dunning delivered coal; Doris made reluctant visits to her mother-in-law with mended stockings; the postman left an occasional card, which Mrs Ruffle could not read, from her married daughter in Canada. The warm June weather turned to a cold and rainy July; water brimmed along the dykes and lay in pools on the sodden marsh and in Mrs Ruffle's garden; predictably, her septic tank began to leak an evil-smelling trickle into the cellar and she sent a message to the council cleansing department asking them to come and pump her out.

And then one day at teatime Wally Turner came to read the electric meter.

It had been a dark, sodden afternoon; rain endlessly trickled off the thatch and overflowed from Mrs Ruffle's rainwater barrel; the saturated sheep huddled together and cried dolefully out on the marsh; Rover dozed in his kennel and Mrs Ruffle sat by a fistful of fire brooding about her empty teapot. Even now, she still sometimes momentarily believed that she might have been mistaken about her loss, and she would take the teapot from the cupboard, lift the lid, and feel wistfully inside, as if a bundle of notes might suddenly materialize there.

When Wally's knock came, Mrs Ruffle was in the back kitchen, putting on the kettle. Accustomed to open the door and walk in if she did not answer, Wally did so on this occasion and made his way through to the narrow passage where the meter was awkwardly sited in a dark corner under the stairs, beside the cellar door.

'Good afternoon, Wally,' Mrs Ruffle's voice behind his shoulder made him start; she was wearing felt slippers and he had not heard her come out of the kitchen.

'Hello, there, Mrs Ruffle,' he said loudly and nervously. 'Not got through quite so much current then, this time, by the look.'

'That's just as well, isn't it? Now all my savings are stolen, I need to cut down on spending.'

'I was sorry to hear about that, Mrs Ruffle,' he shouted.

'Were you, Wally?' She came up close to him and with apparent irrelevance asked, 'How are the pigs, then?' Her nostrils twitched slightly.

'Not so bad, Mrs Ruffle, but they don't like this weather.'

'Who does? I'm worried about my cellar, I can tell you; if the council don't come soon it's going to fill right up. Have a look at it, Wally, and say if you think the water's going to fuse my electric.'

'Oh, it ought to be all right,' he said, 'your wiring doesn't go through the cellar, does it?'

'Just the same, I wish you'd look and see, Wally.'

She unlocked the cellar door and opened it, letting out a dismaying stench of wet decay. With reluctance, Wally peered down the dark steps.

'Can you see where the water's got to?'

'It's too dark,' he said.

'Your eyes'll get used to it in a moment. Take a step down inside.'

He took a step down, she put the end of her stick against his back and gave a powerful shove. Slipping on the wet stone, he fell forward into the dark with a desperate cry, and a splash.

Mrs Ruffle shut and relocked the door.

'That'll teach you to help yourself to other folk's savings,' she shouted through the keyhole, and went back into the kitchen to finish making tea.

Wally, who had broken his leg, managed to drag himself painfully out of two foot of foul-smelling water and up the cellar stairs.

'It wasn't me, it wasn't me!' he moaned, beating on the door with his fists. And then, much later, 'Anyway, you can't prove it, you bloody old hag! You'll never see your money again.'

Mrs Ruffle paid no attention. His shouts were audible only at the back of the cottage, and not very distinctly even there; in any case, she had switched off her hearing-aid, and, after some consideration, dropped it from a height on the brick floor.

Next afternoon she plodded up to the post office, through the rain.

'You'll have to send this thing back to the hospital, George,' she said. 'It's gone wrong again.' She watched impassively while he parcelled and despatched it.

Luke Short was in the shop and she said, 'When's the council going to come and pump out my septic, Luke? The cellar's half full of water as it is; another few days of this weather and it'll be up to the top of the steps.'

'Very sorry, Mrs Ruffle,' Luke bawled at the top of his powerful lungs. 'We've had such a lot of calls, I reckon we're not liable to get round to you for another four or five days at least; say next Thursday.'

Uncertain whether she had understood, he took down the big post-office calendar, held it under her nose, and pointed to Thursday's date. Following his finger, she nodded slowly.

'Thursday? I'll have to be satisfied with that, then, shan't I? Thursday ought to just about do.'

And she hobbled slowly off down the village.

It rained for another week. After three days Mrs Ruffle decided that she would unlock the cellar door. By now the stench was noticeable even when the door was shut.

So she did not bother to open it and look inside.

Furry Night

The deserted aisles of the National Museum of Dramatic Art lay very, very still in the blue autumn twilight. Not a whisper of wind stirred the folds of Irving's purple cloak; Ellen Terry's ostrich fan was smooth and unruffled; the blue-black gleaming breastplate that Sir Murdoch Meredith, founder of the Museum, had worn as Macbeth held its reflections as quietly as a cottage kettle.

And yet, despite this hush, there was an air of strain, of expectancy, along the narrow coconut-matted galleries between the glass cases; a tension suggesting that some crisis had taken or was about to take place.

In the total stillness a listener might have imagined that he heard, ever so faintly, the patter of stealthy feet far away among the exhibits.

Two men, standing in the shadow of the Garrick showcase, were talking in low voices.

'This is where it happened,' said the elder, white-haired man.

He picked up a splinter of broken glass, frowned at it, and dropped it into a litter-bin. The glass had been removed from the front of the case, and some black tights and gilt medals hung exposed to the evening air.

'We managed to hush it up. The hospital and ambulance men will be discreet, of course. Nobody else was there, luckily. Only the Bishop was worried.'

'I should think so,' the younger man said. 'It's enough to make anybody anxious.'

'No, I mean he was *worried*. Hush,' the white-haired man whispered. 'Here comes Sir Murdoch.'

The distant susurration had intensified into soft, pacing

footsteps. The two men, without a word, stepped farther back in the shadow until they were out of sight. A figure appeared at the end of the aisle and moved forward until it stood beneath the portrait of Edmund Kean as Shylock. The picture, in its deep frame, was nothing but a square of dark against the wall.

Although they were expecting it, both men jumped when the haunted voice began to speak.

> You may as well use question with the wolf
> Why he hath made the ewe bleat for the lamb —

A sleeve of one of the watchers brushed against the wall, the lightest possible touch, but Sir Murdoch swung round sharply, his head out-thrust, teeth bared. They held their breath, and after a moment he turned back to the picture.

> Thy currish spirit
> Governed a wolf, who, hang'd for human slaughter,
> Even from the gallows did his fell soul fleet . . .

He paused, with a hand pressed to his forehead, and then leaned forward and hissed:

> Thy desires
> Are wolvish, bloody, starv'd, and ravenous!

His head sank on his chest. His voice ceased. He brooded for a moment, and then resumed his pacing and soon passed out of sight. They heard the steps go lightly down the stairs, and presently the whine of the revolving door.

After a prudent interval the two others emerged from their hiding-place, left the gallery, and went out to a car which was waiting for them in Great Smith Street.

'I wanted you to see that, Peachtree,' said the elder man, 'to give you some idea of what you are taking on. Candidly, as far as experience goes, I hardly feel you are qualified for the job, but you are young and tough, and have presence of mind; most important of all, Sir Murdoch seems to have taken a fancy to you. You will have to keep an unobtrusive eye on him every minute of the day; your job is a combination of secretary, companion, and resident psychiatrist. I have written to Dr Defoe, the local G P at Polgrue. He is old, but you will find him full of practical sense. Take his advice ... I think you said you were brought up in Australia?'

'Yes,' Ian Peachtree said. 'I only came to this country six months ago.'

'Ah, so you missed seeing Sir Murdoch act.'

'Was he so very wonderful?'

'He made the comedies too macabre,' said Lord Hawick, considering, 'but in the tragedies there was no one to touch him. His Macbeth was something to make you shudder. When he said:

> Alarum'd by his sentinel, the wolf,
> Whose howl's his watch, thus with his stealthy pace
> With Tarquin's ravishing strides, towards his design –
> Moves like a ghost –

he used to take two or three stealthy steps across the stage, and you could literally see the grey fur rise on his hackles, the lips drawn back from the fangs, the yellow eyes begin to gleam. It made a cold chill run down your spine. As Shylock and Caesar and Timon he was unrivalled. Othello and Antony he never touched, but his Iago was a masterpiece of villainy.'

'Why did he give it up? He can't be much over fifty.'

'As with other sufferers from lycanthropy,' said Lord Hawick, 'Sir Murdoch has an ungovernable temper. Whenever he flew into a rage it brought on an attack. They grew more and more frequent. A clumsy stagehand, a missed cue, might set him off; he'd begin to shake with rage and the terrifying change would take place.

'On stage it wasn't so bad; he had his audiences completely hypnotized and they easily accepted a grey-furred Iago padding across the stage with the handkerchief in his mouth. But off stage it was less easy; the claims for mauling and worrying were beginning to mount up; Equity objected. So he retired and, for some time, founding the Museum absorbed him. But now it's finished, his temper is becoming uncertain again. This afternoon, as you know, he pounced on the Bishop for innocently remarking that Garrick's Hamlet was the world's greatest piece of acting.'

'How do you deal with the attacks? What's the treatment?'

'Wolf's-bane. Two or three drops given in a powerful sedative will restore him for the time. Of course, administering it is the problem, as you can imagine. I only hope the surroundings in Cornwall will be sufficiently peaceful so that he is not provoked. It's a pity he never married; a woman's influence would be beneficial.'

'Why didn't he?'

'Jilted when he was thirty. Never looked at another woman. Some girl down at Polgrue, near his home. It was a real slap in the face; she wrote two days before the wedding saying she couldn't stand his temper. That began it all. This will be the first time he's been back there. Well, here we are,' said Lord Hawick, glancing out at his Harley Street doorstep. 'Come in and I'll give you the wolf's-bane prescription.'

The eminent consultant courteously held the door for his young colleague.

The journey to Cornwall was uneventful. Dr Peachtree drove his distinguished patient, glancing at him from time to time with mingled awe and affection. Would the harassing crawl down the A30, the jam in Exeter, the flat tyre on Dartmoor bring on an attack? Would he be able to cope if they

did? But the handsome profile remained unchanged, the
golden eyes in their deep sockets stayed the eyes of a man,
not those of a wolf, and Sir Murdoch talked entertainingly,
not at all discomposed by the delays. Ian was fascinated by
his tales of the theatre.

There was only one anxious moment, when they reached
the borders of Polgrue Chase. Sir Murdoch glanced angrily
at his neglected coverts, where the brambles grew long and
wild.

'Wait till I see that agent,' he muttered, and then, half
to himself, 'O, thou wilt be a wilderness again, Peopled
with wolves.'

Ian devoutly hoped that the agent would have a good
excuse.

But the Hall, hideous Victorian-Gothic barrack though it
was, they found gay with lights and warm with welcome.
The old housekeeper wept over Sir Murdoch, bottles were
uncorked, the table shone with ancestral silver. Ian began
to feel less apprehensive.

After dinner they moved outside with their nuts and wine
to sit in the light that streamed over the terrace from the
dining-room french windows. A great walnut tree hung
shadowy above them; its golden, aromatic leaves littered the
flagstones at their feet.

'This place has a healing air,' Sir Murdoch said. 'I should
have come here sooner.' Suddenly he stiffened. 'Hudson!
Who are those?'

Far across the park, almost out of sight in the dusk, figures
were flitting among the trees.

'Eh,' said the housekeeper comfortably, 'they're none
but the lads, Sir Murdoch, practising for the Furry Race.
Don't you worrit about them. They won't do no harm.'

'On my land?' Sir Murdoch said. 'Running across my
land?'

Ian saw with a sinking heart that his eyes were turning to

gleaming yellow slits, his hands were stiffening and curling. Would the housekeeper mind? Did she know her master was subject to these attacks? He felt in his pocket for the little ampoules of wolf's-bane, the hypodermic syringe.

There came an interruption. A girl's clear voice was heard singing:

> Now the hungry lion roars,
> And the wolf behowls the moon —

'It's Miss Clarissa,' said the housekeeper with relief.

A slender figure swung round the corner of the terrace and came towards them.

'Sir Murdoch? How do you do? I'm Clarissa Defoe. My father sent me up to pay his respects. He would have come himself, but he was called out on a case. Isn't it a gorgeous night?'

Sitting down beside them she chatted amusingly and easily, while Ian observed with astonished delight that his employer's hands were unclenching and his eyes were becoming their normal shape again. If this girl was able to soothe Sir Murdoch without recourse to wolf's-bane they must see a lot of her.

But when Sir Murdoch remarked that the evening was becoming chilly and proposed that they go indoors, Ian's embryonic plan received a jolt. He was a tough and friendly young man who had never taken a great deal of interest in girls; the first sight, in lamplight, of Clarissa Defoe's wild beauty came on him with a shattering impact. Could he expose her to danger without warning her?

More and more enslaved, he sat gazing as Clarissa played and sang Ariel's songs. Sir Murdoch seemed completely charmed and relaxed. When Clarissa left, he let Ian persuade him to bed without the topic of the Furry Race coming up again.

Next morning, however, when Ian went down to the

village for a consultation with cheerful, shrewd-eyed old Dr Defoe, he asked about it.

'Heh,' said the doctor. 'The Furry Race? My daughter revived it five years ago. There's two villages, ye see, Polgrue, and Lostmid, and there's this ball, what they call the Furry Ball. It's not furry; it's made of applewood with a silver band round the middle, and on the band is written,

From Lotsmid Parish iff I goe
Heddes will be broke and bloode will flowe.

'The ball is kept in Lostmid and on the day of the race one of the Polgrue lads has to sneak in and take it and get it over the parish boundary before anybody stops him. Nobody's succeeded in doing it yet. But why do you ask?'

Ian explained about the scene the night before.

'Eh, I see; that's awkward. You're afraid it may bring on an attack if he sees them crossing his land? Trouble is, that's the quickest short cut over the parish boundary.'

'If your daughter withdrew her support, would the race be abandoned?'

'My dear feller, she'd never do that. She's mad about it. She's a bit of a tomboy, Clarissa, and the roughhousing amuses her — always is plenty of horseplay, even though they don't get the ball over the boundary. If her mother were still alive now ... Bless my soul!' the old doctor burst out, looking troubled, 'I wish Meredith had never come back to these parts, that I do. You can speak with Clarissa about it, but I doubt you'll not persuade her. She's out looking over the course now.'

The two villages of Lostmid and Polgrue lay in deep adjacent glens, and Polgrue Chase ended on the stretch of high moorland that ran between them. There was a crossroads and a telephone box, used by both villages. A spinney of wind-bitten beeches stood in one angle of the cross, and Clarissa was thoughtfully surveying this terrain. Ian joined her, turning to look back towards the Hall, and noticing with relief that Sir Murdoch was still, as he had been left, placidly knocking a ball round his private golf course.

It was a stormy, shining day. Ian saw that Clarissa's hair was exactly the colour of the sea-browned beech leaves and that the strange angles of her face were emphasized by the wild shafts of sunlight glancing through the trees.

He put his difficulties to her.

'Oh dear,' she said, wrinkling her brow. 'How unfortunate. The boys are so keen on the race. I don't think they'd ever give it up.'

'Couldn't they go some other way?'

'But this is the only possible way, don't you see? In the old days, of course, all this used to be common land.'

'Do you know who the runner is going to be – the boy with the ball?' Ian asked, wondering if a sufficiently heavy bribe would persuade him to take a longer way round.

But Clarissa smiled with innocent topaz eyes. 'My dear, that's never decided until the very *last* minute. So that the Lostmidians don't know who's going to dash in and snatch the ball. But I'll tell you what we *can* do – we can arrange for the race to take place at night, so that Sir Murdoch won't be worried by the spectacle. Yes, that's an excellent idea; in fact it will make it far more exciting. It's next Thursday, you know.'

Ian was not at all sure that he approved of this idea, but just then he noticed Sir Murdoch having difficulties in a bunker. A good deal of sand was flying about, and his employer's face was becoming a dangerous dusky red. 'Here in the sands, Thee I'll rake up,' he was muttering angrily, and something about murderous lechers.

Ian ran down to him and suggested that it was time for a glass of beer, waving to Clarissa as he did so. Sir Murdoch noticed her and was instantly mollified. He invited her to join them.

Ian, by now head over heels in love, was torn between his professional duty, which could not help pointing out to him how beneficial Clarissa's company was for his patient, and a strong personal feeling that the elderly wolfish baronet was not at all suitable company for Clarissa. Worse, he suspected that she guessed his anxiety and was laughing at it.

The week passed peacefully enough. Sir Murdoch summoned the chairmen of the two parish councils and told them that any trespass over his land on the day of the Furry Race would be punished with the utmost rigour. They listened with blank faces. He also ordered man-traps and spring-guns from the Dominion and Colonial Stores, but to Ian's relief it seemed highly unlikely that these would arrive in time.

Clarissa dropped in frequently. Her playing and singing seemed to have as soothing an effect on Sir Murdoch as the songs of the harpist David on touchy old Saul, but Ian had the persistent feeling that some peril threatened from her presence.

On Furry Day she did not appear. Sir Murdoch spent most of the day pacing – loping was really the word for it, Ian thought – distrustfully among his far spinneys, but no trespasser moved in the bracken and dying leaves. Towards evening a fidgety scuffling wind sprang up, and Ian persuaded his employer indoors.

'No one will come, Sir Murdoch, I'm sure. Your notices have scared them off. They'll have gone another way.' He wished he really did feel sure of it. He found a performance of *Caesar and Cleopatra* on TV and switched it on, but Shaw seemed to make Sir Murdoch impatient. Presently he got up, began to pace about, and turned it off, muttering:

And why should Caesar be a tyrant, then?
Poor man ! I know he would not be a wolf !

He swung round on Ian. 'Did I do wrong to shut them off my land?'

'Well,' Ian was temporizing when there came an outburst of explosions from Lostmid, hidden in the valley, and a dozen rockets soared into the sky beyond the windows.

'That means someone's taken the Furry Ball,' said Hudson, coming in with the decanter of sherry. 'Been long enough about it, seemingly.'

Sir Murdoch's expression changed completely. One stride took him to the french window. He opened it, and went streaking across the park. Ian bolted after him.

'Stop! Sir Murdoch, stop!'

Sir Murdoch turned an almost unrecognizable face and hissed, 'Wake not a sleeping wolf!' He kept on his way, with Ian stubbornly in pursuit. They came out by the crossroads and, looking down to Lostmid, saw that it was a circus of wandering lights, clustering, darting this way and that.

'They've lost him,' Ian muttered. 'No, there he goes!'

One of the lights broke off at a tangent and moved away down the valley, then turned and came straight for them diagonally across the hillside.

'I'll have to go and warn him off,' Ian thought. 'Can't let him run straight into trouble.' He ran downhill towards the approaching light. Sir Murdoch stole back into the shade of the spinney. Nothing of him was visible but two golden glowing eye-points.

It was at this moment that Clarissa, having established her red-herring diversion by sending a boy with a torch across the hillside, ran swiftly and silently up the steep road towards the signpost. She wore trousers and a dark sweater, and was clutching the Furry Ball in her hand.

Sir Murdoch heard the pit-pat of approaching footsteps, waited for his moment, and sprang.

It was the thick fisherman's-knit jersey with its roll collar that saved her. They rolled over and over, girl and wolf entangled, and then she caught him a blow on the jaw with the heavy applewood ball, dropped it, scrambled free, and was away. She did not dare look back. She had a remarkable turn of speed, but the wolf was overtaking her. She hurled herself into the telephone box and let the door clang to behind her.

The wolf arrived a second later; she heard the impact as the grey, sinewy body struck the door, saw the gleam of teeth through the glass. Methodically, though with shaking hands, she turned to dial.

Meanwhile Ian had met the red-herring boy just as his triumphant pursuers caught up with him.

'You mustn't go that way!' Ian gasped. 'Sir Murdoch's waiting up there and he's out for blood.'

'Give over that thurr ball,' yelled the Lostmidians.

' 'Tisn't on me,' the boy yelled back, regardless of the fact that he was being pulled limb from limb. 'Caught ye properly, me fine fules. 'Tis Miss Clarissa's got it, and she'm gone backaway.'

'*What?*'

Ian waited for no more. He left them to their battle, in which some Polgrue reinforcements were now joining, and bounded back up the murderous ascent to where he had left Sir Murdoch.

The scene at the telephone box was brilliantly lit by the overhead light. Clarissa had finished her call, and was watching with detached interest as the infuriated wolf threw himself repeatedly against the door.

It is not easy to address your employer in such circumstances.

Ian chose a low, controlled, but vibrant tone.

'Down, Sir Murdoch,' he said. 'Down, sir! Heel!'

Sir Murdoch turned on him a look of golden, thunderous wrath. He was really a fine spectacle, with his eyes flashing, and great ruff raised in rage. He must have weighed all of a hundred and thirty pounds. Ian thought he might be a timber-wolf, but was not certain. He pulled the ampoule from his pocket, charged the syringe, and made a cautious approach. Instantly Sir Murdoch flew at him. With a feint like a bull-fighter's, Ian dodged round the call-box.

'Olé,' Clarissa shouted approvingly, opening the door a crack. Sir Murdoch instantly turned and battered it again.

'Avaunt, thou damned door-keeper!' shouted Ian. The result was electrifying. The wolf dropped to the ground as if stunned. Ian seized advantage of the moment to give him his injection, and immediately the wolf-shape vanished, dropping off Sir Murdoch like a label off a wet bottle. He gasped, shivered, and shut his eyes.

'Where am I?' he said presently, opening them again. Ian took his arm, gently led him away from the door, and made him sit on a grassy bank.

'You'll feel better in a minute or two, sir,' he said, and, since Shakespeare seemed so efficacious, added, 'The cure whereof, my lord, 'Tis time must do.' Sir Murdoch weakly nodded.

Clarissa came out of her refuge. 'Are you all right now, Sir Murdoch?' she asked kindly. 'Shall I sing you a song?'

'All right, thank you, my dear,' he murmured. 'What are you doing here?' and he added to himself, 'I really must not fly into these rages. I feel quite dizzy.'

Ian stepped aside and picked up something that glinted on the ground.

'What's that?' asked Sir Murdoch with awakening interest. 'It reminds me – May I see it?'

'Oh, it's my medallion,' said Clarissa at the same moment. 'It must have come off ...' Her voice trailed away. They both watched Sir Murdoch. Deep, fearful shudders were running through him.

'Where did you get this?' he demanded, turning his

cavernous eyes on Clarissa. His fingers were rigid, clenched on the tiny silver St Francis.

'It was my mother's,' she said faintly. For the first time she seemed frightened.

'Was her name Louisa?' She nodded. 'Then, your father –?'

'Here comes my father now,' said Clarissa with relief. The gnarled figure of the doctor was approaching them through the spinney. Sir Murdoch turned on him like a javelin.

'O thou foul thief!' he hissed. 'My lost Louisa! Stol'n from me and corrupted by spells and medicines.'

'Oh, come, come, come,' said the doctor equably, never slowing his approach, though he kept a wary eye on Sir Murdoch. 'I wouldn't put it quite like that. She came to me. *I* was looking forward to bachelorhood.'

'For the which I may go the finer, I will live a bachelor,' murmured Ian calmingly.

'And I'll tell ye this, Sir Murdoch,' Defoe went on, tucking his arm through that of Sir Murdoch like an old friend, 'you were well rid of her.' He started strolling at a gentle but purposeful pace back towards the Hall, and the baronet went with him doubtfully.

'Why is that?' Already Sir Murdoch sounded half convinced, quiescent.

'Firstly, my dear sir, Temper. Out of this world! Secondly, Macaroni Cheese. Every night till one begged for mercy. Thirdly, Unpunctuality. Fourthly, long, horrifying Dreams, which she insisted on telling at breakfast . . .'

Pursuing this soothing, therapeutic vein, the doctor's voice moved farther away, and the two men were lost in the shadows.

'So that's all right,' said Clarissa on a deep breath of relief. 'Why Ian!'

Pent-up agitation was too much for him. He had grabbed

her in his arms like a drowning man. 'I was sick with fright for you,' he muttered, into her hair, her ear, the back of her neck. 'I was afraid – oh well, never mind.'

'Never mind,' she agreed. 'Are we going to get married?'

'Of course.'

'I ought to find my Furry Ball,' she said presently. 'They seem to be having a pitched battle down below; there's a good chance of getting it over the boundary while everyone's busy.'

'But Sir Murdoch –'

'Father will look after him.'

She moved a few steps away and soon found the ball. 'Come on; through the wood is quickest. We have to put it on the Polgrue churchyard wall.'

No one accosted them as they ran through the wood. Fireworks and shouting in the valley suggested that Lostmid and Polgrue had sunk their differences in happy saturnalia.

'Full surgery tomorrow,' remarked Clarissa, tucking the Furry Ball into its niche. 'Won't someone be surprised to see this.'

When Ian and Clarissa strolled up to the terrace, they found Sir Murdoch and the doctor amiably drinking port. Sir Murdoch looked like a man who had had a festering grief removed from his mind.

'Well,' the doctor said cheerfully, 'we've cleared up some misunderstandings.'

But Sir Murdoch had stood up and gone to meet Clarissa.

'As I am a man,' he said gravely, 'I do think this lady To be my child.'

The two pairs of golden eyes met and acknowledged each other.

'That'll be the end of his little trouble, I shouldn't wonder,' murmured the doctor. 'Specially if she'll live at the Hall and keep an eye on him.'

'But she's going to marry me.'

'All the better, my dear boy. All the better. And glad I shall be to get rid of her, bless her heart.'

Ian looked doubtfully across the terrace at his future father-in-law, but he recalled that wolves are among the most devoted fathers of the animal kingdom. Sir Murdoch was stroking Clarissa's hair with an expression of complete peace and happiness.

Then a thought struck Ian. 'If *he's* her father –'

But Dr Defoe was yawning. 'I'm off to bed. Busy day tomorrow.' He vanished among the dark trees.

So they were married, and lived happily at the Hall. Clarissa's slightest wish was law. She was cherished equally by both father and husband, and if they went out of their way not to cross her in any particular, this was due quite as much to the love they bore her as to their knowledge that they had dangerous material on their hands.

As Gay as Cheese

Mr Pol the barber always wore white overalls. He must have had at least six, for every day he was snowy white and freshly starched as a marguerite, his blue eyes, red face and bulbous nose appearing incongruously over the top of the bib. His shop looked like, and was, a kitchen, roughly adapted to barbering with a mirror, basin and some pictures of beautiful girls on the whitewashed walls. It was a long narrow crack of a room with the copper at one end and a tottering flight of steps at the other, leading down to the street; customers waiting their turn mostly sat on the steps in the sun, risking piles and reading *Men Only*.

Mr Pol rented his upstairs room to an artist, and in the summertime when the customers had been shaved or trimmed they sometimes went on up the stairs and bought a view of the harbour, water or oil, or a nice still life. The artist had an unlimited supply of these, which he whipped out with the dexterity of a card sharper.

Both men loved their professions. When the artist was not painting fourteen by ten inch squares for the trippers, he was engaged on huge, complicated panels of mermaids, sharks, all mixed up with skulls, roses and cabbages, while Mr Pol hung over the heads of his customers as if he would have liked to gild them.

'Ah, I'm as gay as cheese this morning,' he used to say, bustling into his kitchen with a long, gnomish look at the first head of hair waiting to be shorn. 'I'll smarten you up till you're like a new button mushroom.'

'Now I'm as bright as a pearl,' he would exclaim when the long rays of the early sun felt their way back to the copper with an under-water glimmer.

When Mr Pol laid hands on a customer's head he knew more about that man than his mother did at birth, or his sweetheart or confessor – not only his past misdeeds but his future ones, what he had had for breakfast and would have for supper, the name of his dog and the day of his death. This should have made Mr Pol sad or cynical, but it did not. He remained impervious to his portentous gift. Perhaps this was because the destinies of the inhabitants of a small Cornish town contained nothing very startling, and Mr Pol's divinings seldom soared higher or lower than a double twenty or a sprained ankle.

He never cut his own hair, and had no need to, for he was as bald as an egg.

'It was my own hair falling out that started me thinking on the matter,' he told the artist. 'All a man's nature comes out in the way his hair grows. It's like a river – watch the currents and you can tell what it's come through, what sort of fish are in it, how fast it's running, how far to the sea.'

The artist grunted. He was squatting on the floor, stretching a canvas, and made no reply. He was a taciturn man, who despised the trippers for buying his pink and green views.

Mr Pol looked down at the top of his head and suddenly gave it an affectionate, rumpling pat, as one might to a large woolly dog.

'Ah, that's a nice head of hair. It's a shame you won't let me get at it.'

'And have you knowing when I'm going to eat my last bite of bacon? Not likely.'

'I wouldn't tell you, my handsome!' said Mr Pol, very shocked. 'I'm not one to go measuring people for their coffins before they're ready to step in. I'm as close as a false tooth. There's Sam now, off his lorry, the old ruin; I could tell a thing or two about him, but do I?'

He stumped off down the stairs, letting out a snatch of hymn in his powerful baritone.

'And there's some say,' he went on, as he sculpted with his shears round the driver's wicked grey head, 'that you can grow turnip from carrot seed under the right moon. Who'd want to do that, I ask you?'

'Shorter round the ears,' grumbled Sam, scowling down into the enamel basin.

When the night train from Paddington began to draw down the narrow valley towards the sea town, Brian and Fanny Dexter stood up stiffly from the seats where they had slept and started moving their luggage about. Brian was surly and silent, only remarking that it was damned cold and he hoped he could get a shave and a cup of coffee. Fanny glanced doubtfully at her reflection in the little greenish mirror. A white face and narrow eyes, brilliant from lack of sleep, glanced back at her.

'It'll be fine later,' she said hopefully. Brian pulled on a sweater without comment. He looked rough but expensive, like a suede shoe. His thick light hair was beginning to grey, but hardly showed it.

'Lady Ward and Penelope said they'd be getting to Pengelly this week,' Brian observed. 'We might walk along the cliff path later on and see if they've arrived yet. We can do with some exercise to warm us and they'll be expecting us to call.'

'I must do my shopping first. It's early closing, and there's all the food to lay in.'

Brian shot her an angry look and she was reminded that although the ice of their marriage seemed at the moment to be bearing, nevertheless there were frightening depths beneath and it was best not to loiter in doubtful spots.

'It won't take long,' she said hurriedly.

'It was just an idea,' Brian muttered, bundling up a camel-hair overcoat. 'Here we are, thank God.'

It was still only nine in the morning. The town was grey and forbidding, tilted steeply down to a white sea. The fleet was out; the streets smelt of fish and emptiness. After they had had coffee Brian announced that he was going to get his shave.

'I'll do my shopping and meet you,' suggested Fanny.

'No you bloody well won't, or you'll wander off for hours and I shall have to walk half over the town looking for you,' snapped Brian. 'You could do with a haircut yourself, you look like a scotch terrier.'

'All right.'

She threaded her way after him between the empty tables of the café and across the road into Mr Pol's shop. Mr Pol was carefully rearranging his tattered magazines.

'Good morning my handsome,' he cautiously greeted Fanny's jeans and sweater and Eton crop, assessing her as a summer visitor.

'Can you give me a shave and my wife a haircut please?' cut in Brian briskly.

Mr Pol looked from one to the other of them.

'I'll just put the kettle on for the shave, sir,' he answered, moving leisurely to the inner room, 'and then I'll trim the young lady, if you'd like to take a seat in the meanwhile.'

Brian preferred to stroll back and lean against the door-post with his hands in his pockets, while Mr Pol wreathed Fanny's neck in a spotless towel. Her dark head, narrow as a boy's, was bent forward, and he looked benignly at the swirl of glossy hair, flicked a comb through it, and turned her head gently with the palms of his hands.

As he did so, a shudder like an electric shock ran through him and he started back, the comb between his thumb and forefinger jerking upward like a diviner's rod. Neither of the other two noticed; Brian was looking out into the street and Fanny had her eyes on her hands which were locked together with white knuckles across a fold of the towel.

After a moment Mr Pol gingerly replaced his palms on the sides of her head with a pretence of smoothing the downy hair above the ears, and again the shock ran through him. He looked into the mirror, almost expecting to see fish swimming and seaweed floating around her. Death by drowning, and so soon ; he could smell salt water and see her thin arm stretch sideways in the wave.

'Don't waste too much time on her,' said Brian looking at his watch. 'She doesn't mind what she looks like.'

Fanny glanced up and met Mr Pol's eyes in the glass. There was such a terrified appeal in her look that his hands closed instinctively on her shoulders and his lips shaped to form the words:

'There, there, my handsome. Never mind,' before he saw that her appeal was directed, not to him, but to her own reflection's pathetic power to please.

'That's lovely,' she said to Mr Pol with a faint smile, and stood up, shaking the glossy dark tufts off her. She sat on one of his chairs, looking at a magazine while Brian took her place and Mr Pol fetched his steaming kettle.

'You're visiting the town ?' Mr Pol asked, as he rubbed up the lather on his brush. He felt the need for talk.

'Just come off the night train; we're staying here, yes,' Brian said shortly.

'It's a pretty place,' Mr Pol remarked. 'Plenty of grand walks if you're young and active.'

'We're going along to Pengelly by the cliff path this morning,' said Brian.

'Oh, but I thought you only said we *might* –' Fanny began incautiously, and then bit off her words.

Brian shot her a look of such hatred that even Mr Pol caught it, and scuttled into the next room for another razor.

'For Christ's sake *will* you stop being so damned negative,' Brian muttered to her furiously.

'But the groceries –'

'Oh, to hell with the groceries. We'll eat out. Lady Ward and Penelope will think it most peculiar if we don't call – they know we're here. I suppose you want to throw away a valuable social contact for the sake of a couple of ounces of tea. I can't think why you need to do this perpetual shopping – Penelope never does.'

'I only thought –'

'Never mind what you thought.'

Mr Pol came back and finished the shave.

'That's a nice head of hair, sir,' he said, running his hand over it professionally. 'Do you want a trim at all?'

'No thanks,' replied Brian abruptly. 'Chap in the Burlington Arcade always does it for me. Anything wrong?'

Mr Pol was staring at the ceiling above Brian's head in a puzzled way.

'No – no, sir, nothing. Nothing at all. I thought for a moment I saw a bit of rope hanging down, but it must have been fancy.' Nevertheless Mr Pol passed his hand once more above Brian's head with the gesture of someone brushing away cobwebs.

'Will that be all? Thank you, sir. Mind how you go on that path to Pengelly. 'Tis always slippery after the rain and we've had one or two falls of rock this summer; all this damp weather loosens them up.'

'We'll be all right, thanks,' said Brian, who had been walking out of the door without listening to what Mr Pol was saying. 'Come on, Fanny.' He swung up the street with Fanny almost running behind him.

'Have they gone? Damnation, I thought I could sell them a view of the cliffs,' said the artist, coming in with a little canvas. 'Hullo, something the matter?'

For the barber was standing outside his door and staring in indecision and distress after the two figures, now just taking the turning up to the cliff path.

'No,' he said at last, turning heavily back and picking up his broom. 'No, I'm as gay as cheese.'

And he began sweeping up the feathery tufts of dark hair from his stone floor.

Sultan's Splash

'Norman is free, now, Henry,' the secretary said, and gave
him a five-amp smile. Through Norman's open door —
Dobbs-Journeyman Publicity discouraged closed office doors
and were known to ease out executives who were over-keen
on privacy – the Copy Chief had been visible reading the
New Yorker for the last five minutes, but Henry pretended
not to have noticed this. As he entered, Norman began to
scuffle in an important way among the papers on his desk.
Henry patiently studied the familiar props: the fever-pink
carpet, the palm-tree growing upside down from the ceiling
with the Dobbs-Journeyman slogan, 'We can lick Gravity
too', wreathed about its trunk. It needed pruning.

Norman looked up with a dazzling smile.

'Well, Henry! What can we do for you, so early in the
morning?'

'I'd like the day off, Norman, if you don't mind. My
aunt's dying.'

The smile grew infinitesimally less dazzling.

'Rather a *banal* excuse, dear boy?'

Someone had once said in Norman's hearing that if he had
gone into the church he would have made a good cardinal,
and since then he had adopted a subtly paternal attitude towards his staff, giving them inscrutable Monsignor-
like smiles and encouraging them to confide in him by a
manner that combined teasing camaraderie with honest,
manly sympathy. On some people it worked very well. He
slumped back in his swivel chair now and regarded Henry
quizzically; he was a squarely built man with a square
smiling face, a mass of curly black hair, and an unusually

large mouth. His copywriters said that you could see Norman smiling even when you stood behind his back. He wore a white suit and a rosebud in his buttonhole.

'You know, Henry boy, if you take many more days off I shall begin to think you don't *love* us? And since you *have* dropped in, I think I should mention that your work lately has been just a scrap – shall we say – uninspired? Maybe we don't stimulate you enough here, Henry? I wonder if another job, just for a breath of fresh air, might be beneficial? Just for a couple of years, say? Then, *of course*, we'd welcome you back with open arms.'

Of course, Henry thought; if I came with a lot of other people's ideas.

'I'm sure Blather and Pother would *jump* at the chance of securing you,' Norman ended, beaming, his eyes Cheshire-cat slits of fun and friendship. With a strong effort, Henry refrained from putting his hand into the pocket where Blather and Pother's letter regretted they could not avail themselves of his talent at present.

'But to return to your story, dear child. Ah, if only some of this imagination could be canalized!'

'I'm afraid it's the truth,' Henry said stolidly, and held out a telegram. It read: I SHALL DIE TONIGHT AT 10.08 P.M. CAN YOU ARRANGE TO BE THERE? LURLINE HAMMER-STALL.

Norman raised his brows over this. 'Suicide?' he inquired.

'No, she's always said she'd have a presentiment when the time came. She's ninety-five.'

'Lurline Hammerstall,' mused Norman. 'Why does that name ring a bell?'

'She was a romantic novelist in the 'nineties. *A Broken Blossom, Ten days in the Desert, Passion's Oasis.*'

'Of course. And didn't she run off to Constantinople with the Chancellor of the Exchequer?'

'Baghdad with the Foreign Secretary,' Henry corrected.
'Lord Barbilliard. It was a famous scandal.'

'So it was. People sang a song about it, didn't they:

> I'd rather ride on a camel with Barbie
> Than frivol at Ascot or win on the Derby:
> I'd rather spoon by the Sphinx with Lurline
> Than speak to the Commons or chat with the Queen.

What ever became of Barbilliard?'

'He died in the desert in some obscure way; I think it was
said he caught a tropical disease. Lurline subsequently married the Sheikh Ibn al Fuaz el Mezzat al Kebir. When *he*
died, twenty years later, she came back to England with her
three-legged crocodile and settled down in Dorset. I'm her
great-nephew and only living relative.'

'What glamour, my dear! Of course I can see that you
must certainly be at her deathbed. Perhaps she'll leave you
a fortune – her books sold like hot cakes in the 'nineties,
didn't they?'

'She spent all the money on *confort moderne* for the
Sheikh; she has nothing but an annuity.'

'Too bad,' Norman said gaily. 'Well – think over our
chat on your trip, won't you? By the way, I'm moving you
off your present accounts – just for a little change, just for a
breath of fresh air.'

'What are you giving me?' Henry asked, with a horrible
sinking feeling.

'Speedwell Butter.'

'Nothing else?'

'Just to concentrate your abilities, dear child. So be thinking up some *really* scintillating, really creative ideas for
tomorrow, will you, and we'll have a little meeting as soon
as you come in.'

Speedwell Butter! If Norman had thrown a lump of the
stuff at him the news could not have come with a more

dismal squelch. Speedwell Butter, made, allegedly, from residues of several other butters and cooking-fats, had been a non-seller for twenty years, and was among the dregs at the bottom of the Dobbs-Journeyman barrel. Sitting in the train, Henry let his mind teeter distractedly between apprehensions of his aunt's deathbed – what did one do at a deathbed, anyway? – and alarm at the poverty-stricken quality of his ideas about butter. The only thing in Speedwell's favour was that it cost little more than other brands: it had an unpleasant oily taste and tended to disintegrate to a puddle if the thermometer rose more than a few degrees above zero centigrade. Henry saw dismissal staring him in the face; he would not be the first copywriter sped out of Dobbs-Journeyman on a Speedwell slide.

An aged taxi met him at Loose Chippings station; the driver gave the impression of having only just removed a straw from his mouth.

'So the old lady's failing at last?' he said, as they ground along the high-banked lanes. 'Ah, she'll be a sad loss, she will. They don't come like that no more. She'll be missed despert bad in these parts, that's suttin.'

'Oh?' Henry said. 'I'd no idea she was a well-known character.'

'She be mortial clever wi' her unguments and linimations; ah, her linctuary for Megrim of the Bowel have saved many a soul from old Dr Wassop's clutches. Folk comes to her from far and near for poltuses and elixatives.'

If this was so, it was plain that Miss Hammerstall made no great profit from her activities, for her cottage was dilapidated to a degree, and could hardly be seen for the unpruned creepers smothering its exterior. The front garden was overgrown and neglected, but rows of neat plants were visible at the rear, casting long shadows in the light of the setting sun. Miss Hammerstall herself stood by the gate, bidding affectionate good-bye to a pretty dark-haired girl who looked rather tearful and carried a basket.

'Ah, Henry! How good of you to come. Tansy, this is my nephew, Henry Hammerstall; my god-daughter, Tansy Argew. Adieu, then, Tansy, precious girl; I know you will remember all I've told you. Henry, come in; you must be dying for food.'

Aunt Lurline did not look as if she were within four hours of presumptive death; nor did she look ninety-five; she might have been a healthy, wind-browned sixty. Traces of great beauty remained in her delicate, aquiline features and her eyes were remarkable: a dark, Mediterranean blue, unfaded by age.

Over couscous, kebab, and Turkish coffee, she explained why she had asked Henry to come.

'You hear that knocking, dear boy?'

Not being deaf, he could hardly fail to. He had been thinking it an odd time to inaugurate what sounded like extensive repairs to the roof.

'No, it isn't workmen, it's rappings. Spirits, that is to say. I sent you the telegram as soon as it started; Barbie always promised he'd give me twenty-four hours' warning. Dear me, I *am* looking forward to seeing Barbie again; he was always so entertaining, dear fellow! That's why I asked you down, Henry. I fear I am sadly out of touch with public affairs now, and I know Barbie will expect to hear all the latest political gossip, so I want you to spend the next few hours giving me a good briefing. Oh, before you start I should mention that I have made you my literary executor.'

Henry expressed his gratification.

'There's no money in it,' Lurline said frankly. 'All my books have long been out of print – unless you can do something with my unpublished manuscript – *Jottings from a Desert Diary*.' She gave him a large battered black folder crammed with loose and rather grimy pages. 'Tansy, of course, inherits the cottage, which would be no use to you; she will keep on my practice and look after the herbs and the crocodile pool.'

'Pool?'

'In memory of poor Fuaz, you remember him? He died three years ago, faithful fellow; crocodiles do not really thrive in this climate. There's his anklet hanging on the wall.'

Henry remembered that the crocodile had always worn a gold band on his right foreleg.

'But now, Henry, to work! From dear Barbie's rappings I infer he is just as impatient as I for our reunion, so pray, without delay, tell me all the scandals; you are such a young man of affairs! Which party is in power at present, and who is premier?'

The next three hours were almost as exacting for Henry as one of Norman's little meetings, but he came through with fair credit; luckily he took a keen interest in current affairs (he would have liked to go in for politics had he not been under the sad necessity of earning a living) and was friendly with several Fleet Street journalists, so that he was able to give Lurline the inside stories she demanded.

At a few minutes past ten she said, 'Thank you, my dear boy; you have been a great help. Now: I had better just powder my nose – *so* – and a touch of perfume – Fuaz was always so fond of this Attar of Roses.' Henry wondered if she was referring to the crocodile or to her second husband the Sheikh Ibn al Fuaz.

'By the way,' she said, 'if there is anything you don't understand among the jottings, Tansy will help you, but remember – discretion always! There are some powerful –'

Her voice died away. Henry looked at his watch. It was exactly 10.08 p.m. The rappings had ceased and the cottage was extremely quiet. He gently and respectfully covered his aunt's face with a fold of her lace burnous, went up to bed, and slept soundly.

Next day, having left the funeral arrangements in the capable hands of Tansy and Dr Wassop, he caught a train back to London and spent the journey absorbed in Lurline's *Desert Jottings*.

'*June 7th, 1889* By the caravan across Rub' al Khali; at Little Hufhuf Oasis we encountered Sheikh Ibn al Fuaz el Mezzat al Kebir with his retinue. The sheikh v. gracious. Invited us both to sherbet.

'*June 9th* Sheikh I al F. el M. al K. suggested we continue our journey together. I was delighted at prospect, but Barbie less so; he had not altogether taken to Fuaz; says some of his ideas not cricket!! I, however, find the Sheikh a *complete gentleman*. Unfortunately desert life does not really suit Barbie; the insects annoy him terribly & he misses his club.

'*June 18th* Sheikh Fuaz lent me Arab mare, took me on delightful gallop after antelope. Scenery v. romantic!!! A most exhilarating excursion. Barbie, I am sorry to say, remained in tent all day, *sulking*. In evening played chess with S. F.

'*July 4th* Fuaz has given me a collar of pink pearls in requital for rubbing his housemaid's knee. Such a pretty colour! B v. disagreeable; says in any case they will *fade*. Chess again in evening; French defence.'

Here, unfortunately, there came a gap in the journal; all these entries had been written on one sheet, and, search as he would, Henry could not find the continuation. The next sheet began in the middle.

'. . . still miss poor B. sadly. Who would have expected such a result from the immersion?! But perhaps it was for the best. Desert life did *not* suit him & he had repeatedly begged me to return with him to Weybridge. He is happier as it is. Sh. Fuaz *most* gentlemanly & considerate; begs me to look on the Royal Tent as my own, & has presented me with a *delicious* opal-studded belt. Also provided a portable water tank, thoughtful creature! Chess till 2 a.m.'

What could be the use of a portable water tank? Henry wondered. The journal did not declare. He browsed on, finding a thread of narrative here and a thread there, casually mixed among oriental-sounding recipes, purple patches of verse, some unskilled but evocative sketches of camels, robed figures, and palm-trees, remedies for illnesses, historical and topographical notes. In fact a sort of Arabian Mrs Beeton, he mused, reading on:

'The Camel. A useful but ill-condition'd animal which, on account of its curious Stomach, can travel for ??? miles without water at ??? miles per hour. To cure camel-gall: immerse the afflicted part in Hot Tar for half an hour. (Considerable force and resolution are needed.)'

From this time on, it was plain, progress towards matrimony between Lurline and the Sheikh was swift and unimpeded.

'*August 9th* Today I and my dear, *dear* Fuaz became Man & Wife. Oh, how happy it makes me to write these words!!! He has given me a wonderful set of chessmen – rubies and black diamonds – & ordered new carpets for Tent.

'*September 20th* Have been attempting to interest Fuaz in *English cookery*; he is laughably suspicious of such things as our good oatmeal porridge, boiled cod, etc. Tried to convince him that a diet of food cooked largely in rancid oil not *altogether beneficial*.'

A number of recipes followed.

Henry was now mystified by several references to Barbie. Could Barbilliard, after all, be still alive, playing some melancholy gooseberry role? But it soon became clear that the Barbie referred to was, in fact, a pet crocodile belonging to Lurline, the first, presumably, of the dynasty ending with three-legged Fuaz.

'*September 30th* Fuaz has given me a silver chain for dear Barbie. He looks so sweet in it, the links flashing as we toss him fish!

'*October 2nd* Eureka! I have at last found a way to make porridge palatable to Fuaz. Who would have thought it possible to make porridge crisp and crunchy! But it can be done !! And so simply!!! Old Fatima, the great-aunt by marriage, is indeed a treasure-house of lore. I believe this process could also be used on oil & might prevent it turning rancid. Must experiment.'

Several years, it seemed, then elapsed happily and un-eventfully, spent in roaming about the desert from one set of in-laws to another. Only one mishap marred the idyll.

'*August 9th* Horrible catastrophe!! Fuaz had his left hand bitten off by B., whom he was teasing with a piece of fish. I felt oblig'd to point out that if he had not acquired this unkind habit the accident wd not have occur'd. Have dressed the Limb with Hot Tar & Fuaz is well enough but much agitated & has ordered B to be destroyed. I, too, greatly afflicted, indeed a seething ferment of vain regrets. But it is true B hd become rather Large and Dangerous. I shall lose no opportunity in procuring a successor.

'Thinking the matter over, in the light of what F. told me before she died, the accident seems little more than *Poetic Justice*.

'To clarify camel fat . . .'

Henry looked up and found his train entering the ter-minus. Hastily he bundled Lurline's manuscript into his briefcase and dived for a taxi, his mind awhirl with croco-diles, camels, and minarets. What had F. told Lurline before she died? And why was it poetic justice to have your left hand bitten off by a crocodile?

The taxi pulled up outside Dobbs-Journeyman's offices in High Holborn. Henry paid and took the lift up to his office. It was not until he saw the *Urgent* note, signed Norman

Garple, that he remembered his last interview. Good heavens, Speedwell Butter! He had not given it a thought for the last twelve hours.

'*Here's* our wandering boy,' Norman said with his indulgent smile. 'And I've no doubt he's teeming with creative ideas after his little jaunt. I'll just introduce you round the Speedwell group, Henry, and then we're all agog to know what you've thought up for us.'

Henry heard no word of introductions. His mind was, as Lurline would have said, a seething ferment of vain regrets. But there was no use crying over spilt butter. The best thing would be to wait till Norman had finished speaking and then tender a dignified resignation; perhaps he could let it be inferred that Lurline had, after all, left him an unexpected legacy.

'I leave Speedwell Butter in Henry's capable hands,' Norman said, and sat on a corner of a table looking receptive and anticipatory.

Henry stood up to speak.

'We all know what's the matter with Speedwell Butter,' he was surprised to find himself saying. 'The price is okay, but it has a nasty taste and an oily consistency. I suggest that we ignore the taste for the time, but get the client to produce the butter in a crystallized form, and launch an all-out campaign on the theme *Crisp, Crunchy Speedwell Butter Puts the Crunch in Lunch.*'

He paused and looked to see what effect his words were having. The group were gazing at him bug-eyed, open-mouthed, uncertain whether to laugh.

'Dear boy,' Norman said silkily. 'Such a sense of *fun.*'

'I'm serious,' Henry said. 'I have notes of a process here that is guaranteed to crystallize any food with a sloppy, oily consistency. Like butter. Or porridge. Would you like to see it demonstrated?'

He pulled Lurline's recipe out of his briefcase, praying

that it would work as well in the cold English climate as under the hot skies of Arabia.

'You really mean this?' Norman said. 'We don't have to ring for a psychiatrist?'

'Sure I mean it. Have we any butter?'

'Rilla,' said Norman to his secretary, 'bring butter. And porridge. What else will you need?' he asked Henry.

'Tartar – sodium silicate – starch – ice – one or two other things. I'll go over and get them from the Home Economics Department.'

'I'll ring them, dear child – just tell me what you want.' Norman made rapid notes.

An amazing feeling of power and exhilaration took command of Henry. Even Norman now seemed impressed by his confidence. When a girl from the kitchens brought the required ingredients and a portable hotplate he handled them with the certainty of a conjuror.

'Which shall we begin with – butter? I clarify it in a saucepan, add this – this – and this, stir briskly, chill rapidly and – there you have it. Simple, isn't it? Crisp, crunchy butter.'

He shook the saucepan. Sure enough, it was filled with opaque yellow crystals the size of maize kernels.

'Equally delicious on toast, bread, or crackers,' he said, shovelling the crystals on to a sheet of blotting-paper. 'Doesn't affect the flavour at all. It's exactly the same process for porridge, only of course you get grey crystals. Crisp, crunchy porridge ...'

'Boy,' whispered Tom Tocksin, the TV director, 'you've revolutionized the food industry. Just wait till the client hears of this.'

'I think I'd better get on the line to them,' Norman said, looking preoccupied. 'They'll be delighted, I'm sure. It's great stuff, Henry, great! I suggest we all adjourn till after lunch, half past two, everybody? Right.'

Henry floated back to his room on unaccustomed waves of triumph. Most of the Speedwell group came with him and it was natural that they should all float together down to The Fighting Cocks to celebrate Henry's stroke of genius. But after half an hour Tom Tocksin suddenly slammed his glass on the counter and exclaimed.

'Fools that we are! You ought to be down at the Patent Office. Get a taxi, quick!'

'Patent Office?'

'Staking your claim, oaf! Hurry!'

Too late! By the time Henry had found his way to the right department, Patent OOXZA/79658532Q, *Method of Crystallizing Liquescent Foodstuffs*, was already pending, registered under the name of Norman Garple.

Three weeks later Norman left Dobbs-Journeyman to become a director of Speedwell Crunchy Foods Ltd; in six months he was a millionaire.

Henry was pardonably annoyed at this turn of events. True, he had been given a small increase in salary but, by and large, he felt that things had turned out inequitably. The thought of Lurline irritated him so much that he thrust her manuscript into a bottom drawer until a publisher, learning that the world-shaking invention of crunchy butter stemmed from one of her desert recipes, rang up and asked to see *Jottings from a Desert Diary*.

'I'd better put the pages in order and get it typed out first,' Henry said. 'It's in a frightful mess.' With belated caution he had remembered that there might be other epoch-making household hints in the journal.

He began laboriously typing it out, but was soon in difficulties with Lurline's handwriting, particularly over measurements and ingredients in the recipes. At this point he recalled Tansy, Lurline's god-daughter. Perhaps she could help? He sent her a card, inviting himself for a weekend to the pub at Loose Chippings.

Six weeks later Henry rang up Norman Garple and asked if they could meet. Norman was his usual urbane self, but difficult to pin down.

'I'm so busy, dear boy – there's hardly time to breathe. But perhaps I could fit you in just for a few minutes – at my office, say round about six on Thursday evening? That suit?'

'Excellent,' Henry agreed cordially.

The Speedwell Offices were emptying fast when Henry arrived for his appointment. A secretary let him in, put on her hat, and hurried down the stairs. Norman, looking high-level and harassed, nodded to him in a bitten-off fashion.

'The commercial hurly-burly, Henry – it's hideous, really hideous. I can't tell you how I long for the dear old creative days at Dobbs-J. Well, what can I do for you, boy? Anything to help a friend from auld lang syne.'

'I've come to you for advice, really,' Henry said with a diffident air. 'Of course it's cheek but you have such a lot of know-how when it comes to marketing. I thought perhaps you'd have some suggestions about a new product.'

'Which new product is that?' Norman asked alertly.

'It's something else from old Lurline's journal. Really that turns out to be very good value. This new thing is one of her Arabian notions, picked up from an old great-aunt of Ibn al Fuaz. You know the Arabs are great on fancy baths – when they get hold of some water, that is; well, this is a sort of bathfoam powder, invented long before the days of detergents. Fuaz used to have it made up specially; I thought maybe it could be sold as a bath essence for men, called something Arabian Nightish like Sultan's Splash.'

'Sounds a possibility,' said Norman. 'What's it like?'

'Not bad at all,' Henry told him with carefully moderate enthusiasm. 'You put a spoonful in your bath and it really does make you feel a different person. After five minutes soaking you're relaxed and vigorous and wide-awake. Like to try it?'

'Love to, dear boy. You brought some with you? Good show. I'm going straight on to a cocktail party, matter of fact, so I'll just pop a spoonful in the directors' tub . . .'

The police were not inclined to connect the disappearance of Mr Norman Garple with the coincidental discovery of a medium-sized crocodile in the directors' bath at the Speedwell Offices. They did, however, arrest Henry, as the last person known to have seen Garple alive, and he had a difficult time convincing a sceptical Chief Superintendent that he had performed an Arabian-Nights trick on his ex-business associate.

'Look, I can only prove that my story is true by doing it again, can't I?' he said reasonably. 'And who's going to volunteer to be the guinea-pig? No, I can't undo the effects, and so far as Garple's concerned I don't want to. There's no law against turning a man into a crocodile.'

In the end, as the police remained tiresomely intransigent, Henry's lawyers advertised for someone genuinely fed up with life. The thousands of replies were gradually sifted down to one candidate: Albert Weeks, a sad, defeated little ex-swimming instructor whose wife would not let him go in the water in case he had heart-failure. Life had been robbed of meaning for him. When he understood the case he gladly immersed himself in a bathful of Sultan's Splash and became an undoubted crocodile. This convinced the police, Henry was released, and the two crocodiles were given to the Zoo (where they received kind treatment and lived long, socially useful lives).

'I suppose Fuaz the crocodile really was Ibn al Fuaz,' Henry observed to Tansy some days later as they strolled hand-in-hand through the garden at Loose Chippings. 'Lurline must have been annoyed when she discovered the trick he'd played on Barbie, and turned the tables.'

'I think Barbilliard was always her real love,' Tansy said.

'She began to suspect that Fuaz had used a love potion. Oh, excuse me, talking of love potions, I promised to take one along to Dr Wassup's receptionist. I shan't be gone long.'

Henry and Tansy were married the next year. This would have delighted Lurline, who had, indeed, planned it. They lived comfortably; moreover, Lurline's practice and film rights from the *Desert Jottings* provided a steady income and, although Sultan's Splash never went into regular commercial production, Henry achieved his ambition to enter politics by making small quantities of it discreetly available to his own party for the removal of undesirable parliamentary opponents. The number of crocodiles in the Zoo increased materially in the next few years.

Henry's devotion to his wife was undoubted, whether or not it had been boosted by any recourse to love potions on Tansy's part, but, until the end of his life he had a curious phobia about baths, preferring to take them when his wife was out of the house, and always carefully rinsing the bath first with a strong solution of carbolic before venturing to set foot in it.

A Set for Every Sheep

You will be wanting an explanation for the business of the sheep, and here it is.

If ever you saw a little man like a secretary-bird, with large ears and a wisp of distraught grey hair and pale myopic eyes like grapes behind horn-rimmed glasses, sitting in the tube with a thermometer in his mouth, it was probably Lord Dunsinane.

A fortune-teller had foretold that he would meet his downfall either in a pub or in a taxi, and Lord Dunsinane was taking no chances. He was a teetotaller and travelled by tube. He took his temperature every hour and wore shockproof socks and a lightning-conductor pinned to his hearing-aid. Perhaps it was not unfitting that so timid a man should be remembered in connection with sheep.

When he got out of the tube he toddled down Fleet Street a little way until he came to an enormous new white building. Here the doormen bowed, and the telephonists curt-seyed, and Wedge, the editor, locked himself in the cloak-room, for these were the new premises of the *Sunday Spell*, a newspaper devoted almost entirely to prediction, and Lord Dunsinane was the proprietor.

But before he entered the doors he always spared a scowl for the little pub occupying part of the ground premises. It was called The Medusa's Head, and it was old and wizened and black-beamed, and its sooty irregular little shape was wrapped round and contained by the mighty new building as a dirty little bit of grit is embedded in the fibres of a beautiful tree. It was the mote in Lord Dunsinane's eye and the thorn in his side. He would dearly have liked to pull it down; unfortunately the proprietress held it on a 999 years' lease, of which there was still a few months to run.

But when that day came, let her beware! For Lord Dunsinane intended to operate personally the crane which would dash a ten-ton weight clean through the front wall of The Medusa's Head and reduce it to rubble.

Meanwhile the proprietress, pretty Mrs Owen, was not idle. She had written to the Ministry of Antiquities, asking them to include the building in their list of ancient monuments scheduled for preservation, for she claimed that the pub, which had belonged to her family for fifty generations, was of quite as much historical importance as Westminster Abbey. Moreover, if it had not been lost somewhere during the ninth century, the pub would still have had as its sign the original Gorgon's Head, brought from Greece to England by a Phoenician gentleman-adventurer.

The London Museum, called in to arbitrate, was sceptical here, reasoning that a sign guaranteed to turn customers to stone was not the best means of attracting them, and that the pub, once a riverside one before the embankments were built, had originally been called The Mud-User's Hod. But Mrs Owen countered that the Gorgon's Head had become worn with use and only worked on drunken or credulous customers.

The Museum therefore conceded that if she could produce the head, they would fight her case.

So matters stood.

Lord Dunsinane entered his office and summoned his editor.

'Wedge,' he said, 'I've had another letter from this mad Welshman. Will you deal with it, please? Something about sheep. And you can arrange for a suite of rooms to be cleared – I shall take up residence in the Spell Building for the duration of the lift strike.'

Look you, sir, the letter said in passionate and almost illegible writing, *unfair it is that sheep in Newport Isle of Wight should have better treatment than those in Newport Mon. No dentists for sheep are there in Cardiff nor Llanelly nor anywhere in the length and breadth of Wales whatever! Unjust it is on our sheep.*

There was no address or signature on the letter, which was crumpled and rather grubby, as if it had been written with the paper resting on a muddy knee.

'If only he'd given his name,' said Wedge thoughtfully, 'I have a feeling in my bones that there might be the germ of a good campaign here.'

'Pish,' said Lord Dunsinane. 'We don't want campaigns. Horoscopes are what sell the paper, I'll have you remember.'

But Wedge went away muttering, 'Teeth for Foreign Visitors – What About Our Own Sheep?' He did not always see eye to eye with his proprietor.

Cronnet, Lord Dunsinane's butler, had moved into the Spell building with his master. About a week after the beginning of the lift strike – which was due to a prediction in the *Sunday Spell* foretelling a major lift disaster within twenty-three months – Cronnet was startled by a frenzied yell from Lord Dunsinane's room as he was about to take in an early cup of tea.

He found his master sitting bolt upright in bed, staring about him with a haggard look.

'What is it, sir?'

'I had a dream, Cronnet – a ghastly, terrible dream! My heart almost stopped beating!'

'Dear me,' said Cronnet, scratching his head. 'What would the dream have been about, then, sir?'

'That's what I can't remember! All I know is that it was the worst thing that could possibly happen!'

'Well if you don't remember I don't see how it can have been so bad,' said Cronnet rather crossly, for he wanted to get back to his own tea and the sporting predictions. 'Here, have a nice hot cuppa, sir, and look at these pulls –'

Cronnet had no sooner settled down, however, than Lord Dunsinane let out another yell.

'What is it now, then?' grumbled Cronnet, pottering back like an old nanny.

'Look what my horoscope says, Cronnet. "All your dreams will come true!" Suppose *that* dream came true?'

'Then you'd know what it was about, wouldn't you?' pointed out Cronnet reasonably.

Next morning Cronnet found Lord Dunsinane in the same state of agitation.

'Dreaming again, sir?'

'Yes, Cronnet, yes! The same terrible dream!'

'Did you remember it this time, sir?'

'No, but it was just as bad. I have the same feeling here,' Lord Dunsinane thumped his chest – 'as if I had a stone-cold marble cannonball under my ribs. Oh, this is unendurable. Phone Wedge to come in. I must ask his advice.'

Wedge arrived simultaneously with Lord Dunsinane's daughter Janet; the pair of young people gazed at one another sadly while Lord Dunsinane poured out his troubles.

'Father, you worry too much about dreams and predictions,' said Janet. 'You should get out more – into the sunshine, into the country –'

'Not likely!' shuddered her father. 'Why, only last year one of my horoscopes warned me against snakes, and another said Beware of Falling Stones. Nothing would persuade me to go into the country. What I want is something to prevent me from dreaming – or to explain the dreams in a reassuring way.'

'A drop of whisky gives a wonderful peaceful sleep,' said Wedge.

'Or malted milk,' suggested Janet.

'Sleeping tablets?'

'Pillow stuffed with sweet feverfew?'

'Soothing subliminal music?'

But as Lord Dunsinane peevishly rejected all these suggestions, Wedge at length said, 'You say, sir, that you have this dream just before waking?'

'That's what's so horrible,' muttered Lord Dunsinane. 'I wake all of a sweat and a tremble, without knowing why.'

'Then all you need do is get Cronnet to call you five minutes earlier, *before* you have had the dream.'

The other two were struck with the brilliance of this suggestion and Lord Dunsinane, delighted, exclaimed, 'Ah, it was a stroke of genius on my part to pick you as editor! I am a past master at choosing intelligent staff. Your salary is doubled from today.'

'I'd rather marry Janet,' said Wedge quickly.

'Impossible,' Lord Dunsinane snapped. 'Janet shall never marry while I live! You know perfectly well that my 1955 horoscope said that on my daughter's wedding day my monument would be erected in Fleet Street.'

Janet's eyes filled with huge tears and she ran from the room. Wedge, hoping at least that Lord Dunsinane's mood was favourable enough to approve one or two campaigns, hastily submitted a batch of suggestions: 'Make Way for the Tricyclists', 'Make Sunday Granny's Day', and his own favourite, 'Australians! Come back to the Mother Country!'

But Lord Dunsinane would have none of them.

'Sir!' said Wedge desperately. 'You must know that you are paralysing the economic life of the country with all the predictions you publish in the *Spell*. People take them so deadly seriously that no docker will work on a Monday, no trains run on days when the signs of the zodiac are at the cusp (whatever that means), cabinet ministers are chosen for their birth hours, not their abilities –'

But Lord Dunsinane was not listening. He was gazing at the tea leaves in his cup.

'Teeth,' Lord Dunsinane was muttering. 'Quite plainly those tea leaves denote a set of teeth. I must see my dentist. Oh, and by the way, Wedge, there's another letter from the mad Welshman. Take it, will you?'

This time the Welshman had written: *Indeed to goodness if only I could get a right-thinking paper to support the cause of a poor honest sheep farmer there's happy I would be. For here's my poor Blodwen with not a tooth to bite the green grass. Porridge for breakfast every morning I have to make her, gruel for dinner, mash for her tea. Crying shame it is, and the National Health should take the matter on before I will be knocking at the door of Number Ten, demanding fair play for Welsh Sheep!*

As before, no signature.

'Fair play for sheep,' said Wedge wistfully. 'A Health Act with teeth in it. Really, sir, it might be a great campaign.'

'Pish,' said Lord Dunsinane.

For a week, Cronnet woke Lord Dunsinane at ten to eight and the dream did not recur. But on the eighth day as Cronnet poured the tea he heard the same terrible yell, and found Lord Dunsinane tottering along the passage in his striped pyjamas with a glazed look in his eye.

'It's come back, Cronnet! My subconscious must have become used to the earlier hour of waking.' Lord Dunsinane distractedly sniffed his tea and drank some spirits of ammonia. 'Cronnet! From now on you must call me at half past seven.'

'Yes, sir,' said Cronnet resignedly.

But this earned Lord Dunsinane only a brief respite. Soon Cronnet had to wake him at seven, then at six, then at five, in order to forestall the dream. The staff of the *Sunday Spell* had to adjust their working hours accordingly. The time came when Lord Dunsinane had lost an entire twenty-four

hours' sleep, and while everyone else was still in the last day
of May, he had moved on to the first of June.

'Where is this going to end?' lamented Wedge, when he
met Janet for a snatched lunch at ten a.m. one day. 'Your
father is becoming a neurotic wreck – and so are the rest of
us. Something terrible will happen soon. The last *Sunday
Spell* horoscope advised all Virgo subjects to abstain from
both protein and carbohydrate for the forthcoming year.
What will happen to them?'

At this moment they were startled by a solitary 'Ba-aa!'
They saw an elderly man coming from the direction of
Lincoln's Inn fields. He wore a shepherd's smock, and
trousers tied up at the knee with string. He carried a crook
and was accompanied by an equally elderly-looking sheep.

He said to Wedge, 'Will your honour tell me if I am on
the right road for the *Sunday Spell* newspaper?'

Wedge said alertly, 'Can you tell me your business?'

'Me and my poor Blodwen have walked all the way from
Llan Ron in search of fair play for sheep, see. Letter after
letter have I written, and no reply, there is uncivil! Coming
myself I am now, to see justice done.'

'What is your trouble, then, Mr –?'

'Rhys, sir, Dai Rhys is my name and I'm from Llan Ron
which anybody will tell you is the loveliest farm in all North
Wales. Please to tell me, sir, which is the *Sunday Spell*?'

'We are there now,' said Wedge, and led Mr Rhys up
the stairs of the Spell building, where no one was particularly
surprised to see a sheep, since rams, goats, lions and other
signs of the zodiac were a commonplace, live or otherwise.
Blodwen nipped neatly up ahead of them, for she was a
mountain sheep and accustomed to leaping from crag to
crag.

Lord Dunsinane was quite pleased to be distracted from
thoughts of his dream.

'This is Mr Rhys, sir,' said Wedge. 'He wants his cause supported.'

Mr Rhys handed Lord Dunsinane a grubby newspaper cutting. 'Only read that, sir!'

The cutting, which was from the *Guardian*, was headed SHEEP FITTED WITH FALSE TEETH, and reported how an Isle of Wight ewe had put on twenty pounds in a week after having been fitted with a set of dentures.

'Every dentist in Wales have I been to!' said Mr Rhys. 'And not a man of them has ever made a set of dentures for a sheep.'

'Really this is most thought-provoking,' said Lord Dunsinane. 'For I distinctly saw a set of dentures in the tea leaves only last month.'

'Tea leaves!' said Mr Rhys with fearful scorn. 'There is a superstitious old pack of mumbo-jumbo, not fit for a man of sense to put credit in.'

Wedge and Janet held their breath with fright, but Mr Rhys went on, 'Now I, with my back to the Dreaming Stone, and the winds of heaven about my ears, and the majesty of Gwyn Wrtyn mountain under my feet, have dreamed of dentures these seventy nights past.'

'Really?' said Lord Dunsinane, all ears, ignoring the slighting reference to tea leaves. 'Are you an expert on dreams, Mr Rhys?'

'Dreams, is it?' said Mr Rhys. 'Ask if I do not interpret dreams from Llanfair to Pontypridd! And foretell from them, too! More weddings and funerals have I foreseen than there are in the book of Numbers. Rhys the Future, they call me.'

'But this is splendid!' cried Lord Dunsinane in high delight. 'I will strike a bargain with you, Mr Rhys. Am I right in thinking that you want a set of dentures for Blodwen here, and the rest of your flock?'

'Fair play,' said Mr Rhys, 'I am only wanting teeth for

the older sheep. And not charity, mind! Let the Health
Service pay for it, say I! Many's the ewe would be more use
to her country than some old wives I could name, munching
their toast on Government teeth and never yielding a single
pinch of wool.'

'I'll ask my dentist to fit Blodwen with uppers and low-
ers,' said Lord Dunsinane. 'I invite you both to stay here
as my guests for a week till we see whether she really does
put on weight when she can chew. And if this is proved,
I will support your cause in my paper, Mr Rhys – if you,
in the meantime, will help me with a personal dream problem.'

'Indeed,' said Mr Rhys, 'there is glad I will be to help.
What is the nature of the troublesome dream?'

'That's what I can't remember.'

'Difficult it is in that case,' said Mr Rhys. 'Interpret your
dream without hearing its nature is what would be hard
to do, unless I will be having my Dreaming Stone at the back
of me so that I can dream right through my dream and into
yours.'

'Dreaming Stone?' said Lord Dunsinane with an acquisitive gleam in his eye. 'What is that? Is it heavy?'

'Matter of a couple of tons,' said Mr Rhys.

'No trouble to shift,' said Lord Dunsinane. 'If you will
give directions, I will have the stone brought to London –
and taken back to Wales of course when you return,' he
added reluctantly, as a wild light of protest came into Mr
Rhys's eye.

So next day Blodwen, sleeping like a baby under gas, was
fitted with the finest set of porcelain grinders that sheep ever
gnashed, and put out to graze in Lincoln's Inn Fields, where
she soon became as fat as butter.

It was found impossible to fetch the Dreaming Stone for
several days because of an awkward planetary mixture of
Cancer and Gemini, but in the end a British Rail truck

dropped it outside The Medusa's Head and it was man-handled into the front lobby of the *Sunday Spell* building.

Here a difficulty was encountered: no lift to take it up.

'You couldn't do your divining in the vestibule, Mr Rhys?' said Lord Dunsinane.

'Even the prophet Isaiah could not predict anything by there, sir! Too much noise, look you.'

Lord Dunsinane persuaded Cronnet to run the lift, in flat defiance of union rules, which said that no unauthorized person, etc. etc.

Mr Rhys accompanied the stone on its upward journey, in a trance of mystical reunion. All went well until they reached the ninth floor and stepped out; then the weight of the Dreaming Stone suddenly became too much for the lift cables, and the whole thing fell with a fearful and cataclysmic crash down and down, through the teleprinters' floor and the photographic studios and the saloon bar of The Medusa's Head (luckily it was just before opening hours) and the mailing department, into the very bowels of the basement, and buried itself fathoms deep in London clay.

'There is a misfortune,' said Rhys the Future, gloomily.

'It can easily be hoisted out,' Lord Dunsinane assured him. He added hopefully, 'I suppose you didn't – well – *get* anything from the stone on the way up? About my dream?'

'I was only having a first, dim flicker,' said Rhys. 'Time it takes, look you. But this one thing I can tell you – your dream is being put on to you by some person close to you. It is no accident, that dream.'

'*Put on to me?* How disgraceful! Who would do such a thing? Could it be my daughter Janet?'

'That I am not knowing,' said Mr Rhys, and he was so dispirited by the loss of his stone that, clean contrary to his usual abstemious ways, he went down to The Medusa's Head for a rum and milk, while Lord Dunsinane rang for a team of excavators to hoist the stone out of the deep hole it had dug.

'Nice old inn-sign you have there,' said Mr Rhys to pretty Mrs Owen. 'Puts me in mind of my Blod, with the wool curling round her homely face.' He could see at once that Mrs Owen was a kindred spirit.

'Ah, but it's nothing to the one there should be,' said Mrs Owen. Custom was slack – most customers were out watching the cranes delving in the deep pit for the buried Dreaming Stone; so she told Mr Rhys all about her troubles with Lord Dunsinane and the lease, and how the discovery of the real Medusa's Head would save her from eviction.

'But hunt high and hunt low we have, and never a hair of a head have we found.'

An expression of illumination came over Mr Rhys's face. 'It will be you, now, that will have been putting these dreams on Lord Dunsinane?' he asked delicately.

Mrs Owen blushed. 'There's shamed I am,' she said. 'But I couldn't help it, indeed, so worried I've been. And today's the last day of my lease!'

At this simultaneous moment Lord Dunsinane, too, realized that in his preoccupation with sheep and dreams, he had let the 366th day of the 999th year of Mrs Owen's lease creep up on him. A happy gleam came into his eye. He looked out of his window at the cranes in Fleet Street struggling to get a purchase on the massive Dreaming Stone.

'When they have that stone hoisted,' he said, 'I shall use it to deal the first blow at that squalid little pub which defaces the frontage of my beautiful building. I shall go down now and tell Mrs Owen.'

Wedge looked unhappy. He was fond of The Medusa's Head.

'Is it wise?' he suggested hastily. 'What about the prediction that you would – would meet with some mischance in a pub?'

'Aha!' exclaimed Lord Dunsinane. 'But if the lease has expired it is no longer a pub, is it?'

And he went down without more ado. Wedge went too, to have a last beer and gaze sadly at the notice, left over from Ancient British times, which said, ONE FOR THE WOAD? NOT IF YOU'RE THE CHARIOTEER!

Such a commotion was in progress as they entered the bar that they could hardly get inside. Mrs Owen was laughing and crying and kissing her customers and pressing tankards of mead (also left from Ancient British times) on all and sundry.

'Mrs Owen,' said Lord Dunsinane with dignity, 'I have come to inform you –'

But she turned to him, crying, 'It's found, Lord Dunsinane, it was in that deep hole! I've rung the Ministry, and the Museum, and there's a man coming round. Look –' and she held up a most extraordinary object which, under its coat of London clay, could just be recognized as a face with a decidedly severe expression, surrounded by some comatose snakes, the whole thing set in a round yellow tin tray – the sort that often has a brewer's name painted on it.

'Pish –' began Lord Dunsinane, but as he spoke a change came over him – he became even more rigidly dignified, his face turned marble-grey.

'Ah!' exclaimed Rhys the Future in triumph. 'Now I have it, your dream. To be turned to stone by the Medusa!'

Lord Dunsinane was an honourable man according to his lights. In acknowledgement of Rhys's exposition, late though it came, he breathed out his final command. Wedge, entering the public bar, was just in time to catch it.

'New campaign – *Sunday Spell* – a set for every sheep!'

'It will be a fine campaign, sir,' said Wedge, awed and moved. 'It will be a credit to the paper and to your memory.'

He spoke to unheeding ears; Lord Dunsinane had retired into his marble. No one could think quite what to do with him, so he was put on a plinth in Fleet Street, alongside Lord Northcliffe, on the day that Wedge and Janet were married.

Mr Rhys, too, stayed in Fleet Street, rather than be put to the expense of transporting his Dreaming Stone back to Wales. He married pretty Mrs Owen, and Blodwen grazed for the rest of her life in Lincoln's Inn Fields.

Meanwhile the campaign to provide a set for every sheep gathered momentum and overcame all obstacles. And this is the reason why in the year 1983 (due to a slight error of phrasing in the Act and a misunderstanding at Ministerial level) each sheep in the United Kingdom was supplied with a television set of its very own.

Marmalade Wine

'Paradise,' Blacker said to himself, moving forward into the wood. 'Paradise. Fairyland.'

He was a man given to exaggeration; poetic licence he called it, and his friends called it 'Blacker's little flights of fancy,' or something less polite, but on this occasion he spoke nothing but the truth. The wood stood silent about him, tall, golden, with afternoon sunlight slanting through the half-unfurled leaves of early summer. Underfoot, anemones palely carpeted the ground. A cuckoo called.

'Paradise,' Blacker repeated, closed the gate behind him, and strode down the overgrown path, looking for a spot in which to eat his ham sandwich. Hazel bushes thickened at either side until the circular blue eye of the gateway by which he had come in dwindled to a pinpoint and vanished. The taller trees over-topping the hazels were not yet in full leaf and gave little cover; it was very hot in the wood and very still.

Suddenly Blacker stopped short with an exclamation of surprise and regret: lying among the dog's-mercury by the path was the body of a cock-pheasant in the full splendour of its spring plumage. Blacker turned the bird over with the townsman's pity and curiosity at such evidence of nature's unkindness; the feathers, purple-bronze, green, and gold, were smooth under his hand as a girl's hair.

'Poor thing,' he said aloud, 'what can have happened to it?'

He walked on, wondering if he could turn the incident to account. 'Threnody for a Pheasant in May.' Too precious? Too sentimental? Perhaps a weekly would take it. He began choosing rhymes, staring at his feet as he walked, abandoning his conscious rapture at the beauty around him.

> Stricken to death ... and something ... leafy ride,
> Before his ... something ... fully flaunt his pride.

Or would a shorter line be better, something utterly simple and heartful, limpid tears of grief like spring rain dripping off the petals of a flower?

It was odd, Blacker thought, increasing his pace, how difficult he found writing nature poetry; nature was beautiful, maybe, but it was not stimulating. And it was nature poetry that *Field and Garden* wanted. Still, that pheasant ought to be worth five guineas. *Tread lightly past, Where he lies still, And something last ...*

Damn! In his absorption he had nearly trodden on *another* pheasant. What was happening to the birds? Blacker, who objected to occurrences with no visible explanation, walked on frowning. The path bore downhill to the right, and leaving the hazel coppice, crossed a tiny valley. Below him Blacker was surprised to see a small, secretive flint cottage, surrounded on three sides by trees. In front of it was a patch of turf. A deck-chair stood there, and a man was peacefully stretched out in it, enjoying the afternoon sun.

Blacker's first impulse was to turn back; he felt as if he had walked into somebody's garden, and was filled with mild irritation at the unexpectedness of the encounter; there ought to have been some warning signs, dash it all. The wood had seemed as deserted as Eden itself. But his turning round would have an appearance of guilt and furtiveness; on second thoughts he decided to go boldly past the cottage. After all there was no fence, and the path was not marked private in any way; he had a perfect right to be there.

'Good afternoon,' said the man pleasantly as Blacker approached. 'Remarkably fine weather, is it not?'

'I do hope I'm not trespassing.'

Studying the man, Blacker revised his first guess. This was no gamekeeper, there was a distinction in every line of the thin, sculptered face. What most attracted Blacker's attention were the hands, holding a small gilt coffee-cup; they were as white, frail, and attenuated as the pale roots of water-plants.

'Not at all,' the man said cordially. 'In fact you arrive at a most opportune moment; you are very welcome. I was just wishing for a little company. Delightful as I find this sylvan retreat, it becomes, all of a sudden, a little *dull*, a little *banal*. I do trust that you have time to sit down and share my after-lunch coffee and liqueur.'

As he spoke he reached behind him and brought out a second deck-chair from the cottage porch.

'Why, thank you; I should be delighted,' said Blacker, wondering if he had the strength of character to take out the ham sandwich and eat it in front of this patrician hermit.

Before he made up his mind the man had gone into the house and returned with another gilt cup full of black, fragrant coffee, hot as Tartarus, which he handed to Blacker. He carried also a tiny glass, and into this, from a black-currant-cordial bottle, he carefully poured a clear, colourless liquor. Blacker sniffed his glassful with caution, mistrusting the bottle and its evidence of home brewing, but the scent, aromatic and powerful, was similar to that of curaçao, and the liquid moved in its glass with an oily smoothness. It certainly was not cowslip wine.

'Well,' said his host, reseating himself and gesturing slightly with his glass, 'how do you do?' He sipped delicately.

'Cheers,' said Blacker, and added, 'My name's Roger Blacker.' It sounded a little lame. The liqueur was not curaçao, but akin to it, and quite remarkably potent; Blacker who was very hungry, felt the fumes rise up inside his head as if an orange tree had taken root there and was putting out leaves and golden glowing fruit.

'Sir Francis Deeking,' the other man said, and then Blacker understood why his hands had seemed so spectacular, so portentously out of the common.

'The surgeon? But surely you don't live down here?'

Deeking waved a hand deprecatingly. 'A week-end retreat. A hermitage, to which I can retire from the strain of my calling.'

'It certainly is very remote,' Blacker remarked. 'It must be five miles from the nearest road.'

'Six. And you, my dear Mr Blacker, what is your profession?'

'Oh, a writer,' said Blacker modestly. The drink was having its usual effect on him; he managed to convey not that he was a journalist on a twopenny daily with literary yearnings, but that he was a philosopher and essayist of rare quality, a sort of second Bacon. All the time he spoke, while drawn out most flatteringly by the questions of Sir Francis, he was recalling journalistic scraps of information about his host: the operation on the Indian Prince; the Cabinet Minister's appendix; the amputation performed on that unfortunate ballerina who had both feet crushed in a railway accident; the major operation which had proved so miraculously successful on the American heiress.

'You must feel like a god,' he said suddenly, noticing with surprise that his glass was empty. Sir Francis waved the remark aside.

'We all have our godlike attributes,' he said, leaning forward. 'Now you, Mr Blacker, a writer, a creative artist – do you not know a power akin to godhead when you transfer your thought to paper?'

'Well, not exactly then,' said Blacker, feeling the liqueur moving inside his head in golden and russet-coloured clouds. 'Not *so* much then, but I do have one unusual power, a power not shared by many people, of foretelling the future. For instance, as I was coming through the wood, I *knew* this house would be here. I knew I should find you sitting in front of it. I can look at the list of runners in a race, and the name of the winner fairly leaps out at me from the page, as if it was printed in golden ink. Forthcoming events – air disasters, train crashes – I always sense in advance. I begin to have a terrible feeling of impending doom, as if my brain was a volcano just on the point of eruption.'

What was that other item of news about Sir Francis Deeking, he wondered, a recent report, a tiny paragraph that had caught his eye in *The Times*? He could not recall it.

'*Really?*' Sir Francis was looking at him with the keenest interest; his eyes, hooded and fanatical under their heavy lids, held brilliant points of light. 'I have always longed to know somebody with such a power. It must be a terrifying responsibility.'

'Oh, it is,' Blacker said. He contrived to look bowed under the weight of supernatural cares; noticed that his glass was full again, and drained it. 'Of course I don't use the faculty for my own ends; something fundamental in me rises up to prevent that. It's as basic, you know, as the instinct forbidding cannibalism or incest –'

'Quite, quite,' Sir Francis agreed. 'But for another person you would be able to give warnings, advise profitable courses of action –? My dear fellow, your glass is empty. Allow me.'

'This is marvellous stuff,' Blacker said hazily. 'It's like a wreath of orange blossom.' He gestured with his finger.

'I distil it myself; from marmalade. But do go on with what you were saying. Could you, for instance, tell me the winner of this afternoon's Manchester Plate?'

'Bow Bells,' Blacker said unhesitatingly. It was the only name he could remember.

'You interest me enormously. And the result of today's Aldwych by-election? Do you know that?'

'Unwin, the Liberal, will get in by a majority of two

hundred and eighty-two. He won't take his seat, though. He'll be killed at seven this evening in a lift accident at his hotel.' Blacker was well away by now.

'Will he, indeed?' Sir Francis appeared delighted. 'A pestilent fellow. I have sat on several boards with him. Do continue.'

Blacker required little encouragement. He told the story of the financier whom he had warned in time of the oil company crash; the dream about the famous violinist which had resulted in the man's cancelling his passage on the ill-fated *Orion*; and the tragic tale of the bullfighter who had ignored his warning.

'But I'm talking too much about myself,' he said at length, partly because he noticed an ominous clogging of his tongue, a refusal of his thoughts to marshal themselves. He cast about for an impersonal topic, something simple.

'The pheasants,' he said. 'What's happened to the pheasants? Cut down in their prime. It – it's terrible. I found four in the wood up there, four or five.'

'Really?' Sir Francis seemed callously uninterested in the fate of the pheasants. 'It's the chemical sprays they use on the crops, I understand. Bound to upset the ecology; they never work out the probable results beforehand. Now if *you* were in charge, my dear Mr Blacker – but forgive me, it is a hot afternoon and you must be tired and footsore if you have walked from Witherstow this morning – let me suggest that you have a short sleep . . .'

His voice seemed to come from farther and farther away; a network of sun-coloured leaves laced themselves in front of Blacker's eyes. Gratefully he leaned back and stretched out his aching feet.

Some time after this Blacker roused a little – or was it only a dream? – to see Sir Francis standing by him, rubbing his hands, with a face of jubilation.

'My dear fellow, my dear Mr Blacker, what a *lusus naturae*

you are. I can never be sufficiently grateful that you came my way. Bow Bells walked home – positively *ambled*. I have been listening to the commentary. What a misfortune that I had no time to place money on the horse – but never mind, never mind, that can be remedied another time.

'It is unkind of me to disturb your well-earned rest, though; drink this last thimbleful and finish your nap while the sun is on the wood.'

As Blacker's head sank back against the deck-chair again, Sir Francis leaned forward and gently took the glass from his hand.

Sweet river of dreams, thought Blacker, fancy the horse actually winning. I wish I'd had a fiver on it myself; I could do with a new pair of shoes. I should have undone these before I dozed off, they're too tight or something. I must wake up soon, ought to be on my way in half an hour or so . . .

When Blacker finally woke he found that he was lying on a narrow bed, indoors, covered with a couple of blankets. His head ached and throbbed with a shattering intensity, and it took a few minutes for his vision to clear; then he saw that he was in a small white cell-like room which contained nothing but the bed he was on and a chair. It was very nearly dark.

He tried to struggle up but a strange numbness and heaviness had invaded the lower part of his body, and after hoisting himself on to his elbow he felt so sick that he abandoned the effort and lay down again.

That stuff must have the effect of a knockout drop, he thought ruefully; what a fool I was to drink it. I'll have to apologize to Sir Francis. What time can it be?

Brisk light footsteps approached the door and Sir Francis came in. He was carrying a portable radio which he placed on the window sill.

'Ah, my dear Blacker, I see you have come round. Allow me to offer you a drink.'

He raised Blacker skilfully, and gave him a drink of water from a cup with a rim and a spout.

'Now let me settle you down again. Excellent. We shall soon have you – well, not on your feet, but sitting up and taking nourishment.' He laughed a little. 'You can have some beef tea presently.'

'I am so sorry,' Blacker said. 'I really need not trespass on your hospitality any longer. I shall be quite all right in a minute.'

'No trespass, my dear friend. You are not at all in the way. I hope that you will be here for a long and pleasant stay. These surroundings, so restful, so conducive to a writer's inspiration – what could be more suitable for you? You need not think that I shall disturb you. I am in London all week, but shall keep you company at week-ends – pray, pray don't think that you will be a nuisance or *de trop*. On the contrary, I am hoping that you can do me the kindness of giving me the Stock Exchange prices in advance, which will amply compensate for any small trouble I have taken. No, no, you must feel quite at home – please consider, indeed, that this *is* your home.'

Stock Exchange prices? It took Blacker a moment to remember, then he thought, Oh lord, my tongue has played me false as usual. He tried to recall what stupidities he had been guilty of. 'Those stories,' he said lamely, 'they were all a bit exaggerated, you know. About my foretelling the future. I can't really. That horse's winning was a pure coincidence, I'm afraid.'

'Modesty, modesty.' Sir Francis was smiling, but he had gone rather pale, and Blacker noticed a beading of sweat along his cheekbones. 'I am sure you will be invaluable. Since my retirement I find it absolutely necessary to augment my income by judicious investment.'

All of a sudden Blacker remembered the gist of that small paragraph in *The Times*. Nervous breakdown. Complete rest. Retirement.

'I – I really must go now,' he said uneasily, trying to push himself upright. 'I meant to be back in town by seven.'

'Oh, but Mr Blacker, that is quite out of the question. Indeed, so as to preclude any such action, I have amputated your feet. But you need not worry; I know you will be very happy here. And I feel certain that you are wrong to doubt your own powers. Let us listen to the nine o'clock news in order to be quite satisfied that the detestable Unwin did fall down the hotel lift shaft.'

He walked over to the portable radio and switched it on.

Our Feathered Friends

Major Teape was passionately fond of tidiness; had a perfect reverence for it. He was not very tidy himself, but he was logical and irascible, qualities which, he felt, made up for any little lack of complete order in his house. He and his dog Rover were so tall, so spare and un-cheerful that his tenant, Miss Murdeigh, always felt a strong desire to snip a bit off them and put them in a vase of warm water with a penny in it, to revive them.

In money matters the Major was rigidly impeccable and on any day in the month could tell where his money was to the last halfpenny, not to mention the money in the organ fund, the brass band takings, the men's club subscriptions and the various separate accounts he himself kept in the local bank for poultry profits, rates, emergencies and pocket money.

Naturally with all this his house was a bit untidy, for the machines were always breaking down and having to be repaired, so of course the dining-room table was covered with the components of the water-softener, neatly arranged (the table was never used anyway); the diesel pump and lawn mower were in for repair too, but nevertheless *you could walk*, it was not like some people's houses. The engine that supplied the electricity was giving trouble too.

One could not be sure of finding a hammer in the Major's house, or a bit of fuse-wire or the pliers, without delving through four or five tables and work-benches covered with valves, spanners, springs, sparking-plugs and long oily bits of cable; but it was a dead certainty that in Miss Murdeigh's no hammer would ever be found at all, though the original score of an unpublished Haydn symphony might come to light. If Miss Murdeigh wanted to hammer in a nail, which was seldom, she did it with a brick; and she had no need for electricity because she preferred candles.

The Major often said with restraint that Miss Murdeigh's house was very untidy: very untidy indeed.

His main cause for complaint against her was what he called her unreliability in money-matters. She had been installed as his tenant in Orchard Cottage during the war when the Major's back was, so to speak, turned; and when he had leisure to deal with her he found it impossible, simply impossible, to get her to understand that he wished his rent to be in *cash,* and not in any form that occurred to the inventive mind of Miss Murdeigh.

She frequently pointed out to him that he was the gainer in these transactions, since the actual value of a first edition, or an original Hogarth drawing or three pounds of Jersey cream was more than the rent. Cash played a negligible part in her life. Subsisting, as she did, almost entirely off her smallholding, she found it much more convenient to pay him in kind; but the Major did not see eye to eye with her over this. He wanted tangible coins or notes that he could place in one of a series of cashboxes labelled Orchard Cottage Accounts, and he told Miss Murdeigh so, patiently, or fairly patiently, ever so many times.

'But honey is so good for you,' Miss Murdeigh said in a mild tone, standing with the untidy greaseproof-paper parcel in her hands. 'I'm sure you don't get enough sugar into your system.'

'Sell it to me, then,' screamed the Major, at the end of his tether, 'and pay the rent with the proceeds.'

'Fifty pence, if you must, but it doesn't seem the same thing,' she sighed, watching as he violently unlocked a cashbox labelled Poultry Profits and shovelled out five ten p. pieces. Four of them she handed back to him and he threw them into the Orchard Cottage box. 'I wish to goodness,' he said savagely as he put the keys in an envelope, 'I wish to goodness you'd buy Orchard Cottage, and then I could get it out of my mind. I couldn't in decency ask more than two hundred for it, and I shall never be able to let it again. I suppose the roof is leaking, isn't it?'

'Do you suppose so?' said Miss Murdeigh vaguely.

'Bound to be. I'll send Hutton over on Monday.'

'I don't think I could buy it,' Miss Murdeigh went on, consideringly. 'I very much doubt if I could do that. I have only seven pounds at present.'

The Major made a gesture of despair, and Miss Murdeigh took her departure. But his remark bore fruit for, about a week later when he returned from Boy Scouts, he found that his tenant had called while he was absent. On the kitchen table (his daughter Sally made him keep this clear) she had left a most extraordinary article – a glass dome, covering two of the shabbiest, seediest stuffed birds he had ever seen in his life, with lacklustre eyes and hardly a feather between them. They were seated on an elaborate erection something like the Albert Memorial, in attitudes of indescribably rakish abandon. At any minute, it seemed, they might burst into a dance.

A note in Miss Murdeigh's handwriting, propped against the glass case, said: *Dear Major Teape, since our conversation last week I have been turning over in my mind the question of buying Orchard Cottage, and I have hit on this solution. My friend Constantia Lambrette the harpist, who is staying with me at the moment, assures me that this set is worth at least five hundred pounds, and I therefore suggest that you take it in exchange for Orchard Cottage. It is an early and authentic piece by Liefmehr, in full working order, except that I have unfortunately lost the key. Pray accept the difference in price as a token of good-neighbourhood, and in requital for all the trouble I have caused you, and your many kindnesses.*

The Major nearly burst a blood vessel at this missive. He

hardly waited to fling on his duffle-coat again before stamping out with the early Liefmehr (it weighed a good ten pounds) clasped in his arms. But then he reflected that in five minutes it would be Rover's feeding-time, so he slammed back again for two handfuls of dog biscuits, which he thrust into his pockets, and then once more set out for Orchard Cottage with Rover following at his heels.

What made it so much more annoying was that he had taken rather a fancy to the Liefmehr. He had a passion for alarm clocks; so long as they went. The house was full of dust-covered dead clocks and one or two large live ones, which tocked out solemnly the steps to eternity. (The small ones, somehow, never seemed to stand the strain for long.) And there were also pingers and chronometers, sundials and barometers; anything that went round was dearly liked by the Major. Plainly Miss Murdeigh's treasure was some sort of musical-box, and the Major's fingers itched to investigate it. But the principles of an English gentleman and a landlord restrained him.

The path to Orchard Cottage lay, not surprisingly, through the orchard. The door was open but nobody seemed to be about. The Major went in and waited, restraining his disapproval with such an effort that he began to sweat slightly.

The brick floor was thick with dust. Two ghostly shapes, swathed in parachute nylon, were Miss Murdeigh's Bechstein and Miss Lambrette's harp. Narrow lanes led to them through the furniture, which was plentiful. A table by the window held manuscripts, matches, bits of sealing-wax, shallots, garden tools, dirty plates and coffee cups, candlesticks, a chianti bottle or two, embroidery catalogues, some Christmas cards, two bowls of narcissi, and piles of books. The Major ruthlessly swept these things to one side and set down his burden: then, consulting his watch, he called Rover and scattered the dog biscuits on the front doorstep.

Fuming, he sat down on an oak settle. He knew that his hostess could not be long, for it was nearly milking-time and her two Jerseys were standing in the cabbage-plot near the house; unmethodical Miss Murdeigh might be, but the Major knew that with her consideration to animals was a creed. It was her only characteristic of which he wholeheartedly approved.

While he waited he heard a mysterious rumbling on the floor. At first he could not locate it. Could it be deathwatch? but no, it was too loud for that. Whenever he moved, it stopped.

At last he was able to trace it to one corner under a cluttered Chippendale desk. Squatting on hands and knees he discovered that one of Rover's biscuits had been rolled into the extreme angle of the wall, and when he moved this he saw a mouse's face staring at him, with hostility it seemed, out of two beady black eyes.

'Damn it all!' said the Major violently. 'Must m'dog's biscuits be pilfered under my very nose?' At this the mouse took fright and reversed, leaving a long, very long tail in view. Obeying a primeval instinct of the chase the Major pounced on this tail, and whisked the mouse, dangling, into the air. For an instant he held it in triumph, then it turned, ran up its own tail, as it were, and bit his thumb. He dropped it and it darted under the table and out of sight.

'Perdition take it, the place is like a zoo,' said the Major furiously, and he wrapped a handkerchief round his thumb. Now he began to understand why plates of food were mysteriously poised on the tops of tall vases. He went out on to the doorstep, where Rover was finishing the biscuits in a hurried manner, unbefitting to so large and dignified a hound.

When Miss Murdeigh and Miss Lambrette appeared the Major was pacing like a caged lion.

'Ah, my dear Major Teape,' said Miss Murdeigh. 'May I introduce my friend Constantia Lambrette?'

The Major quailed a little as an unbelievably frail, bent, grey figure approached him, and a pair of eyes, bluer than the June sky, slowly swam up to peer at him. He was re minded of the brilliant, mysterious gaze of some rare water-bird. He knew that Miss Lambrette had an international reputation; even Harpo Marx had been awed by her remarkable presence when they played together at a Victory concert.

Under that penetrating blue gaze, with the pressure of that fragile claw on his hand, the Major stammered a few words to the effect that he could not, of course, accept the Liefmehr birds without having them valued by an expert, and he suggested young George Thorless.

'Ah yes, poor George,' said Miss Murdeigh. 'Ah, yes indeed, poor George. Very well, then, my dear friend, you ring him up. In that way, perhaps, we shall kill *several* birds with one stone. And until then we are pleased to be reunited with our feathered friends again, for a short spell.'

The Major fled back to his own house, leaving the two old creatures gazing after him like astronomers who have seen an unusual, but predicted, comet swing past.

'I will milk, dear one, while you do your practising,' Miss Murdeigh said, after a moment or two. 'The cows do enjoy it so.'

Presently, therefore, the sweet and accomplished twangling of the harp stole out into the summer dusk while the Jerseys stood flapping their thoughtful ears and drinking it in.

Meanwhile in his garage the Major was having his daily battle with the engine that supplied his electricity. Poking about in the dim light he first turned on the petrol, which began to drip down at a great rate and leak into a rusty cocoa-tin. Then, cursing and panting, he repeatedly pulled a switch for about ten minutes until the engine, for no discernible reason, suddenly gave a hoarse asthmatic wheeze and coughed itself into riotous life. The house at once leapt out of the gloom in a torrential flood of light, every window blazing.

After waiting a moment or two to make sure that it was not going to die again at once (a frequent occurrence) the Major switched over the engine to tractor vaporizing oil and stumped off indoors, where his daughter Sally had supper ready for him.

He looked and felt cross – heaven knew there were enough things in life to plague him, with that infernal engine which would probably drop to bits before the electric grid reached them, the state of his tenant's house, and her cockeyed notions about payment.

He strode to the telephone and dialled.

'That you, George?' he yelled. 'How are you keeping? It's been a long time. I know, I know, you're busy, so are we busy, but you ought to look us up sometimes. It must be two years. No, no, far too busy to call on *you*, keeping things going here. Better when this miserable electricity comes, if it ever does. Got a job for you, George, a valuation job. Want you to come up to Orchard Cottage and look at a kind of musical box old Miss Murdeigh's offering me. Pair of birds under a glass case. But you'll have to bring some keys or bits of wire, she's lost the key, needless to say.'

He listened for a moment, shouted, 'Good-bye,' thumped down the receiver, came over to the table and began to drink his soup.

Damn, said Sally to herself inwardly. Damn, damn, double damn. Oh well, I shall fix to be out when he comes. I can be getting on with Goldenrod's portrait.

'Funny thing how George can hear quite well on the phone,' the Major said, starting on his boiled eggs and cold ham, the supper he ate every day, year in, year out, 'when you think he's deaf as a post to speak to. He thinks the thing might be worth quite a bit. If they did buy Orchard Cottage and we had some money in hand we could sell the rotary scythe and put down the first payment on a cultivator. And we could get all sorts of things when the electricity comes.'

He fell to brooding pleasantly over his tea.

Machinery, thought Sally. You'd think people would be wise to it by now. Spoiling your ability to do things for yourself, and then going wrong when you've come to depend on it. If it doesn't electrocute you first, or cut you in half.

She often wondered how her father managed to survive, but he seemed to bear a charmed life among his temperamental Sorcerer's Apprentices. Unlike George Thorless.

It was two years since George's tragedy. Sally's pity and grief for him still burned in her so painfully that her mind swung away like a shying horse from the thought of him.

George had been training as an auctioneer and valuer when the war came. He had taken to flying with enthusiasm, and became a civil air pilot when hostilities ended. He fell in love with a very beautiful girl, Dilys Heron, who became an air hostess in order to see as much of him as possible, and she was on board the ill-fated airliner that was accidentally shot down by Chinese guerrillas on its way out to Japan. Dilys was killed and George survived, with one leg and permanent total deafness.

Sally had become used to meeting George and Dilys sometimes about the lanes, and to battening down her agony of unspoken love. She had known at eighteen, and she knew now at twenty-four, that she wanted no one else in the world but George, and that she might as well hanker after Cleopatra's Needle. But what was still more unendurable was to see, nowadays, George's look of clenched, icy reserve and the bitter line of his mouth, shut like a trap. His deafness prevented his taking up his original job of auctioneer, and he had bought the old forge and lived on his pension, occasional odd jobs of valuation, and a bit of smithing and ornamental ironwork.

'It's a mysterious thing, you know,' old Doctor Coulthurst

had said to Sally once in an expansive moment, 'there's no organic reason for George's deafness so far as I can discover; if I was one of those psychologists, which thank God I'm not, I'd say he was deliberately shutting himself off from mankind. He needs some sort of a shock.'

Sally did her best to avoid George. Pride had kept her calm and heart-whole to all appearance in the face of George's overwhelming attachment to Dilys, and pride now helped her to live her life with courage and good sense.

Next day accordingly she took her paints and easel into the paddock where Goldenrod the pig lived, and began painting his portrait which was, in due course, to become the new signboard for the Pig and Whistle.

It was a pleasant occupation. Goldenrod rootled and grunted; when he moved too far away Sally flung down a handful of pignuts to tempt him back, but he was a sociable creature and mostly stayed near at hand while she roughed in his luscious curves and the spreading Landrace ears that earned him his nickname of Dumbo in the village.

After an hour or so Goldenrod pricked the ear that was pointing towards the garden gate and Sally saw her father coming along pushing the rotary scythe. Once through the gate he stooped, puffed, swore, and pulled the starter-string thirty or forty times. Letting out a roar of vindictive noise the machine then tore itself loose from him and launched off towards Goldenrod who, thoroughly alarmed, broke away and dashed through the orchard hedge into the lane. There was a shout from the other side of the hedge, a horse's terrified whinny, a fusillade of squeals and a thudding of hoofs, all faintly to be heard above the noise of the scythe which, with the bit between its teeth, had come up against a tree and was chattering in impotent rage.

'Turn that thing off, Sally,' shouted the Major. 'Someone's in trouble in the lane.'

Sally approached the motor and switched it off while her

father pushed through the hedge, shouting, 'Are you all right?' Then there was an ominous hush, save for the sound of Goldenrod, peacefully grunting among the Queen Anne's Lace.

'It's George!' the Major shouted. 'He's been thrown!'

Hollow with suspense, Sally hesitated, and then peered through the hedge to see her father supporting George, who looked sick and dazed.

'Thanks,' he was saying icily, 'of course it was stupid of me to ride up here on a raw colt that I'd just shod for the first time.'

'But are you all right, my dear chap?' the Major shouted again anxiously. 'How about the leg?'

'The good one's all right. The tin one's twisted round the wrong way.'

Listening to George's tone Sally dug her nails into her hands and prayed that her father would leave the subject. He did so.

'We'd better go up to the cottage – it's nearer than my place. I expect Miss Murdeigh will have a bit of brandy – so long as there isn't a dead mouse floating in it, ha ha! Now, how are we to manage? Sally,' he yelled, 'where are you? Come and take George's other arm, will you?'

'I'm all right, I can manage perfectly well like this.'

The walk up to the cottage was fortunately brief.

Sally said nothing – the difficulties of communicating with George were too great. She kept her eyes averted from him. She was in terror of the scene with the two old ladies, but, oddly enough, their attentions did not seem to distress George.

Miss Murdeigh quietly sat him down, looked at his knee, put a cold compress on it and said it would be all right in a few minutes. She did not fuss or exclaim, and George seemed strangely at ease looking round him at the unbelievable clutter, with the bitter lines for once smoothed from his face.

Miss Lambrette had tottered off and now reappeared with a crystal decanter, very dusty.

'No brandy, I am afraid,' Miss Murdeigh said. 'But perhaps a little Tio Pepe –?'

'I oughtn't to,' the Major said longingly when it was offered him. 'With my liver . . . but I can't resist it.'

Sally sipped her sherry quietly, listening to the muted flutter of the swallows that were nesting under the mantelpiece and watching from the corner of her eye a golden reflection dance from his drink on to George's lean jaw. How peaceful it would be, she mused, if George and I were paying a morning call on the old ladies, and afterwards we'd stroll back to the forge and he'd clink and clank on the anvil or grind away at the bellows while I cut bread and cheese and drew a jugful of cider.

She shut her eyes, seduced by this fancy, but opened them again when she heard George's hesitant voice:

'Is that the piece you wanted me to see? Perhaps I could be having a look at it.'

Sally suppressed a smile at her first sight of the birds but George took them seriously enough. He removed the glass case, turned the whole contraption upside down, and studied it carefully. Then he brought out from his pocket various keys and bits of wire and began trying them in the little keyhole.

'It's a Liefmehr, without a doubt,' he said politely to Miss Murdeigh, who was watching him with a lock of grey hair falling over her bright eyes. 'Do you know its history?'

'It was given me by the Duke of Medina Sidonia,' she told him. 'Of its history before it came into his possession I know nothing.'

'Speak up,' the Major muttered, 'don't forget the feller's deaf.'

'It's supposed to have an unusual gift,' Miss Murdeigh

went on in a piercing voice, 'that of granting a wish to any person hearing it for the first time.'

'Bosh,' grunted the Major to himself, and he said sceptically, 'Has it ever granted a wish for you, Miss Murdeigh?'

Miss Murdeigh shook her head. 'But then I have never played it,' she added. 'I lost the key in Madrid. And then, you know, I am so contented that I really have nothing left to wish for.'

'Ah,' said George suddenly. A click sounded from the interior of the mechanism. He began winding with a piece of bent wire, turning it carefully and slowly. His glance just brushed Sally, silent in her corner, and then all at once he smiled. I haven't seen *that* smile for five years, Sally thought. It was like unexpectedly meeting an old friend in the streets of a foreign city. She found that she was holding on tightly to the arms of her chair.

'You should all shut your eyes,' Miss Murdeigh commanded. Obediently they did so.

Oh, thought Sally, all her mind, her being, clenched on the one object. *Make him better, make him better.*

Dilys. George's mind went on its accustomed track. *If only I could forgive myself for letting you come. If only I could be sure you hadn't suffered.*

Unaware that he did so, he moved his head like someone trying to avoid unbearable pain.

That damned electric light, grumbled the Major to himself. *Bound to come some year, I suppose.*

The old ladies' eyes met, smiling across the birds as George's fingers finished their winding. Miss Murdeigh looked round the littered room contentedly, and she pushed a crumb of cheese nearer to a confiding mouse who was sitting at her elbow.

Then the birds began their dance. It was the sound of the music, so astonishingly like laughter, that first penetrated George's darkness. He couldn't help it; he opened his eyes.

And then kept them open, watching with incredulous pleasure the extraordinary galvanic hopping jig the birds were performing.

Sally heard the ludicrous sweet piping, and then she heard George laugh. She opened her eyes and saw him throw himself back in his chair, helpless and crowing with mirth, wiping the tears from his eyes. They were all laughing; Sally's ribs seemed to have ached all her life and she thought she would never breathe again; frail Miss Lambrette gave vent to an astonishing sonorous guffaw, even the upright Major was choking and mopping his eyes. There was something perfectly irresistible about the innocent, sugary tune accompanying that frantic flapping dance.

Oh, don't let it stop, don't let it ever stop, Sally begged, but already the birds were slowing down, and one of them suddenly flung itself forward in a last frenzied effort, right off its perch and on to the floor, while the other fell backward in an attitude of drunken exhaustion, and with a grinding jerk the music came to an end.

'By Jove,' said the Major. 'Don't know when I've laughed like that. Comical little beggars. But I'm afraid it's done it no good to play it, Miss Murdeigh.'

'Alas, I fear it was their swansong,' Miss Murdeigh agreed philosophically. 'Has the mainspring gone, Mr Thorless?'

He nodded. 'I'm sorry. I very much doubt if it can be repaired now – it's just shaken itself to bits.'

'And so we shall have, after all, to continue paying you rent,' said Miss Murdeigh to the Major, but she did not seem dismayed at the prospect. Indeed Sally thought there was a glint of amusement in her eye.

'Maybe it's as well,' the Major grunted heavily. 'Roof would be like a sieve and you'd probably be living in two foot of water without noticing it if I didn't give you a once-over from time to time.'

'Well, I must be going back,' Sally murmured, 'I left

some lentils in the oven.' Then she suddenly stood still. '*George!*'

He looked at her, smiling.

'You heard what Miss Murdeigh said! About the main-spring! And she wasn't shouting.'

'I suppose I did,' he agreed.

'You're hearing me!' He nodded again, looking a little shamefaced this time.

'Oh, you are irritating!' exclaimed Sally. Violently, inexplicably, she burst into tears and ran from the room. Wordlessly answering Miss Murdeigh's raised eyebrow, George limped rapidly after her.

'Well,' muttered the Major, 'I suppose it was that fall that did it. Most remarkable thing, most. I say, though, Miss Murdeigh, are you sure you wouldn't like Orchard Cottage as a gift? It seems such a damned shame about those birds being broken.'

Miss Murdeigh gave him her sweet, inscrutable smile. 'Really, do you know, I'd sooner go on paying you rent.'

' 'Fraid I haven't always been a very good neighbour,' the Major went on awkwardly. 'But I tell you what, as soon as the electricity comes along I'm going to sell Goldenrod and get a TV set, and then you must come up and watch whenever you like.'

He stumped off home, to the long blue envelope that awaited him with its undreamed-of mechanical possibilities.

Miss Murdeigh and Miss Lambrette fed the mice and sat down comfortably to play a sonata by Pousset.

Postman's Knock

It all began when Marilyn, feeling about in the post-office box to make sure her parcel had fallen through, found her hand taken in a warm, firm clasp, and a pair of lips gently, yet ardently pressed against it.

Or, no, it began when Fred Hwfa, pushing his red bike up the hill with two soap coupons addressed to The Lady of the House and a form from the Ministry of Agriculture relating to fowl pest, looked over a wall and saw an enchantingly pretty girl picking rhubarb.

Or perhaps it began when the entire sixth form of St Imelda's School for Girls, having been to a matinée of his play *Medea*, burst in on the dramatist in his London home just as he was triumphantly hammering down the first two lines of a new tragedy entitled (without any marked orginality) *Antigone*.

Really, of course, the whole thing originated with Fred's great-uncle the Nabob and his Arabian jar. The jar was not a particularly large one, but it was rather attractive in appearance, rounded and solid, and made of some blue stone with a faint sheen on it like alabaster. It was too small to be used for pot-plants, too large for an ash-tray, but Fred kept it on his desk, since it was the only personal possession his great-uncle had left him, apart from a hundred and fifty thousand pounds and the London house. But you cannot classify these as personal bequests, whereas the jar had been specifically mentioned. 'All I die possessed of and my blue Arabian jar to my great-nephew Frederick Sebastian Hwfa . . .'

The money was, if anything, an inconvenience, since, before his plays had become so successful, Fred had achieved a most adequate technique for living on cheese and carrots, which he was perfectly prepared to continue indefinitely. The house was a mausoleum in that part of London which might be called Chutney, falling as it does somewhere between Chelsea and Putney. He felt in duty bound to live in it, and at once fell prey to his admirers.

For by some mysterious spring-tide of public opinion, Fred's tragedies had become immensely popular. Glasses of stout, small ports, pints of beer stood untasted on saloon bars, while his heart-broken lines sobbed and muttered out of radio or television sets, and customers listened spellbound.

Poor Fred was shy to the roots of his eyelashes. He detested public notice. He had taken a dive into the font at his christening rather than face the scrutiny of all his aunts, and his behaviour since then had been of a similar pattern, culminating in his deliberate choice of playwriting as a career, for it had never occurred to him that he might become a *successful* playwright.

When the thirty hockey-playing prefects from St Imelda's burst into his study he was appalled. He looked round frantically for a means of escape. There was no second door, but his eye lit on the blue jar by his typewriter. Something about it beckoned him – an infinitesimal blue nod passed over its surface – and the next moment, neat as ninepence, he had climbed inside it, and the autograph hunters were looking about the room in perplexed disappointment.

'I could have sworn I saw him over Rosalie's shoulder –'

'*I* thought he was here –'

'If he's not in this room, ladies, then he's out,' said the butler, who, having been overborne by the first assault wave, was now making a comeback. And he marshalled them back down the stairs past the Nabob's engravings of the Acropolis under fire.

Presently Fred raised a cautious eye above the rim of the jar and, finding peace restored, clambered happily out to immerse himself once more in Antigone's troubles. That was

a most useful legacy of Uncle Swithin's he reflected; hither-
to he had not appreciated its worth, but from now on he was
never going to be parted from it by more than three feet.

He found it so useful, indeed, and spent so much time in it
dodging his fans, that at last his doctor, surveying him
sternly, told him that his lungs would atrophy from lack of
use unless he found some outdoor occupation.

It was at this point that Fred thankfully gave up his uncle's
house and took a job as postman in a remote and backward
district where it was to be hoped that no one would have
heard of him. A postman's life, he thought, should be ideal,
since it was solitary, healthy, and contained plenty of opportunity for those long, brooding walks during which the creative spirit begins to work and ferment. Moreover postmen
are seldom required to communicate with their fellow-men
save by the medium of raps on doors.

Naturally, though, he took his jar with him.

One of the first things he did, and this was completely
outside the programme he had laid down for himself, was to
fall in love.

In the country, of course, people do not take letters for
granted as city dwellers do. They know that writing a letter
entails coming in out of the garden, finding the ink in its nest
among bast and seed-potatoes, and a pen from the drawer
under the chick-incubators; then paper has to be procured,
and finally the letter has to be taken six miles to the post and
then carried up hill and down dale, through rain and shine,
by the devoted postman. So Fred soon found that he was
being handed clutches of eggs and vegetable marrows in exchange for pools-coupons and poultry-feed advertisements.

Next, he began to find his mind freewheeling ahead of
him to the white cottage by the millpool and his gifts of
rhubarb from Marilyn Gillan.

There was nothing out of the common about Marilyn,
save that she was pretty as a sea-pink, curvilinear as a sea-

shell, and had a very poor memory for faces, particularly male faces. Psychologists could have traced this to the fact that Marilyn was the elder sister of identical triplet brothers. Owing to the early death of her mother she had had the care of the triplets, Matthew, Mark, and Luke, since she was twelve years old. As their faces were indistinguishable, she had formed the habit of identifying them by their legs, since Matthew's were bandy, Mark's knock-kneed, and Luke's spindly as ballpoint pens. This worked all right until they went into long trousers; after that Marilyn gave up trying to tell them apart. In the meantime she had lost the knack of distinguishing faces and had to rely on her memory for legs, which, when confronted by the trousered male sex, was little help to her.

She had worked in London up to the time when her firm was taken over by new management. Marilyn tried in vain to memorize the faces of the new directors so that she could be civil to them when she met them in the lift. She constantly held doors open for surprised electricians and messengers, but was not sacked until she asked the managing director to whistle her up a taxi.

Much relieved, Marilyn rented a cottage in the wilds and began taking in paying guests, which suited her perfectly. People wrote booking rooms for specific dates, and so, when they arrived, she had no doubt as to who they were. She was so friendly, and her beds were so soft, and her cottage-pie so delicious, that departing guests invariably booked for the same week next year, and when they returned, Marilyn, after consulting her booking diary, was able to say, 'How nice to see you again, Mr and Mrs Hardcastle,' without giving away the fact that, to the best of her recollection, she had never seen their faces before.

Somehow when Fred first saw her over the wall, she reminded him of his jar; perhaps it was the blueness of her eyes, or the delicate and yet sturdy curve of the hip on which the basket of rhubarb was poised. There was something both reassuring and tantalizing about her appearance, and Fred longed to know her better.

He soon found, however, that she was a puzzle. For instance the first time he knocked on her door with a letter she called out,

'Who's there?'

'Fred.'

'Fred who?'

'Fred Hwfa.'

'Hwfa loaf is better than no bread,' said this enigmatic girl (who had acquired some regrettably schoolboyish habits from her brothers).

While Fred stood scratching his head over this, she opened the door fully, noticed his uniform, beamed, said, 'You must be the new postman, Fred. Fred any good books lately?' and invited him in for a glass of cherry wine. After that his heart was lost for ever.

When Marilyn learned that he was the author of *Medea*, *Orion*, and the rest of them, which he was soon tempted to confess, she evinced a becoming respect, but did not burst into hysterical fan giggles. Instead she remarked, 'Keep Orion the ball,' with her disconcerting grin.

But what puzzled Fred most of all was that, on the occasions when she met him out of uniform, or in the streets of Poldickery, the market town where postmen were two a penny, she would pass him without a smile or sign of recognition. It was all very mysterious, and added to her elusive charm.

Fred himself was vague and absent enough, in all conscience, for his new play was carrying him along like a velocipede, and he rode on his postman's rounds knee-deep in blank verse, kicking unwanted lines out of the way like dead leaves, and sometimes having to go back miles in order to deliver forgotten letters. On one occasion, indeed, when he knocked on Marilyn's door and she called out her usual 'Who's there?' before opening, he was so absorbed that, absently gazing at her hand on the door-jamb with its green signet-ring, he answered, 'Antigone.'

There was a baffled silence inside the door, and then Marilyn's voice suggested tentatively, 'Antigone rain no more, no more?'

Fred was so bewildered by this gambit that he put her soap coupon back in his satchel and went on his way in perplexity. When Marilyn looked out he had gone round the corner and there was no one in sight.

Ill consequences were to come of this. One of them was that Marilyn had to walk into Poldickery to post six letters accepting bookings (which normally she would have handed to Fred) and a parcel of rhubarb she was sending to her aunt Edith at Skegness. It was while she was reassuring herself about this parcel's safe arrival in the box that she felt the mysterious postal kiss deposited on her hand like a frank, or an impassioned postmark.

Marilyn let out a faint shriek, and her fingers were instantly released. She drew them out and gazed at them wonderingly. Her first notion, that there was a poltergeist in the postbox, was replaced by the correct one, that a postman had been clearing the cage inside at the moment her hand had entered the slot. But – and here Marilyn's heart went a pit-a-pat – *which* postman? Was it Fred? for whom, all secretly, she was beginning to feel a melting, burgeoning tenderness, like the upcurling rose-coloured fronds of the rhubarb in her garden? And if it was Fred, had he known it was her hand? It was true that she wore the green signet-ring, but had he recognized it?

With unparalleled courage, Marilyn walked into the post-office, asked for a packet of stamped postcards, and blushingly glanced about her. To her dismay there were no less than five postmen in the place, sorting mail, emptying sacks, and filling in various kinds of forms. She beat a discomfited retreat. Had one of them been Fred? Impossible to say. All their faces were alike.

Fred, on his side, had been so alarmed at his rash act that he hardly dared lift his eyes to Marilyn's face from then on. When, as he handed her an income-tax return next day, she turned a becoming pink and asked him in for a glass of cherry wine, he murmured that really he must not stop, and went on his way in a sad turmoil. His tragedy about Antigone faltered, lagged, and came to a standstill; he was unable to get his wretched heroine married off to Haemon.

Things had come to a pretty pass.

Marilyn, however, was not lacking in energy and resolution. She took to walking into Poldickery every day, and always posted her letters at the time when a postman cleared the mailbox. Twice more her fingers were kissed in its discreet depths. There must, she thought be *some* way by which she could discover the identity of her mail admirer; could she slip a noose over the hand, fasten it to a nearby tree, and then dart into the post-office while he stood captive?

She shrank, though, from the publicity and excitement this course would arouse; besides, even then, with her lover on a string, how would she be able to discover, without asking him straight out, and thus revealing her disability, whether he was indeed Fred? The only way to be sure of Fred's identity was to encounter him on his regular round.

Then the solution came to her – simple, masterly, leaving no room for doubt on either side.

Next day she loosened her signet-ring with a little soap, so that it would glide off easily, and when she posted her letters and the kiss was printed on her palm, she slid off the ring with her thumb and little finger (this was not easy, but she had devoted much practice to it) and deposited it, gently and confidingly, in the hand that held hers. Then, palpitating, she fled away. What if her admirer were not Fred?

What if some total stranger misconstrued her gesture and began to pursue her? She would have lost her precious ring in vain, and be subjected to a lot of inconvenience, too.

Next day at post-time she could hardly bear her anxiety. She was making rhubarb jam to distract her mind, and the whole cottage was full of the sweet, hot, amorous fragrance of boiling fruit and sugar.

A knock sounded on the door.

'Wh – who's there?' Marilyn murmured in trembling tones.

'Fred!' came the answer – ringing, confident, joyful. Her heart leapt.

'Bring the letters in!' she called. 'My hands are all jammy.'

He opened the door and came in. When she looked at his face, and then at his hand, Marilyn's doubts were all resolved. His face was ablaze with happiness; his hand, carrying a picture-postcard from Skegness, bore her ring. He laid the postcard on the table, gently took the jammy spoon from her hand, and folded her in the embrace that had been waiting for so long.

Hours seemed to pass; the jam boiled over; Antigone sat on her funeral pyre unregarded the afternoon postal collections were grievously late, and still these lovers remained as if fused together.

'My Andromeda, my Hebe, my Deianeira! Marry me! Be the post-mistress of my heart!'

'Oh, Fred,' Marilyn whispered, overcome. Then she became practical. 'Promise me that you will never, never take that ring off your little finger.'

'It needed no asking. my angel.'

Thus, after a slight superficial scrutiny, Marilyn was able to recognize her lover when she met him in the streets of Poldickery, and ran no risk of lavishing her embraces on no doubt equally deserving but less familiar postmen. By the winter, with its hazard of gloves, they would have been safely married for some time and she might have discovered some other landmark by which to recognize him; in any case, if you cut your husband in the street, the situation is not so desperate.

It was agreed that they should continue to live in the mill cottage. Fred endowed Marilyn with his hundred and fifty thousand, to buy a few more articles of furniture. He moved in his own possessions, which consisted of various manuscripts, a few dozen reams of foolscap paper, and his great-uncle's jar. Basking in the society of the delicious Marilyn, he felt less and less need for the reassurance of the jar, but still it might come in useful, and it looked pleasing on the mantelpiece of the blue and white kitchen.

Marilyn would no longer take in paying guests; financially there was now no need for it, and she decided that she would feel more secure – and there would be no possible chance of mistake – if Fred was the only man about the house.

They were married, and who shall speak of the raptures of the wedding night of Fred Hwfa and his bride? Suffice it to say that when Fred woke at seven next morning, his mind was a tumbling, inspired ferment of blank verse and love, Antigone, funeral pyres, Haemon, Marilyn, rhubarb, and rings. His first impulse was to leap out and grab his pen and some paper; his second, more decisive impulse was to wake his sleeping love.

He tapped lightly on her half-averted cheek, and she smiled in her sleep and began to turn to him.

'Who's there?' she said.

Alas for poor Fred, all bemused with love! He answered absently, 'Haemon,' and Marilyn shot up in the bed, gave him one startled glance, and shrieked, 'Haemon? I didn't marry *you*!'

Fred gazed at her, too dumbfounded to speak.

'How dare you lie there, in my bed, stroking my collar-bone?' she stormed. 'Leave my room at once!'

Fred, hungry, confused, at a loss, and wearing the less operative half of a pyjama-suit, felt in no case to argue. He crept mournfully down the stairs, and, finding the world altogether too complicated for him, climbed into his jar. There, being supplied with enough raw material for at least five acts, he curled up and sank into a trance of composition.

Weeks passed. Poor Marilyn was in despair. She searched in vain for her bridegroom; she haunted the post-office, she scrutinized every male hand. No ring to be seen.

Her Aunt Edith in Skegness, finding Marilyn's letters more and more dejected, and the parcels of rhubarb becoming very inferior in quality, came down on a visit to see what ailed her niece.

The loss of a new husband seemed light in Aunt Edith's eyes, when set against the background of a hundred and fifty thousand pounds; being a managing woman herself she decided that plenty of work was all that was needed to set Marilyn to rights, and she encouraged her niece to begin bottling rhubarb. Bottle after bottle, jar after jar, they indefatigably filled with pink and pearly segments, until the shelves in the storeroom resembled some museum of marine monstrosities. But still Marilyn drooped and pined, and Aunt Edith was not satisfied.

'We must bottle more,' she declared. 'There is still plenty of rhubarb.'

'No jars left,' sighed Marilyn, for the very thought of rhubarb was linked in her mind with that of Fred.

'Three pickle-bottles, a ginger-jar, and that thing on the mantelpiece,' announced Aunt Edith after a round-up of the house. 'That will be sufficient for this small bundle of rhubarb, at all events.'

'Fred's jar! I couldn't use that!'

'Nonsense,' Aunt Edith said masterfully. 'Why ever not?

He left you flat; at least you can make some use of the few odds and ends he brought you. Take down the jar; it will hold quite a nice lot of rhubarb.' And she stirred her boiling brew.

Marilyn took down the jar, but her hand shook as she thought of her wandering Fred, and she knocked it against the table-edge. A surprised voice from inside the jar called out,

'Who's there?'

Hardly daring to believe her ears, she whispered, 'M-Marilyn!'

Among the other fruits of Fred's meditations in the jar was a solution to Marilyn's puzzling responses to the question 'Who's there?'

Now, triumphantly, he remarked:

'Marilyn, Marilyn, shall I live now,
Under the blossom that hangs on the bough',

and stepping out of the jar, he took his bride in his arms.

Aunt Edith, unaccustomed to sudden and inexplicable appearances of young men in the less operative halves of pyjama-suits, screamed and went hastily out into the garden to pick more rhubarb.

'Fred!' Marilyn murmured (having identified him by the ring). 'Darling, where have you been all this time?'

'In the jar, of course,' he said. 'You just try it!' And he kissed her again, picked her up, and climbed back into jar with her.

They lived happily ever after.

The Cold Flame

I was asleep when Patrick rang up. The bell sliced through a dream about this extraordinary jampot factory, a kind of rose-red brick catacomb, much older than time, sunk deep on top of the Downs, and I was not pleased to be woken. I groped with a blind arm and worked the receiver in between my ear and the pillow.

'Ellis? Is that you?'

'Of course it is,' I snarled. 'Who else do you expect in my bed at three a.m.? Why in heaven's name ring up at this time?'

'I'm sorry,' he said, sounding muffled and distant and apologetic. 'Where I am it's only half past something.' A sort of oceanic roar separated us for a moment, then I heard him say, '... rang you as soon as I could.'

'Well, where are you?'

Then I woke up a bit more and interrupted as he began speaking again. 'Hey, I thought you were supposed to be dead! There were headlines in the evening papers – a climbing accident. Was it a mistake then?'

'No, I'm dead right enough. I fell into the crater of a volcano.'

'What were you doing on a *volcano*, for goodness' sake?'

'Lying on the lip writing a poem about what it looked like inside. The bit I was lying on broke off.' Patrick sounded regretful. 'It would have been a good poem, too.'

Patrick was a poet, perhaps I should explain. Had been a poet. Or said he was. No one had ever seen his poetry because he steadfastly refused to let anybody read his work, though he insisted, with a quiet self-confidence not otherwise habitual to him, that the poems were very good indeed.

In no other respect was he remarkable, but most people quite liked Patrick; he was a lanky, amusing creature with guileless blue eyes and a passion for singing sad, randy songs when he had had a drink or two. For some time I had been a little in love with Patrick. I was sorry to hear he was dead.

'Look, Patrick,' I began again. 'Are you sure you're dead?'

'Of course I'm sure.'

'Where are you, then?'

'Lord knows. I've hardly had time to look round yet. There's something on my mind; that's why I contacted you.'

The word contacted seemed inappropriate. I said, 'Why ring up?'

'I could appear if you'd prefer it.'

Remembering the cause of his death I said hastily, 'No, no, let's go on as we are. What's on your mind?'

'It's my poems, Ellis. Could you get them published, do you think?'

My heart sank a bit, as anybody's does at this sort of request from a friend, but I said, 'Where are they?'

'At my flat. A big thick stack of quarto paper, all hand-written. In my desk.'

'Okay. I'll see what I can do. But listen, love – I don't want to sound a gloomy note, but suppose no publisher will touch them – what then? Promise you won't hold me responsible? Keep hanging around, you know, haunting, that kind of thing?'

'No, of course not,' he said quickly. 'But you needn't worry. Those poems are good. There's a picture at the flat as well, though, behind the wardrobe, with its face to the wall. As a matter of fact it's a portrait of my mother. It's by Chapdelaine – done before he made his name. About seven years ago I got him to paint her for her birthday present (this was before I quarrelled with Mother, of course). But she didn't like it – said it was hideous – so I gave her a bottle of scent instead. Now, of course, it's worth a packet. You can get Sowerby's to auction it, and the proceeds would certainly pay for the publication of the poems, if necessary. But only in the last resort, mind you! I'm convinced those poems can stand on their own. I'm only sorry I didn't finish the volcano one – maybe I could dictate it –'

'I really must get some sleep,' I broke in, thinking what a good thing it was they hadn't got S T D yet between this world and the next. 'I'll go round to your flat first thing tomorrow. I've still got the key. Good-bye, Patrick.'

And I clonked back the receiver on its rest and tried to return to my lovely deep-hidden jampot factory among the brooding Downs. Gone beyond recall.

Next day at Patrick's flat I found I had been forestalled. The caretaker told me that a lady, Mrs O'Shea, had already called there and taken away all her son's effects.

I was wondering how to inform Patrick of this development – he hadn't left a number – when he got through to me again on his own phone. At the news I had to relate he let out a cry of anguish.

'Not Mother! God, what'll we do now? Ellis, that woman's a vulture. You'll have the devil's own job prising the poems out of her.'

'Why not just get in touch with her direct – the way you did with me – and tell *her* to send the poems to a publisher?' I said. 'Suggest trying Chatto first.'

'You don't understand! For one thing, I couldn't get near her. For another, she has this grudge against me; when I gave up going home it really dealt her a mortal blow. It'd give her the most exquisite pleasure to thwart me. No, I'm afraid you'll have to use all your tact and diplomacy, Ellis; you'd better drive down to Clayhole tomorrow –'

'But look here! Supposing she won't –'

No answer. Patrick had disconnected.

So next afternoon found me driving down to Clayhole. I had never been to Patrick's home – nor had Patrick, since the quarrel with his mother. I was quite curious to see her, as a matter of fact; Patrick's descriptions of her had been so conflicting. Before the breach she was the most wonderful mother in the world, fun, pretty, sympathetic, witty – while after it, no language had been too virulent to describe her, a sort of female Dracula, tyrannical, humourless, bloodsucking.

One thing I did notice as I approached the house – up a steep, stony, unmetalled lane – the weather had turned a bit colder. The leaves hung on the trees like torn rags, the ground was hard as iron, the sky leaden.

Mrs O'Shea received me with the utmost graciousness. But in spite of this I retained a powerful impression that I had arrived at an awkward moment; perhaps she had been about to bath the dog, or watch a favourite programme, or start preparing a meal. She was a small, pretty Irishwoman, her curling hair a beautiful white, her skin a lovely tea-rose pink, her eyes the curious opaque blue that goes with real granite obstinacy. One odd feature of her face was that she appeared to have no lips; they were so pale they disappeared into her powdered cheeks. I could see why Patrick had never mentioned his father. Major O'Shea stood beside his wife, but he was a nonentity; a stooped, watery-eyed, dangling fellow, whose only function was to echo his wife's opinions.

The house was a pleasant Queen Anne manor, furnished in excellent taste with chintz and Chippendale, and achingly, freezingly cold. I had to clench my teeth to stop them chattering. Mrs O'Shea in her cashmere twinset and pearls, seemed impervious to the glacial temperature, but the Major's cheeks were blue; every now and then a drop formed at the tip of his nose which he carefully wiped away with a spotless silk handkerchief. I began to understand why Patrick had been keen on volcanoes.

They stood facing me like an interview board while I explained my errand. I began by saying how grieved I had been to hear of Patrick's death, and spoke of his lovable nature and unusual promise. The Major did look genuinely grieved, but Mrs O'Shea was smiling, and there was something about her smile that irritated me profoundly.

I then went on to say that I had received a communication from Patrick since his death, and waited for reactions. They were sparse. Mrs O'Shea's lips tightened fractionally, the Major's lids dropped over his lugubrious milky-tea-coloured eyes; that was all.

'You don't seem surprised,' I said cautiously. 'You were expecting something of the kind perhaps?'

'No, not particularly,' Mrs O'Shea said. She sat down, placed her feet on a footstool and picked up a circular embroidery frame. 'My family is psychic, however; this kind of thing is not unusual. What did Patrick want to say?'

'It was about his poems.'

'Oh yes?' Her tone was as colourless as surgical spirit. She carefully chose a length of silk. Her glance flickered once to the object she was using as a footstool: a solid pile of papers about a foot thick, wrapped up clumsily in an old grey cardigan which looked as if it had once lined a dog-basket; it was matted with white terrier-hairs.

My heart sank.

'I believe you have his poems now? Patrick is most anxious that they should be published.'

'And I'm not at all anxious they should be published,' Mrs O'Shea said with her most irritating smile.

'Quite, quite,' the Major assented.

We argued about it. Mrs O'Shea had three lines of argument: first, that no one in her family had ever written poetry therefore Patrick's poems were sure to be hopeless; second, that no one in her family had ever written poetry and, even in the totally unlikely event of the poems being any good, it was a most disreputable thing to do; third, that Patrick was conceited, ungrateful, and self-centred, and it would do him nothing but harm to see his poems in print. She spoke as if he were still alive.

'Besides,' she added, 'I'm sure no publisher would look at them.'

'You have read them?'

'Heavens, no!' she laughed. 'I've no time for such rubbish.'

'But if a publisher did take them?'

'You'd never get one to risk his money on such a venture.'

I explained Patrick's plans regarding the Chapdelaine portrait. The O'Sheas looked sceptical. 'You perhaps have it here?' I asked.

'A hideous thing. Nobody in their senses would give enough money for that to get a book published.'

'I'd very much like to see it, all the same.'

'Roderick, take Miss Bell to look at the picture,' Mrs O'Shea said, withdrawing another strand of silk.

The picture was in the attic, face down. I saw at once why Mrs O'Shea had not liked it. Chapdelaine had done a merciless job of work. It was brilliant – one of the best examples of his early Gold Period. I imagined it would fetch even more than Patrick hoped. When I explained this to the Major an acquisitive gleam came into his eye.

'Surely that would more than pay for the publication of the poems?'

'Oh, certainly,' I assured him.

'I'll see what my wife has to say.'

Mrs O'Shea was not interested in cash. She had a new line of defence. 'Of course you've no actual proof that you come from Patrick, have you? I don't really see why we should take your word in the matter.'

Suddenly I was furious. My rage and the deadly cold were

simultaneously too much for me. I said, as politely as I could, 'Since I can see you are completely opposed to my performing this small service for your son I won't waste any more of our time,' and left them abruptly. The Major looked a little taken aback, but his wife calmly pursued her stitchery.

It was good to get out of that icy, lavender-scented morgue into the fresh, windy night.

My car limped down the lane pulling to the left but I was so angry that I had reached the village before I realized I had a flat tyre. I got out and surveyed it. The car was slumped down on one haunch as if Mrs O'Shea had put a curse on it.

I went into the pub for a hot toddy before changing the wheel and while I was in there the landlord said, 'Would you be Miss Bell? There's a phone call for you.'

It was Patrick. I told him about my failure and he cursed, but he did not seem surprised.

'Why does your mother hate you so, Patrick?'

'Because I got away from her. That's why she can't stand my poetry – because it's nothing to do with her. Anyway she can hardly read. If my father so much as picks up a book she gets it away from him as soon as she can and hides it. Well, you can see what he's like. Sucked dry. She likes to feel she knows the whole contents of a person's mind, and that it's entirely focused on *her*. She's afraid of being left alone; she's never slept by herself in a room in her life. If ever he had to go away she'd have my bed put in her room.'

I thought about that.

'But as to your authority to act for me,' Patrick went on. 'We can easily fix that. Have a double whisky and get a pen and paper. Shut your eyes.'

Reluctantly I complied. It was an odd sensation. I felt Patrick's light, chill clutch on my wrist, moving my hand. For a moment, the contrast with the last time I had held his hand made a strangling weight of tears rise in my throat; then I remembered Mrs O'Shea's icy determination, and realized that Patrick resembled her in this; suddenly I felt free of him, free of sorrow.

When I opened my eyes again, there was a message in Patrick's odd, angular script, to the effect that he authorized me to sell his Chapdelaine picture and use the proceeds to pay for the publication of his poems, if necessary.

The drinks had fortified me, so I got a garage to change my wheel and walked back up the lane to Clayhole. The O'Sheas had just finished their supper. They invited me civilly, but without enthusiasm, to drink coffee with them. The coffee was surprisingly good, but stone-cold, served in little gold-rimmed cups the size of walnut shells. Over it Mrs O'Shea scanned Patrick's message. I glanced round – we were in the arctic dining-room – and noticed that Chapdelaine's picture had now been hung on the wall. It smiled at me with Mrs O'Shea's own bland hostility.

'I see; very well,' she said at last. 'I suppose you must take the picture then.'

'And the poems, too, I hope.'

'Oh no. Not yet,' she said '*When* you've sold the picture, for this large sum you say it will fetch, *then* I'll see about letting you have the poems.'

'But that's not –' I began, and then stopped. What was the use? She was not a logical woman, no good reasoning with her. One step at a time was as fast as one could go.

The sale of an early Chapdelaine portrait made quite a stir, and the bidding at Sowerby's began briskly. The picture was exhibited on an easel on the auctioneer's dais. From my seat in the front row I was dismayed to notice, as the bids rose past the four-figure mark, that the portrait was beginning to fade. The background remained, but by the time twenty-five hundred had been reached, Mrs O'Shea had vanished completely. The bidding faltered and came to a stop; there were complaints. The auctioneer inspected the portrait, directed an accusing stare at me, and declared the sale null. I had to take the canvas ignominiously back to my flat, and the evening papers had humorous headlines: *Where did the colours run to? No bids for Chapdelaine's White Period.*

When the telephone rang I expected that it would be Patrick and picked up the receiver gloomily, but it was a French voice.

'Armand Chapdelaine here. Miss Bell?'

'Speaking.'

'We met, I think once, a few years ago, in the company of young Patrick O'Shea. I am ringing from Paris about this odd incident of his mother's portrait.'

'Oh yes?'

'May I come and inspect the canvas, Miss Bell?'

'Of course,' I said, slightly startled. 'Not that there's anything to see.'

'That is so kind of you. Till tomorrow, then.'

Chapdelaine was a French Canadian: stocky, dark, and full of *loup-garou* charm.

After carefully scrutinizing the canvas he listened with intense interest to the tale about Patrick and his mother.

'Aha! This is a genuine piece of necromancy,' he said, rubbing his hands. 'I always knew there was something unusually powerful about that woman's character. She had a most profound dislike for me; I recall it well.'

'Because you were her son's friend.'

'Of course.' He inspected the canvas again and said, 'I shall be delighted to buy this from you for two thousand five hundred pounds, Miss Bell. It is the only one of my pictures that has been subjected to black magic, up to now.'

'Are you quite sure?'

'Entirely sure.' He gave me his engagingly wolfish smile.

'Then we will see what shot Madame Mère fetches out of her locker.'

Mrs O'Shea was plainly enjoying the combat cver Patrick's poems. It had given her a new interest. When she heard the news that two thousand five hundred pounds was lodged in a trust account, ready to pay for the publication of the poems if necessary, her reaction was almost predictable.

'But that wouldn't be honest!' she said. 'I suppose Mr Chapdelaine bought the canvas out of kindness, but it can't be counted as a proper sale. The money must be returned to him.' Her face set like epoxy and she rearranged her feet more firmly on the footstool.

'On no account will I have it back, madame,' Chapdelaine riposted. He had come down with me to help persuade her; he said he was dying to see her again.

'If you won't then it must be given to charity. I'm afraid it's out of the question that I should allow money which was obtained by what amounts to false pretences to be used to promote that poor silly boy's scribblings.'

'Quite, quite,' said the Major.

'But it may not be necessary –' I began in exasperation. An opaque blue gleam showed for an instant in Mrs O'Shea's eye. Chapdelaine raised a hand soothingly and I subsided. I'd known, of course, that I too was an object of her dislike, but I had not realized how very deep it went; the absolute hatred in her glance was a slight shock. It struck me that, unreasonably enough, this hate had been augmented by the fact that Chapdelaine and I were getting on rather well together.

'Since Madame does not approve of our plan I have another proposition,' said Chapdelaine, who seemed to be taking a pleasure in the duel almost equal to that of Mrs O'Shea. I felt slightly excluded. 'May I be allowed to do a second portrait, and two thousand five hundred shall be the sitter's fee?'

'Humph,' said Mrs O'Shea. 'I'd no great opinion of the last one ye did.'

'Hideous thing. Hideous,' said the Major.

'Oh, but this one, madame, will be quite different!' Chapdelaine smiled, at his most persuasive. 'In the course of seven years, after all, one's technique alters entirely.'

She demurred for a long time but in the end, I suppose, she could not resist this chance of further entertainment. Besides he was extremely well known now.

'You'll have to come down here, though, Mr Chapdelaine; at my age I can't be gadding up to London for sittings.'

'Of course,' he agreed, shivering slightly; the sittingroom was as cold as ever. 'It will be a great pleasure.'

'I think the pub in the village occasionally puts up visitors,' Mrs O'Shea added. 'I'll speak to them.' Chapdelaine shuddered again. 'But they only have one bedroom, so I'm afraid there won't be room for *you*, Miss Bell.' Her tone expressed volumes.

'Thank you but I have my job in London,' I said coldly. 'Besides I'd like to be getting on with offering Patrick's poems; may I take them now, Mrs O'Shea?'

'The? – Oh, gracious, *no* – not till the picture's finished! After all,' she said, with a smile of pure, chill malice, 'I may not like it when it's done, may I?'

'It's a hopeless affair, hopeless!' I raged, as soon as we were away from the house, 'She'll always find some way of slipping out of the bargain; she's utterly unscrupulous. The woman's a fiend! Really I can't think how Patrick could ever have been fond of her. Why do you bother to go on with this?'

'Oh, but I am looking forward to painting this portrait immensely!' Chapdelaine wore a broad grin. 'I feel convinced this will be the best piece of work I ever did. I shall have to get that house warmed up, though, even if it means myself paying for a truckload of logs; one cannot work inside of a deep-freeze.'

Somehow he achieved this; when I took down a photographer to get a story, with pictures, for the magazine on which I work, we found the sitting-room transformed, littered with artists' equipment and heated to conservatory temperature by a huge roaring fire. Mrs O'Shea, evidently making the most of such unaccustomed syberitude, was seated close by the fire, her feet, as ever, firmly planted on the blanket-wrapped bundle. She seemed in high spirits. The Major was nowhere to be seen; he had apparently been banished to some distant part of the house. Chapdelaine, I thought, did not look well; he coughed from time to time, complained of damp sheets at the pub, and constantly piled more logs on the fire. We took several shots of them both, but Mrs O'Shea would not allow us to see the uncompleted portrait.

'Not till it's quite done!' she said firmly. Meanwhile it stood on its easel in the corner, covered with a sheet, like some hesitant ghost.

During this time I had had numerous calls from Patrick, of course; he was wildly impatient about the slow progress of the painting.

'Do persuade Armand to go a bit faster, can't you, Ellis? He used to be able to dash off a portrait in about four sittings.'

'Well, I'll pass on your message, Patrick, but people's methods change, you know.'

When I rang Clayhole next day, however, I was unable to get through; the line was out of order, apparently, and remained so; when I reported this to the local exchange the girl said, 'Double four six three ... wait a minute; yes, I thought so. We had a nine-nine-nine call from them not long ago. Fire brigade. No, that's all I can tell you, I'm afraid.'

With my heart in my suède boots I got out of the car and drove down to Clayhole. The lane was blocked by police trucks, fire engines, and appliances; I had to leave my car at the bottom and walk up.

Clayhole was a smoking ruin; as I arrived they were just carrying the third blackened body out to the ambulance.

'What began it?' I asked the chief.

'That'll be for the insurance assessors to decide, miss. But it's plain it started in the lounge; spark from the fire, most likely. Wood fires are always a bit risky, in my opinion. You get that green apple wood —'

A spark, of course; I thought of the jersey-wrapped pile of poems hardly a foot away from the crackling logs.

'You didn't find any papers in that room?'

'Not a scrap, miss; that being where the fire started, everything was reduced to powder.'

When Patrick got through to me that evening he was pretty distraught.

'She planned the whole thing!' he said furiously. 'I bet you, Ellis, she had it all thought out from the start. There's absolutely nothing that woman won't do to get her own way. Haven't I always said she was utterly unscrupulous? But I shan't be beaten by her, I'm just as determined as she is — *Do* pay attention Ellis!'

'Sorry, Patrick. What were you saying?' I was very low-spirited, and his next announcement did nothing to cheer me.

'I'll dictate you the poems, it shouldn't take more than a month or so if we keep at it. We can start right away. Have you a pen? And you'll want quite a lot of paper. I've finished the volcano poem, so we may as well start with that — ready?'

'I suppose so.' I shut my eyes. The cold clutch on my wrist was like a fetter. But I felt that, having gone so far, I owed this last service to Patrick.

'Right – here we go.' There followed a long pause. Then he said, with a good deal less certainty:

> 'On each hand the flames
> Driven backward slope their pointing spires –'

'That's from *Paradise Lost*, Patrick,' I told him gently.

'I know . . .' His voice was petulant. 'That isn't what I meant to say. The thing is – it's starting to get so cold here. Oh, God, Ellis – it's so *cold* . . .'

His voice petered out and died. The grasp on my wrist became freezing, became numbing, and then, like a melted icicle, was gone.

'Patrick?' I said. 'Are you there, Patrick?'

But there was no reply, and indeed, I hardly expected one. Patrick never got through to me again. His mother had caught up with him at last.

Lodging for the Night

'This sewing-machine will last you over sixty years without needing repair or maintenance,' said Henry Dulge. He took a quick look at the housewife; that should see her well into her hundred-and-twenties. 'It is rustless, foolproof, perfectly insulated, five pounds down, and a hundred-and-forty-eight payments of ninety-nine-and-a-half. I'll leave it with you for a week's trial, shall I? Or will you sign right away, here's the form . . .'

'It's ever so kind of you,' she said faintly. 'But in your advert that I saw it said – what I wrote up for was –'

'And of course that entitles you to free service and repair for the first two months, not that you are going to need that with an O-Sew-matic, ha ha!'

'You did say in your advert that you had reconditioned models for sale for eight pounds,' she persisted timidly.

His face changed. 'Oh, well, of course, if you want *that* sort of stuff – We did have just a few, but they're trash, let me assure you, madam, trash! Why, you'd only use one for a few days before you'd be begging me to change it for an O-Sew-matic. Now, this lovely model here, you can make all your children's clothes on it, curtains, quilts, it's like a dream to handle –'

'Haven't you one of the £8 models in your van that I could just look at?' she pleaded.

He hesitated. But it was pouring with rain, and she looked the sort that could be browbeaten – a pale, pulpy little woman with hair like tangled raffia. 'No I haven't, as a matter of fact,' he snapped. 'Sold the last one to a silly old fool who didn't know a bad bargain when she saw one. Now you be sensible, madam, you take my advice, you'll never regret it –'

She wavered. 'Well – I do want to get on with my husband's winter shirts –'

He handed her the pen.

At this critical moment her husband came home, beer-flavoured and hungry for his supper.

'What the blazes is going on here ?' he growled, taking in the whole situation – the poised pen, the form with its mass of small print, the seductive glitter of the O-Sew-matic and Henry Dulge's truculence suddenly turned ingratiating.

'I was just explaining to your good lady here –'

She gave her husband an alarmed, pleading smile, but he was wasting no time.

'Out! And take your flaming machine with you. I'll have no never-never in my house. *Out!*'

The rain blattered against the front window. Henry Dulge was not a coward. He rallied for a last try – but the husband moved towards him so threateningly that he abandoned the hope, picked up the O-Sew-matic, said, with an angry, pitying laugh, 'Well, I'm afraid you're going to be very, very sorry for this, madam. You won't often get the chance of such a bargain,' and departed, letting the wind slam the door behind him.

Rain sluiced over the aluminium cover of the O-Sew-matic, and he had to rub it dry, cursing, before he drove off into the drenching dusk. He was so annoyed at having missed what promised to be an easy sale that, instead of finding a hotel for the night, as he had intended, he drove straight through the town and on along the coast road towards Crowbridge.

The rain spun down in his headlights, thick as thatch, and bounced off the shingle-spattered road. Every half-mile or so illuminated signs by the roadside warned 'This Road impassable during Spring Tides when tide is high.'

Dulge had no notion whether the tide was at springs or neaps, but in any case it was satisfactorily far out – only occasionally when the road curved up over a bluff did he catch a glimpse of tossing, menacing whitecaps, far to his right.

He passed a solitary, plodding walker, a tramp, to judge from his pack and ragged coat, and took a mean pleasure in cutting close past the man to spray him with mud and sand from the wheels. The fellow must be soaked through, anyway ; a bit extra wouldn't make much odds.

Ten miles farther on he overtook another pedestrian, this time a girl. She was wearing a dark rain-cape but the headlights picked out the white kerchief over her hair. Henry's chivalry came to the fore, and he pulled in beside her and opened the door.

'Hop in, mermaid,' he said jovially. She seemed startled, but thanked him, and settled quietly beside him. He let in the clutch, pleased with such a piece of luck : this girl was a peach, a real contest-winner, looked a bit chilled with the wet and cold – what the devil was she doing walking along the coast road at this time of night? – but a topnotch figure, what he could see of it, and classy, too, with that pale-gold hair trained back from a high forehead.

'Dangerous along here, didn't you know?' he said. 'Wouldn't want the tide to come in and wash away a pretty girl like you.'

'Oh, I often walk this way,' she said carelessly. 'There is no danger if you know the state of the tide.'

'Live in Crowbridge?'

'Yes, I have a house there.'

'All on your own?'

She nodded. His eyes widened. This seemed an unbelievably promising situation.

'That makes two of us, then. Here's me, a poor bachelor, don't know a soul in the town. How about cheering me up? Have dinner with me at the Ship?'

'You are kind,' she said, 'but I never eat at inns.'

'How about inviting me round to your place, then? Take pity on the stranger, eh?'

She looked at him oddly. 'I never invite guests. Those who wish for my hospitality must find the way themselves.'

They had entered the small port of Crowbridge and were climbing the main street towards the upper town. Street lamps, wildly swinging from their brackets, threw shifting gleams of light on tudor gables and brickwork.

'I won't be shy in finding the way, darling, believe me. What's your name? Where's your house?'

'I live near here,' she said, 'if you will be so kind as to put me down.'

'Ah, come on now, darling. At least have a quick one with me at the old Ship, to keep out the wet.'

'Thank you no, I –'

But he drove on. He was forced to stop, though, at the traffic lights, and to his annoyance she somehow managed to slip out – heaven knew how she did it, for he thought he had locked the door and that catch was the devil to shift anyway. Before he could let out a word or curse she was gone, following the flutter of her kerchief into the dark rainy night. The lights changed to green and a furious hooting from behind forced him on, damning her whole-heartedly, the artful bitch! But Crowbridge was a small town, maybe someone at the pub would know who she was.

He made straight for the bar and had three doubles in quick succession to sink the memory of the missed sale and the mislaid pick-up. Then he inquired about a bed for the night.

'Sorry, sir. I'm afraid we're full right up.'

'Full up? In October? Are you crazy?'

'It's the annual conference of the N.A.F.F.U., sir. Always held in Crowbridge. I'm afraid you won't find a bed in the town. I know for a fact they're full at the Crown and the George, we've had people come on from there.'

'For Pete's sake! Isn't there anywhere in the town I can get a bed – digs, boarding-house, anything?' He appealed to the other drinkers in the bar. 'Can't any of you gentlemen suggest somewhere? It's thirty miles on to Castlegate.'

They hesitated. 'The road's flooded, too, between here and Castlegate,' put in the barman. 'I doubt you'd not get through that way.'

'Well,' said one man after a pause, 'he could sleep at the old Dormer House.'

'What's that?' Henry's hopes rose. 'A hostel?'

'No, it's a private house. As a matter of fact it's empty now – due for demolition. Work starts tomorrow. The Council's been itching to get it out of the way for years, but they couldn't touch it till the last of the family died, which she did a couple of months back – an old lady of ninety-three. Historic sort of place, some society's been protesting about the demolition, but the house sticks right out into a crossroads, makes a very dangerous corner.'

'Ah well, some of these old places have to come down, can't keep 'em all,' Henry agreed. 'But I can't stay there if it's empty, can I? I don't fancy sleeping on bare boards.'

'Ah, you see, that's the point. It's a kind of a celebrated house, the old Dormer – you're sure you haven't heard of it?'

'No, never.'

'There's a tradition that if anyone asks to stay, the family will allow them to – Hardisty, the family name was, belonged to the Hardistys since the first Queen Elizabeth's time – and give them free fire and bedding. A clause in the old lady's will, the Miss Hardisty who just died, said this custom was to be kept up till demolition began. So you'll find fires and beds there.'

'Free fire and bedding? Sounds too good to be true! Maybe my luck's changing. And about time, too.'

'There's another thing.'

'Well?'

'Anyone who stays there till eight o'clock next morning has a right to claim a thousand pounds from the Estate.'

'A *thousand pounds*? What do you think I am? A sucker?'

But all the men in the bar assured him that this was perfectly true. They were quite serious. Henry, studying the faces, began to believe them.

'But has nobody claimed it yet?'

'Not one. It's haunted, you see.'

'Haunted? What by?' Henry looked sceptical. 'I'd like to see the ghost that could shift *me* out of a free bed and a thousand quid.'

'By one of the family, a girl called Bess Hardisty who lived in the first Elizabeth's time. The story goes that her young man fell in love with the Queen. He was so dazzled that he went off and forgot Bess, sailed to discover the Indies and never came back. She turned bitter and sour, lived to be very old, and was finally burned as a witch. Since then no one but members of the family can sleep in the house – she gives people terrible dreams.'

Henry burst out laughing. 'She'll be clever if she can give me dreams! Why, it's a cinch. Can you do me dinner here?' he asked the barman.

'Why yes, sir, we can manage that.'

'All right, you give me some dinner, and then tell me where to find this place. By the way,' he added, remembering, 'can you tell me the name of a girl who lives on her own here, very pretty girl, about twenty-five, pale blonde hair?'

'No sir, I can't say I can call her to mind,' said the barman. 'But I haven't been here long.' The other men shook their heads. Did some of them look at Henry oddly? It was probably his hunger that made him imagine them suddenly pale and remote, as if seen through glass; he would pursue the matter of the girl when he'd had a good dinner.

The Ship dinner was excellent, but the service was slow. It was near closing-time when Henry returned to the bar, and by now he was feeling tired. The men who had been there before were gone now, and the barman seemed pre-occupied. Why bother about the girl? If she was lost, she was lost, no sense whining over her. He had a couple more drinks fairly fast, put his car in the town car-park, and took the direction the barman had given him.

The rain had let up a little, but it was still too dark to see much of the old Dormer House, and he was in no mood to linger. He pushed open the heavy door and climbed the stairs. No electricity, but he had his powerful car-torch, and from somewhere above he could see the glow and hear the comfortable crackle of a blazing fire.

A few rooms he looked into were empty, already stripped of their furniture, but, following the firelight, he found a big stately bedroom with a carpet and chairs and a blue-silk-hung fourposter. It smelt delicious, of applewood and laven-der. Henry dumped his wet case on the carpet with a grunt of content and punched the mattress.

'This certainly beats the old Ship,' he said to himself with satisfaction. 'I bet Queen Elizabeth never slept on *that*.'

Apart from himself, the house seemed empty. He un-dressed, leisurely, by the leaping fire, replenished it from a basket of logs, bolted the door, and got into bed. The bed was even warm – you might have thought one of those Elizabethan things, what did they call them, warming-pans, had just been taken out of it.

And when he was more than halfway into the mist of sleep a pair of warm arms came round his neck and a voice said gently in his ear,

'Did you think you weren't going to see me again? I knew you'd find your way here.'

'Is that you, darling?' Henry murmured sleepily. 'My luck surely has turned. But how did you get in? I could have sworn there was no one in the place.'

'I was here already. Don't you see? I live here . . .'

It was after him. It was gaining on him. A hundred, five hundred people, women mostly were watching him with hating eyes, cheering it on, and it was plunging along the road behind him, its great wheel letting off blue sparks as it whirled round, the gigantic needle munching steadily towards him, cutting the tar of the road as if it were cheese. Now it was right alongside him and he was paralysed, unable to stir, and the needle was above him, vibrating, poised for the terrible downward thrust that would pierce from brain to groin, pinning him to the bed like a butterfly –

He woke sweating, screaming, struggling with the bed-clothes. Instinctively he turned to seek the comfort of his bedmate but she was gone. Could he feel something metallic, hard and ice-cold among the sheets? He leapt out as if he had found a snake in the bed. The grip of nightmare was still on him and he started pulling on his clothes with frantic trembling haste, all other considerations lost in the urge to get out of there. He kept glancing haggardly at the ceiling, as if he expected the great bright needle to come plunging through to impale him. The fire burned bright, but he never noticed the portrait on the wall of a pale, gilt-haired girl smiling primly above her ruff, he overlooked the scatter of clothes on a chair, the brocade skirts, the little square-toed shoes with jewelled buckles. He unbolted the door with shaking hands, stumbled down the stairs, and ran for the car-park like a hunted thing. The rain had stopped but dead leaves like packs of wolves scurried down the street after him and the wind shook and grappled him. Not a soul stirred; it was the dead hour of night.

He found a board across the Castlegate road: 'Floods.

Impassable,' and turned back the way he had come, along the coast road to Trowchester. The tide was nearly full now, he could hear the roar of the waves like a thousand sewing-machines, and he cast a nervous glance in the rear mirror, half wondering if he would see *It* coming steadily along behind, munching up the miles. What a hell of a dream. He would have to pack in the job if he had many more like that.

When he turned his eyes back to the road ahead he found the girl sitting in the car beside him.

He gasped something incoherent. His hands shook and slipped on the wheel.

'You didn't think I'd stay behind, did you?' she said. 'I'm coming with you. They're pulling my house down tomorrow, I shall have nowhere to live. It was lucky you came to see me tonight. Now I can come and live in *your* house.'

'You can't — you can't!' he gabbled. 'I've a wife — children—'

He jabbed his foot on the accelerator, and the car swooped up over a bluff, following the old, winding coast road. But on the far side of the bluff there was no road, only the white-capped waves, warring with the dark of the night, grinding like a thousand sewing-machines against the shingle bank. His car ran smoothly in among the crests and disappeared.

At about the same time two policemen were interrogating a tramp in the streets of Crowbridge.

'Let's have a look at that pack of yours,' one of them said, mistrusting the raggedness of the man and the suspicious weight of the pack.

'I object,' the tramp said with dignity. 'It's starting to rain again and I don't want my things all wet.'

'You'll have to come along to the station then.'

He accompanied them without protest. He was a blue-eyed, weatherbeaten man who might have been any age between forty and seventy. His pack, opened at the police station, proved to contain sheets of paper covered with handwriting, and a number of books.

'Russian,' whispered one of the constables. 'Think he's a spy, sarge?'

'That's Greek, you ignorant thick,' said the sergeant, who had been on Crete. 'All right, you can go. Be a bit more cooperative another time.'

'It's coming down hard now,' the tramp said mildly. 'I suppose you can't put me up for the night in a cell?'

'Sorry, mate, cells all full up with trade union members sleeping it off.'

'He could go to the Old Dormer,' the constable said.

'Where's that?' the tramp asked.

The sergeant said, doubtfully, 'Well, I suppose it won't do no harm.'

They told him how to get there.

It was raining hard again. The tramp made haste to get indoors but then, instead of going upstairs, found the big stone flagged kitchen with its massive table, and pulled up a chair. He took a piece of paper, a pencil, and a lump of cheese from his pack, and began writing, slowly, with many crossings-out, absently taking a bite of cheese from time to time.

About half an hour later he jumped violently, as he suddenly became aware that someone was looking over his shoulder.

'Why don't you come upstairs?' she said. 'There's a fire upstairs.'

'Blimey, you gave me a start,' he said. 'I never heard you come in.'

'Come up by the fire?' she repeated.

'All right, miss. That's very kind of you. I'll just finish this.'

He wrote for another ten minutes, and then followed her up to the room with the fourposter. The bed was smoothly made, the fire leaping. 'Nice place,' he said, with appreciation, looking round. He sat by the fire.

'Wouldn't you like to go to bed?' she asked.

'Well, thanks, miss, but I'm not sleepy. Had a good kip under a hedge this afternoon. I think I'll read for a bit, unless you feel like a chat.'

'That was a sonnet you were writing, wasn't it? Why do you write sonnets?'

'I dunno, really. I just took a fancy to. That's why I'm on the roads. I used to be a seaman, radio technician, till I retired and had me own little business. Then I took this fancy to write sonnets and learn languages. Well, after all, you've only got one life, got to please yourself sometimes, haven't you? So my daughter and son-in-law that I lived with, they got fed up and gave me the push.'

'Your own daughter turned you out?' she said, shocked.

'You couldn't blame her, lass, with me not bringing in any money. Matter of fact I've been happier since then than ever in me life. No worries, got my transistor if ever I feel lonely. Like a bit of music?'

He turned a switch and suddenly the room was filled with sweet, orderly sound.

'Cood, isn't it? That's Hamburg. Made the set myself.'

'But that is a galliard!' she said, her face lighting up. 'We used to dance to it. Like this!'

She rose and began turning and gliding before him, holding up her brocade skirts so that the jewels in her buckled shoes glittered in the firelight.

'Brayvo!' he said. 'That's as good as Sadlers' Wells!'

'You dance, too!' She caught at his hand. 'Oh, what a long time it is since I danced!'

'Me, lass? I don't know how. All I ever learned was the two-step.'

'I can show you. See how easy it is? The music carries you.'

And indeed it did seem that the music was guiding him through the intricate courtly pattern of the dance. He stepped erectly, his blue eyes shone at her as she moved and dipped, graceful as a ship under full sail. One dance followed another, and yet he was not tired, or conscious of any incongruity in their dancing together. At last the music ended and she swept him a deep curtsey.

'See,' she said, 'we have danced so long that dawn is breaking. I never thought to dance again.'

'So we have. So we have. And yet I don't feel tired at all. I believe I could walk sixty miles this very minute, and never notice.'

He looked out of the window. A wild and ragged dawn was breaking over the wet roofs of the town. Pointed gables gleamed in the first light.

'I'd best be off, I reckon. Thank you kindly for the night's shelter, lass.'

'There's a thousand pounds for you if you wait here till eight o'clock,' she said. 'Stay a bit longer.'

He looked blank, then laughed. 'What good is a thousand to me? They better build themselves a new school or do something useful with it. No, thank you all the same – I'll be on the move –'

He was halfway along the coast road, where the shingle lay in gleaming heaps, scattered by the receding tide, when he heard her light step behind him.

'I've a mind to come along. Will you let me come with you?' she called.

'And welcome, lass, if you want to.'

She tucked her arm through his. 'Can we have a bit of music?'

A coastguard, coming out early to survey the storm damage, saw the tramp but not the girl. Till the end of his days he carried a memory of the man with ragged clothes and clear blue eyes, who went free as the air along the battered coast road, stepping out briskly to the music of Mr William Byrd.

Safe and Soundproof

There she sat, pretty as a bumble-bee with her gold eyes and brown hair, attracting even more attention than men with hydraulic grabs on building sites. She sat behind a sheet of plate glass in Dowbridge's window, at a desk that was all made of glass, and she had a mighty mirror behind her.

At her side was a dear little electric furnace, all in white, and on the desk was a guillotine; not the sort fed by tumbrils full of aristos, but a handy paper-cutting size. With this she was demolishing stacks and stacks of documents, cutting them into slivers like bacon, and then turning them round and repeating the process crossways until she had a mound of confetti. When it was knee-high she slid the whole heap into a plastic basket and shot it into the furnace.

Pile after pile of paper the furnace wolfed down with the barest flicker of acknowledgement, and Roger Mauleverer, watching through the window, thought of pine forests in Sweden and Canada, vast stretches of spruce and redwood towering majestically in snow and sunshine, all destined to total extinction after this girl had done with them. He felt quite cross about it, for he liked trees. But he had to admit that the girl was very attractive.

Over her head, right across the plate glass, he could read the inscription:

CONFIDENTIAL RECORDS EFFECTIVELY
DESTROYED UNDER GUARANTEE

For the first two weeks that Ghita Waring sat in the window, her boss, who had a flair for publicity, tied a bandage over her eyes so that it was plain she couldn't read the documents she was chopping. But she cut her finger three times.

The following week he put her in dark glasses, but he had to admit that the gold eyes were a loss. So the fourth week he contented himself with a notice on the front of her desk:

SHE ONLY READS MUSIC
YOUR SECRETS ARE SAFE WITH HER

Ghita's old headmistress, who happened to pass by and see this, was very annoyed about it and complained that it was a poor advertisement for her school, but Ghita merely laughed and said she didn't mind; anyway, it was almost true. Though she added that she could read cookery books if the words weren't too long. She managed to conceal her really dangerous gift; if it had been discovered she would hardly have landed the job.

It was a never-failing pleasure for passers-by to stop and watch her, and wonder what she was cutting up now.

'That's a will,' muttered Sidey Curtiss to Bill Brewer. 'Bang goes the long-lost blooming heir. Now what's she got?'

'Might be an agreement. See the red seal?'

'There goes a confidential file; some bloke's past history smoking up the chimbley. Pity she couldn't chop up your record, Bill, eh? Just phone police headquarters and tell 'em to send it along in a plain van.'

Bill took this bit of humour coldly. 'Why not ask 'er to chop off your fingerprints while she's at it?'

A van drew up beside them; not a plain one. It was one of Pickering and Pumphrey's expensive-looking utilities. Beside the driver sat Miss Inglis, the gaunt, severe secretary of old Mr Pumphrey himself. She got out of the van with dignity and marched inside, carrying a large roll of paper. She talked for a short time with the golden-eyed girl at the desk and then came out again, leaving the document behind her. She stepped back into the van and was buzzed away down to the immense and gleaming new office building that Pickering and Pumphrey had just erected at the other end of the square.

'Wonder what they're getting rid of?' speculated Sidey.

'Something old Pumphrey doesn't want to be blackmailed about,' suggested Bill. 'Cor, here comes a smasher.' He stared approvingly at a sapphire-and-mink blonde who burst out of a taxi like a ray of sunshine coming out of a cloud. 'Bet *she's* got some compromising letters.'

The blonde sailed inside, and presently the two watchers saw her pull a bundle of letters from her magnificent hand-bag and pass them across to the girl at the desk. They saw her talking vigorously.

'It really does seem a shame to destroy them,' was what she was saying. 'They're so romantic. I can't bear for someone not to see them. You read them, ducky. You must get bored chopping away all the time and never a chance of a peep. And Roger's letters are as good as Shakespeare; they're so poetic they always make me cry. It's like murdering a child to have them guillotined.' She dabbed at her eyes. 'But he says I've got to. See, in the last letter.'

Ghita looked at the top one. *Dear Rosemary*, it said baldly, *in view of developments, please destroy all my letters. I am returning yours herewith.*

'That's not very poetic, surely,' Ghita said.

'Ah, but look at the earlier ones, ducky.'

It certainly was rather a treat for Ghita to be allowed to read a document before destroying it, and she glanced at one or two of the letters towards the bottom of the pile. When she read them her golden eyes became larger and rounder and mistier.

'Why, they're beautiful,' she breathed.

'Aren't they,' said Rosemary with satisfaction. 'I do miss

him, you know. No one else has ever said such beautiful things to me.' She dabbed her eyes again. 'Oh, would you mind giving me a testimonial, or whatever you call it, saying you've destroyed them? Roger is so fierce, and he's been beastly enough to me as it is. I don't want any more trouble.' Her lip quivered.

The man must be a brute, Ghita thought indignantly. Fancy writing letters like that to a girl, and then making her destroy them; demanding it so curtly, too.

I hereby certify, she wrote, *that I have destroyed twenty handwritten letters to Miss Rosemary Trench-Giddering from 'Roger', Quincetree Cottage, Broken End, Hazeldean.*

Why, she thought to herself in sudden enlightenment, he must be the young architect that Mother's always talking about, who's taken Quincetree Cottage. I shouldn't have thought he'd been there long enough to write twenty letters. And then he asks her to destroy them. What a trifler! What a snake in the grass!

'That will be one pound, please,' she said.

'Thank you, ducky,' said Rosemary. She gave a last dab to her eyes, a lingering glance at the last letter coming under the headsman's axe. 'Ah well ...' She straightened her shoulders with a billowing glitter of mink, dazzled Ghita with her smile, and ran out to the taxi, which was still stolidly ticking up three pences.

'Now 'e won't be able ter prove a thing,' muttered Sidey to Bill. The drama had gone out of the window, but they still lingered in the spring sunshine watching Ghita, who had pulled towards her the large scroll left by Miss Inglis.

Absently she scanned it, and then blushed pink as she realized that she had violated professional ethics. Being allowed to read Rosemary's letters had led her astray.

She glanced up, scowled at the two seedy watchers outside, and grabbed her guillotine. In her confusion she let the scroll slip and it rolled to the floor, displaying its contents. She pounced on it and minced it into ribbons as if it had bitten her. Anyway it was only a blueprint; no possible harm could come from her having glanced at it.

'Did you see what that was?' said Bill to Sidey. 'It was the plans of Pickering and Pumphrey's new office building.'

'Well, what of it?' said Sidey. 'Come on, I'm getting cold. I want a cuppa.'

'What of it, you daft fool, what *of* it? Why don't you see ...?'

He was talking urgently as they moved off to the Bide-Awile Café.

It was bad luck on Ghita that she had a photographic memory.

'Some people are coming in for drinks,' Mrs Waring said when Ghita went home on Friday. 'That nice young Mr Mauleverer who's taken Quincetree Cottage will be here. I think I've mentioned him before.'

'Only about forty times,' said Ghita, but she said it to herself. She knew, and her mother knew that she knew, and she knew that her mother knew that she knew, that Mrs Waring disapproved of Ghita's chopping documents by day in order to put herself through music school at night. Both these occupations were nonsensical, Mrs Waring considered; the sort of fandangle that a girl who was engaged, say to a nice young architect, would soon put behind her.

Nice young Mr Mauleverer indeed, Ghita thought, hugging her mother affectionately. I could tell you a thing or two about that two-faced fiend in human form if I weren't a model of professional discretion. Just don't let him try his come-hither tactics on me, that's all.

Nice young Mr Mauleverer had a somewhat familiar face. After a little thought Ghita identified him as the tall, dark young man who had passed by her shop window nine or

ten or eleven times in the course of the last few days. So that's
who you are, is it, she thought, and she gave him such a flash
of her eye, along with one of her mother's walnut canapés,
that he staggered as if he had been stabbed with an eighteen-
carat tie-pin.

'I hear you are studying music,' he said, recovering. 'I
compose a little myself.'

'Oh, do you?' Ghita said, interested in spite of herself.
'What sort of things?'

'Songs,' Roger Mauleverer said, and for some mysterious
reason he chuckled. 'I write songs.'

The chuckle incensed Ghita. 'I shouldn't think you have
a great deal of time for writing songs,' she said icily. 'Writing letters must be such an engrossing occupation.' She gave
him a menacing look, and he eyed her warily.

'Am I to infer that my ex-fiancée has been to you professionally?'

'Miss Trench-Giddering has confided in me and has all
my sympathy. But my lips are sealed,' Ghita said firmly.
And that's settled *him*, she thought with satisfaction. Now
we know where we stand with one another.

She darted another disapproving, golden flash at him; was
pleased to see that it appeared to leave him quite prostrated;
and went on to offer her walnut canapés with the utmost
grace and charm to ninety-year-old Great Uncle Wilber-
force.

On Wednesday, when Ghita was having her elevenses
over the local paper, in between spells of guillotining, her
satisfaction was given a jolt, and she was more than a little
disconcerted to read a report of the wedding of Miss Rosemary Trench-Giddering to Mr Cecil Quayle, M.P., with
eight bridesmaids and all the trimmings. There were several
photographs, and it was easy to see that Mr Quayle, pros-
perous though he seemed – and as Ghita knew him to be, for
he owned the town's largest factory – was about three times

the age of the bride, who could hardly be seen behind the enormous diamond she wore.

Ghita began to feel a little contrite and remorseful. Lifting her eyes to the window she thought that supposing, just supposing, Roger Mauleverer were to pass by, as he had done some eight or nine or ten times in the last few days, there would be no harm in giving him a friendly smile. But there was nobody outside the window except those two seedy-looking toughs who seemed to have spent a lot of time loitering round there lately.

She turned back to the paper and a familiar name caught her eye: Roger Mauleverer, A.R.I.B.A.

Roger Mauleverer, A.R.I.B.A., was, it appeared, the architect responsible for the large new office building recently erected in the town's main square on behalf of the local firm of Pickering and Pumphrey; the building had just been completed and the ceremonial tape cut by Mrs Pumphrey, wife of the Managing Director.

An unusual feature of the building was the hidden safe-deposit room concealed on one of its nine floors. No one knew the whereabouts of this soundproof room except Mr Pumphrey, Mr Harris the chief cashier, and the architect himself. Even the plans of the building had been destroyed so that unauthorized persons could not stumble on the information. The door of the room was opened by the newest form of electronic device; it would respond only to a code word spoken outside it. Needless to say, this code word was known to only three people, Mr Pumphrey, Mr Harris the chief cashier, and to the architect.

And to me, Ghita thought in cold terror. The type of the newspaper swam before her guilty eyes. Never, never, she thought, would she look at another document, however innocuous it appeared; no, not if fifty people begged her to on their bended knees. She knew now what that blueprint had been; she knew which floor the room was on, she knew which door led to it, and worst of all she knew, for it had been written in the margin, the code word that would open the door.

What ought she to do? Hasten to Mr Pumphrey and tell him that his secret was discovered? Consult a psychiatrist and ask if there was any way of expunging the guilty knowledge from her mind? Or go to Roger Mauleverer and ask his advice?

Something about the simplicity of the last course commended itself. I'll ask him on Saturday, she thought – for her mother had artlessly invited him to Saturday supper. Nothing much can happen between now and then.

She was very, very wrong.

If she had read the Stop Press column in the evening paper, she would have seen the item headed MISSING MANAGING DIRECTOR. But she did not. She had a class on Diminished and Augmented Triads at half past six, and, hellbent to get to it, she thrust the evening paper in among her shopping and ran like a doe to the City Literary Institute in Tennyson Street.

It was late when she came out; late and dark and quiet. Tennyson Street, all foggy and cobbled, looked like a set from a French film, and it looked still more like one when two shadowy figures came up swiftly and menacingly behind Ghita and slipped a sack over her head. Her hands were tied behind her back and she was whisked into an alley that led as she knew, to the river.

'Don't yell, *don't*,' a hoarse voice said warningly in her ear, 'because if you do we'll have to treat you rough. Just you keep quiet. We only want you to tell us something and then we'll let you go.'

'What do you want?' Ghita gasped inside the bag. A cold premonition had already told her the answer.

'We was watching you the other day a-reading of a blue-

print,' the voice said ingratiatingly. 'We saw your beautiful
eyes a-taking of it in. All we want from you is the whereabouts of that there famous secret room at Pickering's what's
got a million of di'monds shut away in it; and the code word
for opening the door. That's all we want.'

'I shan't tell you,' said Ghita.

'Now, duck, don't you be so hasty. If you do tell us, who's
to know it was you passed on the information? No one but
us knows you read the plan. But if you *don't* tell us –'

'What?' Ghita said uneasily, for he had paused.

'Why, then I'm afraid we shall have to take you to the end
of this alley and drop you in the river. Runs powerful fast
the river does hereabouts,' the voice said reflectively.

Ghita shivered. She had never tried swimming with her
hands tied behind her back, but she didn't think she would
excel at it.

An idea struck her. 'I can't possibly explain where the
door is,' she said. 'It's much too complicated. I can tell you
the password. It's Lancashire Hot-Pot. Now will you let me
go?'

'Not likely,' said Sidey. 'You'll have to come with us and
show us. Once you get inside the building you'll know
where you are. Coming? Or do we have to drop you in the
water?'

'All right, I'm coming,' Ghita said sadly. 'The room's
in the basement.'

The route they took to Pickering and Pumphrey's was
circuitous, and entailed climbing some fences, crossing a
bomb site, and cutting through a warehouse. At length they
arrived in a wide, dark basement area next to a car-park.
Sidey, scouting ahead, picked a lock and let them in
through a service door.

Ghita saw nothing of all this, for her head was still in the
sack, but now they took it off and let her look round and get
her bearings. Unerringly she led them along a red-and-white

tiled corridor in which floated a haunting and evocative smell of stew. It ended at double red doors, chromium handled, and labelled DIRECTORS' CANTEEN. They were locked.

'Here you are,' Ghita whispered. 'That notice is a blind. It isn't really the canteen, that's on the first floor. Now you must stand here and say Lancashire Hot-Pot. But you have to say it in a particular tone of voice, and that's what I don't know, because I only saw it written down. You'll have to keep on trying till you hit the right pitch.'

'Got it all pat, ain't she,' Bill whispered admiringly. 'You oughter come into the profession, miss; you'd do champion at it. Now then, Sidey, you try first, tenor and counter-tenor. Then I'll try bass and baritone.'

'Lancashire Hot-Pot,' said Sidey.

At about the twentieth attempt, when they were getting really enthusiastic, Ghita slipped quietly away round the corner to the little block where LIFTS had been marked on the ground-plan.

Yes, here they were; and in such a modern building they were sure to be automatic. She pressed a button. Luckily they'd had to untie her hands to climb the fences. A lift came gliding down, and she tiptoed in and wafted herself up to the ninth floor where, among other things, she remembered having noticed the switchboard room. Thank goodness, the police station was only a couple of blocks away!

But when she stepped out of the lift she was thunderstruck to find lights burning, footsteps clattering, and an atmosphere of hectic activity, very unexpected in an office building at ten minutes to midnight.

Three men hurried past her, distraught and preoccupied.

'Hey!' Ghita said. 'There are two burglars in the basement, trying to get into the safe-deposit room.'

'Those aren't burglars, my good girl,' one of the men said testily. 'The building's full of 'em. The Managing Director's got himself stuck inside the strongroom and no one knows where it is. Everybody's trying to find him.' Evidently he took her for a member of the staff.

'What about Mr Harris, the chief cashier?' suggested Ghita, very much taken aback by this new development.

'He's having his spring week sailing in the Baltic.'

'Well then, what about . . .?'

But they hurried away, calling, 'Throgmorton, Throgmorton, have you tried the mezzanine floor?'

'Wait!' Ghita called. She chased them and caught them at the head of the stairs. 'I can tell you where the safe-deposit room is!'

'*You* can?' They turned and regarded her with suspicion. 'How?'

'Well, never mind that for now,' Ghita said. 'It's on this floor, the fourth door to the right from the auditors' room.'

By this time a group had assembled.

'I tried to get the architect, Mr Throgmorton,' someone panted. 'I tried five times. But there's no reply from his number.'

'This young person seems to think she knows where the door is,' Mr Throgmorton said with awful majesty.

Ghita's feeling of guilt and confusion intensified. She went tremblingly up to the fourth door and pointed at it. 'That should be the one, and the password's Pickled Pumpkins.'

Mr Throgmorton gave her a look which, although she was ice-cold with fright, chilled her still further. He placed himself directly in front of the door, looked at it commandingly, and uttered the words, Pickled Pumpkins, in a sonorous voice.

Nothing happened.

Ghita began to wish that she could fall down the lift-shaft, or, failing that, just drop dead. She wondered what had gone wrong. And now that her password had failed, how was she ever going to introduce the topic of the two safe-breakers in the basement? But at that moment, she noticed that Roger Mauleverer was behind her.

'Ah, Mr Mauleverer,' Throgmorton said reprovingly. 'It took you a very long time to get here.'

'Long time?' Roger said, puzzled. 'I came just as fast as I possibly could. Is Miss Waring all right?' He looked anxiously at Ghita.

'Miss Waring? I am not aware that she has been in any trouble. It is Mr Pumphrey we are concerned with. Mr Pumphrey is immured in the strongroom.'

'Oh, is that all?' Roger said cheerfully. 'We can soon get him out of there.'

He stepped up to the door and serenaded it in a pleasing tenor:

> Safe, my dear, list and hear!
> None but I is standing near.

This seemed an inaccuracy to Ghita, but everybody else was dead serious.

> None can pry, none can see,
> Open wide your door to me.

The door swung open and revealed Mr Pumphrey, indignant and ravenous, ensconced in a nest of diamonds and securities.

'I forgot the tune,' he said accusingly to Roger. 'That's the trouble with these fancy gimmicks!'

'Well, sir,' said Roger, 'it was your idea to have a tune. If you recall, I was in favour of the simple words Pickled Pumpkins, and it was you who said that you'd look like a fool if one of your staff found you in the corridor saying Pickled Pumpkins, and it would be better if you had a verse that you could sing.'

'You must think of something else tomorrow,' snapped Mr Pumphrey. 'Have to, anyway, now half the staff's heard it.'

He glared round, explosive as a turkeycock. 'Let alone this young lady who's not a staff member. What's she doing here?'

'She told us where the strongroom was,' Throgmorton said.

'What? How the devil did she know that?'

Tremblingly, Ghita confessed how she had come by her knowledge.

'I shall ring up Dowbridge's,' Mr Pumphrey said, with the quiet menace of an impending avalanche. 'That's the last of my business they handle. And what, pray, were you doing in my building at this time of night?'

'I was b-brought here by two burglars,' Ghita faltered. 'They're down in the basement saying L-Lancashire Hot-Pot outside the Directors' Canteen.'

'I beg your pardon?'

But, thank heaven, Roger seemed to have grasped the situation. He murmured something to Throgmorton and the other two men. They shot away in the lift, found Sidey and Bill trying Hot-Pot for the seventy-seventh time in A alt and middle C, and nobbled them. The two burglars, hoarse and exhausted, were glad to go quietly.

'Where is Miss Waring?' Roger asked, when they led the captives before Mr Pumphrey, who had the telephone in his hand.

'She took her departure,' Mr Pumphrey said severely, 'after I had issued her a warning.' He put down the receiver.

Poor Ghita crept to her office next morning more dead than alive. Instead of the usual pile of documents awaiting destruction there was one envelope on her desk. It said, *Please read before destroying*. Inside was a week's salary and notice of dismissal from her boss, who had been rung by Mr Pumphrey at ten minutes past midnight.

Two large tears trickled down Ghita's cheeks and splashed

on the glass desk. Absently she slid her notice into the guillotine and sliced it into spills. Then she looked up and saw Roger outside the window. She glared at him. Undeterred, he came in.

'It's all your fault,' Ghita stormed at him. 'If I hadn't been inveigled into reading your letters I'd never have looked at that blueprint. And now I've got the sack, and I'll probably go to p-prison, and I'll never be able to afford to finish learning about Diminished and Augmented Triads, and what do *you* care?'

'I do care,' Roger said. 'Very much. I *love* Augmented Triads.' Something about the way in which he said this, coupled with the fact that he was holding Ghita in a close embrace at the time, carried instant conviction.

He went on, 'I explained to Mr Pumphrey that you'd been shanghai'd, and he says he's sorry he misunderstood the situation and he'll put it right with your boss.'

'But how do you know about it?' Ghita said, wiping her eyes on his lapel, regardless of the interested spectators outside.

'I was lecturing on architecture at the City Literary Institute last night, and I looked out of the window and saw them putting your head in the bag. By the time I'd dashed out you were gone, but I guessed where they'd be making for.'

'It was nice of you to bother,' Ghita said, and added in a small voice, 'I owe you an apology about Miss Trench-Giddering. Did you mind terribly when she married Mr Quayle?'

'Frankly, no,' said Roger, very cheerfully for a rejected suitor. 'She was grand for practising my literary style on. But I wouldn't want to spend my life with somebody who sleeps all day and spends the hours between ten p.m. and five a.m. in half a dozen night clubs. I hate ear-splitting music.'

Ghita drew back a couple of inches and looked at him nervously.

'What about piano-playing?'

'The minute we're married,' he said, 'I shall design us a house with a soundproof room in the middle, where you can pile up the Augmented Triads to your heart's content.'

Sonata for Harp and Bicycle

'No one is allowed to remain in the building after five p.m.,' Mr Manaby told his new assistant, showing him into the little room that was like the inside of an egg carton.

'Why not?'

'Directorial policy,' said Mr Manaby. But that was not the real reason.

Gaunt and sooty, Grimes Buildings lurched up the side of a hill towards Clerkenwell. Every little office within its dim and crumbling exterior owned one tiny crumb of light – such was the proud boast of the architect – but towards evening the crumbs were collected, absorbed and demolished as by an immense vacuum cleaner, and yielded to an uncontrollable mass of dark that came tumbling in through windows and doors to take their place. Darkness infested the building like a flight of bats returning willingly to roost.

'Wash hands, please. Wash hands, please,' the intercom began to bawl in the passages at four-forty-five. Without much need of prompting the staff hustled like lemmings along the corridors to the green- and blue-tiled washrooms that mocked the encroaching dusk with an illusion of cheerfulness.

'All papers into cases, please,' the Tannoy warned, five minutes later. 'Look at your desks, ladies and gentlemen. Any documents left lying about? Kindly put them away. Desks must be left clear and tidy. Drawers must be shut.'

A multitudinous shuffling, a rustling as of innumerable bluebottles might have been heard by the attentive ear after this injunction, as the employees of Moreton Wold and Company thrust their papers into briefcases, hurried letters and invoices into drawers, clipped statistical abstracts together and slammed them into filing cabinets; dropped discarded copy into wastepaper baskets. Two minutes later, and not a desk throughout Grimes Building bore more than its customary coating of dust.

'Hats and coats on, please. Hats and coats on, please. Did you bring an umbrella? Have you left any shopping on the floor?'

At three minutes to five the home-going throng was in the lifts and on the stairs; a clattering staccato-voiced flood momentarily darkened the great double doors of the building, and then as the first faint noises of St Paul's came echoing faintly on the frosty air, to be picked up near at hand by the louder chime of St Biddulph's on the Wall, the entire premises of Moreton Wold stood empty.

'But why is it?' Jason Ashgrove, the new copywriter asked his secretary. 'Why are the staff herded out so fast in the evenings? Not that I'm against it, mind you, I think it's an admirable idea in many ways, but there is the liberty of the individual to be considered, don't you think?'

'Hush!' Miss Golden, casting a glance towards the door, held up her felt-tip in warning or reproof. 'You mustn't ask that sort of question. When you are taken on to the Established Staff you'll be told. Not before.'

'But I want to know now,' said Jason in discontent. 'Do you know?'

'Yes I do,' Miss Golden answered tantalizingly. 'Come on, or we shan't have done the Oat Crisp layout by a quarter to.' And she stared firmly down at the copy in front of her, lips folded, candyfloss hair falling over her face, lashes hiding eyes like peridots, a girl with a secret.

Jason was annoyed. He rapped out a couple of rude and witty rhymes which Miss Golden let pass in a withering silence.

'What do you want for Christmas, Miss Golden? Sherry? Fudge? Bath cubes?'

'I want to go away with a clear conscience about Oat Crisps,' Miss Golden retorted. It was not true; what she chiefly wanted was Mr Jason Ashgrove, but he had not realized this yet.

'Come on, don't be a tease! I'm sure you haven't been on the Established Staff that long,' he coaxed her. 'What happens when one is taken on, anyway? Does the Managing Director have us up for a confidential chat? Or are we given a little book called The Awful Secret of Grimes Buildings?'

Miss Golden wasn't telling. She opened her desk drawer and took out a white towel and a cake of rosy soap.

'Wash hands, please! Wash hands, please!'

Jason was frustrated. 'You'll be sorry,' he said. 'I shall do something desperate.'

'Oh no, you mustn't!' Her eyes were large with fright. She ran from the room and was back within a couple of minutes, still drying her hands.

'If I took you out to dinner, wouldn't you give me just a tiny hint?'

Side by side Miss Golden and Mr Ashgrove ran along the green-floored corridors, battled down the white marble stairs, among the hundred other employees from the tenth floor, and the nine hundred from the floors below.

He saw her lips move as she said something, but in the clatter of two thousand feet the words were lost.

'. . .f-f-fire-escape,' he heard, as they came into the momentary hush of the coir-carpeted entrance hall. And '. . . it's to do with a bicycle. A bicycle and a harp.'

'I don't understand.'

Now they were in the street, chilly with the winter-dusk smells of celery on barrows, of swept-up leaves heaped in faraway parks, and cold layers of dew sinking among the withered evening primroses in the building sites. London lay about them wreathed in twilit mystery and fading against the barred and smoky sky. Like a ninth wave the sound of traffic overtook and swallowed them.

'Please tell me!'

But, shaking her head, she stepped on to a scarlet home-bound bus and was borne away from him.

Jason stood undecided on the pavement, with the crowds dividing round him as round the pier of a bridge. He scratched his head and looked about him for guidance.

An ambulance clanged, a taxi screeched, a drill stuttered, a siren wailed on the river, a door slammed, a van hooted, and close beside his ear a bicycle bell tinkled its tiny warning.

A bicycle, she had said. A bicycle and a harp.

Jason turned and stared at Grimes Buildings.

Somewhere, he knew, there was a back way in, a service entrance. He walked slowly past the main doors, with their tubs of snowy chrysanthemums, and on up Glass Street. A tiny furtive wedge of darkness beckoned him, a snicket, a hacket, an alley carved into the thickness of the building. It was so narrow that at any moment, it seemed, the over-topping walls would come together and squeeze it out of existence.

Walking as softly as an Indian, Jason passed through it, slid by a file of dustbins, and found the foot of the fire-escape. Iron treads rose into the mist, like an illustration to a Gothic fairytale.

He began to climb.

When he had mounted to the ninth storey he paused for breath. It was a lonely place. The lighting consisted of a dim bulb at the foot of every flight. A well of gloom sank beneath him. The cold fingers of the wind nagged and flut-tered at the edges of his jacket, and he pulled the string of the fire-door and edged inside.

Grimes Buildings were triangular, with the street forming the base of the triangle, and the fire-escape the point. Jason could see two long passages coming towards him, meeting at an acute angle where he stood. He started down the left-hand one, tiptoeing in the cave-like silence. Nowhere was there any sound, except for the faraway drip of a tap. No night-watchman would stay in the building; none was needed. No precautions were taken. Burglars gave the place a wide berth.

Jason opened a door at random; then another. Offices lay everywhere about him, empty and forbidding. Some held lipstick-stained tissues, spilt powder, and orange-peel; others were still foggy with cigarette smoke. Here was a director's suite of rooms — a desk like half an acre of frozen lake, inch-thick carpets, roses, and the smell of cigars. Here was a conference room with scattered squares of doodled blotting-paper. All equally empty.

He was not sure when he first began to notice the bell. Telephone, he thought at first, and then he remembered that all the outside lines were disconnected at five. And this bell, anyway, had not the regularity of a telephone's double ring: there was a tinkle, and then silence: a long ring, and then silence: a whole volley of rings together, and then silence.

Jason stood listening, and fear knocked against his ribs and shortened his breath. He knew that he must move or be paralysed by it. He ran up a flight of stairs and found himself with two more endless green corridors beckoning him like a pair of dividers.

Another sound now: a waft of ice-thin notes, riffling up an arpeggio like a flurry of sleet. Far away down the passage it echoed. Jason ran in pursuit, but as he ran the music receded. He circled the building, but it always outdistanced him, and when he came back to the stairs he heard it fading away on to the storey below.

He hesitated, and as he did so, heard once more the bell: the bicycle bell. It was approaching him fast, bearing down on him, urgent, menacing. He could hear the pedals, almost see the shimmer of an invisible wheel. Absurdly, he was reminded of the insistent clamour of an ice-cream vendor, summoning children on a sultry Sunday afternoon.

There was a little fireman's alcove beside him, with buckets and pumps. He hurled himself into it. The bell stopped beside him, and then there was a moment while his heart tried to shake itself loose in his chest. He was looking into two eyes carved out of expressionless air; he was held by two hands knotted together out of the width of dark.

'Daisy? Daisy?' came the whisper. 'Is that you, Daisy? Have you come to give me your answer?'

Jason tried to speak, but no words came.

'It's *not* Daisy! Who are you?' The sibilants were full of threat. 'You can't stay here! This is private property.'

He was thrust along the corridor. It was like being pushed by a whirlwind – the fire door opened ahead of him without a touch, and he was on the openwork platform, clutching the slender railing. Still the hands would not let him go.

'How about it?' the whisper mocked him. 'How about jumping? It's an easy death compared with some.'

Jason looked down into the smoky void. The darkness nodded to him like a familiar.

'You wouldn't be much loss, would you? What have you got to live for?'

Miss Golden, Jason thought. She would miss me. And the syllables Berenice Golden lingered in the air like a chime. Drawing on some unknown deposit of courage he shook himself loose from the holding hands, and ran down the fire escape without looking back.

Next morning when Miss Golden, crisp, fragrant and punctual shut the door of Room 92 behind her, she stopped short by the hat-pegs with a horrified gasp.

'Mr *Ashgrove*! Your *hair*!'

'It makes me look very distinguished, don't you think?' he said.

It did indeed have this effect, for his Byronic dark cut had changed to a stippled silver.

'How did it happen? You've not –' her voice sank to a whisper –'*You've not been in Grimes Buildings after dark?*'

'What if I have?'

'Have you?'

'Miss Golden – Berenice,' he said earnestly. 'Who was Daisy? I can see that you know. Tell me her story.'

'Did you see him?' she asked faintly.

'Him?'

'William Heron – the Wailing Watchman. Oh,' she exclaimed in terror, 'I can see that you must have. Then you are doomed – doomed!'

'If I'm doomed,' said Jason, 'let's have coffee and you tell me about it.'

'It all happened over fifty years ago,' said Berenice, as she spooned out coffee powder with distracted extravagance. 'Heron was the night-watchman in this building, patrolling the corridors from dusk to dawn every night on his bicycle. He fell in love with a Miss Bell who taught the harp. She rented a room – this room – and gave lessons in it. She began to reciprocate his love, and they used to share a picnic supper every night at eleven, and she'd stay on a while to keep him company. It was an idyll, among the fire-buckets and the furnace-pipes.

'On Christmas Eve he had summoned up the courage to propose to her. The day before he had told her that he was going to ask her a very important question. Next night he came to the Buildings with a huge bunch of roses and a bottle of wine. But Miss Bell never turned up.

'The explanation was simple. Miss Bell, of course, had been losing a lot of sleep through her nocturnal romance, as she gave lessons all day, and so she used to take a nap in her music-room between seven and ten every evening to save going home. In order to make sure that she would wake up, she persuaded her father, a distant relation of Graham Bell who shared some of the more famous Bell's mechanical ingenuity, to install an alarm device, a kind of telephone, in her room which called her every evening at ten. She was far too modest and shy to let Heron know that she spent those hours actually in the building and to give him the chance of waking her himself.

'Alas! On this important evening the gadget failed and she never woke up. Telephones were in their infancy at that time, you must remember.'

'Heron waited and waited. At last, mad with grief and jealousy, having rung up her home and discovered that she was not there, he concluded that she had rejected him, ran to the fire-escape and cast himself off it, holding the roses and the bottle of wine. He jumped from the tenth floor.

'Daisy did not long survive him, but pined away soon after; since that day their ghosts have haunted Grimes Building, he vainly patrolling the corridors on his bicycle in search of her, she playing her harp in the small room she rented. *But they never meet.* And anyone who meets the ghost of William Heron will himself within five days leap down from the same fatal fire-escape.'

She gazed at him with tragic eyes.

'In that case we mustn't lose a minute,' said Jason and he enveloped her in an embrace as prolonged as it was ardent. Looking down at the gossamer hair sprayed across his shoulder, he added, 'Just the same, it is a preposterous situation. Firstly, I have no intention of jumping off the fire-escape –' here, however, he repressed a shudder as he remembered the cold, clutching hands of the evening before – 'and secondly, I find it quite nonsensical that those two inefficient ghosts have spent fifty years in this building without coming across each other. We must remedy the matter, Berenice. We must not begrudge our new-found happiness to others.'

He gave her another kiss so impassioned that the electric typewriter against which they were leaning began chattering to itself in a frenzy of enthusiasm.

'This very evening,' he went on, looking at his watch, 'we will put matters right for that unhappy couple and then, if I really have only five more days to live, which I don't for one moment believe, we will proceed to spend them together my bewitching Berenice, in the most advantageous manner possible.'

She nodded, spellbound.

'Can you work a switchboard?' She nodded again. 'My love, you are perfection itself. Meet me in the switchboard room, then, at ten this evening. I would say, have dinner with me, but I shall need to make one or two purchases and see an old R.A.F. friend. You will be safe from Heron's curse in the switchboard room if he always keeps to the corridors.'

'I would rather meet him and die with you,' she murmured.

'My angel, I hope that won't be necessary. Now,' he said sighing, 'I suppose we should get down to our day's work.' Strangely enough, the copy they wrote that day, although engendered from such agitated minds, sold more packets of Oat Crisps than any other advertising matter before or since.

That evening when Jason entered Grimes Buildings he was carrying two bottles of wine, two bunches of red roses, and a large canvas-covered bundle. Miss Golden, who had concealed herself in the telephone exchange before the offices closed for the night, gazed at these things with interest.

'Now,' said Jason after he had greeted her, 'I want you first of all to ring our own extension.'

'No one will reply, surely.'

'I think *she* will reply.'

Sure enough, when Berenice rang Extension 170 a faint sleepy voice, distant and yet clear, whispered, 'Hullo?'

'Is that Miss Bell?'

'... Yes.'

Berenice went a little pale. Her eyes sought Jason's and, prompted by him, she said formally, 'Switchboard here, Miss Bell. Your ten o'clock call.'

'Thank you,' whispered the telephone.

'Excellent,' Jason remarked, as Miss Golden replaced the receiver with a trembling hand. He unfastened his package and slipped its straps over his shoulders. 'Now, plug in the intercom.'

Berenice did so, and then announced, loudly and clearly,

'Attention. Night watchman on duty, please. Night watchman on duty. You have an urgent summons to Room 92. You have an urgent summons to room 92.'

Her voice echoed and reverberated through the empty corridors, then the Tannoy coughed itself to silence.

'Now we must run. You take the roses, sweetheart, and I'll carry the bottles.'

Together they raced up eight flights of stairs and along the green corridors to Room 92. As they neared the door a burst of music met them – harp music swelling out, sweet and triumphant. Jason took one of the bunches of roses from Berenice, opened the door a little way, and gently deposited the flowers with the bottle, inside the door. As he closed it again Berenice said breathlessly,

'Did you see anything?'

'No,' he said. 'The room was too full of music.' His eyes were shining.

They stood hand in hand, reluctant to move away, waiting for they hardly knew what. Suddenly the door flew open again. Neither Berenice nor Jason, afterwards, cared to speak of what they saw then, but each was left with a memory, bright as the picture on a Salvador Dali calander, of a bicycle bearing on its saddle a harp, a bottle of wine, and a bouquet of red roses, sweeping improbably down the corridor and far, far away.

'We can go now,' said Jason. He led Berenice to the fire door, tucking the other bottle of Mâcon into his jacket pocket. A black wind from the north whistled beneath, as they stood on the openwork iron platform, looking down.

'We don't want our evening to be spoilt by the thought of that curse hanging over us,' he said, 'so this is the practical thing to do. Hang on to the roses.' And holding his love firmly, Jason pulled the ripcord of his R.A.F. friend's parachute, and leapt off the fire-escape.

A bridal shower of rose-petals adorned the descent of Miss Golden, who was possibly the only girl to be kissed in mid air in the district of Clerkenwell at ten minutes to midnight on Christmas Eve.

Searching for Summer

Lily wore yellow on her wedding day. In the 'seventies people put a lot of faith in omens, and believed that if a bride's dress was yellow her married life would be blessed with a bit of sunshine.

It was years since the bombs had been banned but still the cloud never lifted. Whitish grey, day after day, sometimes darkening to a weeping slate-colour, or, at the end of an evening, turning to smoky copper, the sky endlessly, secretively brooded.

Old people began their stories with the classic, fairytale opening: 'Long, long ago, when I was a liddle un, in the days when the sky was blue ...' and children, listening, chuckled among themselves at the absurd thought, because, *blue*, imagine it! How could the sky ever have been *blue*? You might as well say 'In the days when the grass was pink'.

Stars, rainbows, and all other such heavenly sideshows had been permanently withdrawn, and if the radio announced that there was a blink of sunshine in such and such a place, where the cloud-belt had thinned for half an hour, cars and coaches would pour in that direction for days in an unavailing search for warmth and light.

After the wedding, when all the relations were standing in the church porch, with Lily shivering prettily in her buttercup nylon, her father prodded the dour and withered grass on a grave – although it was August the leaves were hardly out yet – and said, 'Well, Tom, what are you aiming to do now eh?'

'Going to find a bit of sun and have our honeymoon in it,'

said Tom hardily. There was a general laugh from the wedding party.

'Don't get sunburnt,' shrilled Aunt Nancy.

'Better start off Bournemouth way. Paper said they had a half hour of sun last Wednesday week,' Uncle Arthur weighed in heavily.

'We'll come back brown as – as this grass,' said Tom, and ignoring the good-natured teasing from their respective families, the two young people mounted on their scooter, which stood ready at the churchyard wall, and chugged away in a shower of golden confetti. When they were out of sight, and the yellow paper had subsided on the grey and gritty road, the Whitemores and the Hoskinses strolled off sighing to eat wedding-cake and drink currant wine, and old Mrs Hoskins spoiled everyone's pleasure by bursting into tears as she thought of her own wedding-day when everything was so different.

Meanwhile Tom and Lily buzzed on hopefully across the grey countryside, with Lily's veil like a gilt banner floating behind. It was chilly going for her in her wedding things, but the sight of a bride was supposed to bring good luck and so she stuck it out, although her fingers were blue to the knuckles. Every now and then they switched on their portable radio and listened to the forecast. Inverness had seen the sun for ten minutes yesterday, and Southend for five minutes this morning, but that was all.

'Both those places are a long way from here,' said Tom cheerfully. 'All the more reason we'd find a nice bit of sunshine in these parts somewhere. We'll keep going south. Keep your eyes peeled, Lil, and tell me if you see a blink of sun on those hills ahead.'

But they came to the hills and passed them, and a new range shouldered up ahead and then slid away behind, and still there was no flicker or patch of sunshine to be seen anywhere in the grey, winter-ridden landscape. Lily began to get discouraged, so they stopped for a cup of tea at a pull-up.

'Seen the sun lately, mate?' Tom asked the proprietor. He laughed shortly. 'Notice any coaches or caravans round here? Last time I saw the sun was two years ago September; came out just in time for the wife's birthday.'

'It's stars I'd like to see,' Lily said, looking wistfully at her dust-coloured tea. 'Ever so pretty they must be.'

'Well, better be getting on, I suppose,' said Tom, but he had lost some of his bounce and confidence. Every place they passed through looked nastier than the last, partly on account of the dismal light, partly because people had given up bothering to take a pride in their boroughs. And then, just as they were entering a village called Molesworth, the dimmest, drabbest, most insignificant huddle of houses they had come to yet, the engine coughed and died on them.

'Can't see what's wrong,' said Tom, after a prolonged and gloomy survey.

'Oh, Tom!' Lily was almost crying. 'What'll we do?'

'Have to stop here for the night, s'pose.' Tom was short-tempered with frustration. 'Look, there's a garage just up the road. We can push the bike there and they'll tell us if there's a pub where we can stay. It's nearly six anyway.'

They had taken the bike to the garage, and the man there was just telling them that the only pub in the village was the Rising Sun, where Mr Noakes might be able to give them a bed, when a bus pulled up in front of the petrol pumps.

'Look,' the garage owner said, 'there's Mr Noakes just getting out of the bus now. Sid!' he called.

But Mr Noakes was not able to come to them at once. Two old people were climbing slowly out of the bus ahead of him: a blind man with a white stick, and a withered, frail old lady in a black satin dress and hat. 'Careful now, George,' she was saying, 'mind ee be careful with my son William.'

'I'm being careful, Mrs Hatching,' the conductor said patiently, as he almost lifted the unsteady old pair off the bus platform. The driver had stopped his engine, and everyone on the bus was taking a mild and sympathetic interest, except for Mr Noakes just behind who was cursing irritably at the delay. When the two old people were on the narrow pavement the conductor saw that they were going to have trouble with a bicycle that was propped against the kerb just ahead of them; he picked it up and stood holding it until they had passed the line of petrol pumps and were going slowly off along a path across the fields. Then, grinning, he put it back, jumped hurriedly into the bus, and rang his bell.

'Old nuisances,' Mr Noakes said furiously. 'Wasting public time. Every week that palaver goes on, taking the old man to Midwick Hospital Out Patients and back again. I know what *I'd* do with 'em. Put to sleep, that sort ought to be.'

Mr Noakes was a repulsive-looking individual, but when he heard that Tom and Lily wanted a room for the night he changed completely and gave them a leer that was full of false goodwill. He was a big, red-faced man with wet, full lips, bulging pale-grey bloodshot eyes, and a crop of stiff greasy black hair. He wore tennis shoes.

'Honeymooners, eh?' he said, looking sentimentally at Lily's pale prettiness; 'want a bed for the night, eh?' and he laughed a disgusting laugh that sounded like thick oil coming out of a bottle, heh-heh-heh-heh, and gave Lily a tremendous pinch on her arm. Disengaging herself as politely as she could, she stopped and picked up something from the pavement. They followed Mr Noakes glumly up the street to the Rising Sun.

While they were eating their baked beans Mr Noakes stood over their table grimacing at them. Lily unwisely confided to him that they were looking for a bit of sunshine.

Mr Noakes's laughter nearly shook down the ramshackle building.

'Sunshine! Oh my gawd! That's a good 'un! Hear that Mother?' he bawled to his wife. 'They're looking for a bit of sunshine. Heh-heh-heh-heh-heh-heh! Why,' he said banging on the table till the baked beans leapt about, 'if I could find a bit of sunshine near here, permanent bit that is, dja know what I'd do?'

The young people looked at him inquiringly across the bread and marge.

'Lido, caravan-site, country-club, holiday camp – you wouldn't know the place. Land round here is dirt-cheap, I'd buy up the lot. Nothing but woods. I'd advertise – I'd have people flocking to this little dump from all over the country. But what a hope, what a hope, eh? Well, feeling better? Enjoyed your tea? Ready for bed? Heh-heh-heh-heh, bed's ready for you.'

Avoiding one another's eyes, Tom and Lily stood up.

'I – I'd rather go for a bit of a walk first, Tom,' Lily said in a small voice. 'Look, I picked up that old lady's bag on the pavement, I didn't notice it till we'd done talking to Mr Noakes, and by then she was out of sight. Should we take it back to her?'

'Good idea,' said Tom, pouncing on the suggestion with relief. 'Do you know where she lives, Mr Noakes?'

'Who, old Ma Hatching? Sure I know. She lives in the wood. But you don't want to go taking her bag back, not this time o' the evening you don't. Let her worry. She'll come asking for it in the morning.'

'She walked so slowly,' said Lily, holding the bag gently in her hands. It was very old, made of black velvet on two ring-handles, and embroidered with beaded roses. 'I think we ought to take it to her, don't you ,Tom?'

'Oh, very well, very well, have it your own way,' Mr Noakes said, winking at Tom. 'Take that path by the garridge, you can't go wrong. I've never been there meself but they live somewhere in that wood back o' the village, you'll find it soon enough.'

They found the path soon enough, but not the cottage. Under the lowering sky they walked forward endlessly among trees that carried only tiny and rudimentary leaves, wizened and poverty-stricken. Lily was still wearing her wedding sandals, which had begun to blister her. She held on to Tom's arm, biting her lip with pain, and he looked down miserably at her bent brown head; everything had turned out so differently from what he had planned.

By the time they reached the cottage Lily could hardly bear to put her left foot to the ground, and Tom was gentling her along: 'It can't be much farther now, and they'll be sure to have a bandage. I'll tie it up and you can have a sit-down. Maybe they'll give us a cup of tea. We could borrow an old pair of socks or something ...' Hardly noticing the cottage garden, beyond a vague impression of rows of runner beans, they made for the clematis-grown porch and knocked. There was a brass lion's head on the door, carefully polished.

'Eh, me dear!' It was the old lady, old Mrs Hatching, who opened the door, and her exclamation was a long-drawn gasp of pleasure and astonishment. 'Eh, me dear! 'Tis the pretty bride. See'd ye s'arternoon when we was coming home from hospital.'

'Who be?' shouted a voice from inside.

'Come in, come in, me dears. My son William'll be glad to hear company; he can't see, poor soul, nor has this thirty year, ah, and a pretty sight he's losing this minute –'

'We brought back your bag,' Tom said, putting it in her hands, 'and we wondered if you'd have a bit of plaster you could kindly let us have. My wife's hurt her foot –'

My wife. Even in the midst of Mrs Hatching's voluble welcome the strangeness of these words struck the two young people, and they fell quiet, each of them, pondering, while Mrs Hatching thanked and commiserated, all in a breath, and asked them to take a seat on the sofa and fetched a basin of water from the scullery, and William from his seat in the chimney corner demanded to know what it was all about.

'Wot be doing? Wot be doing, Mother?'

''Tis a bride, all in's finery,' she shrilled back at him, 'an's blistered her foot, poor heart.' Keeping up a running commentary for William's benefit she bound up the foot, every now and then exclaiming to herself in wonder over the fineness of Lily's wedding-dress which lay in yellow nylon swathes round the chair. 'There, me dear. Now us'll have a cup of tea, eh? Proper thirsty you'm fare to be, walking all the way to here this hot day.'

Hot day? Tom and Lily stared at each other and then round the room. Then it was true, it was not their imagination, that a great dusty golden square of sunshine lay on the fireplace-wall, where the brass pendulum of the clock at every swing blinked into sudden brilliance? That the blazing geraniums on the window-sill housed a drove of murmuring bees? That, through the window the gleam of linen hung in the sun to whiten suddenly dazzled their eyes?

'The sun? Is it really the sun?' Tom said, almost doubtfully.

'And why not?' Mrs Hatching demanded. 'How else'll beans set, tell me that? Fine thing if sun were to stop shining, that ilt.' Chuckling to herself she set out a Crown Derby tea-set, gorgeously coloured in red and gold, and a baking of saffron buns. Then she sat down and, drinking her own tea began to question the two of them about where they had come from, where they were going. The tea was tawny and hot and sweet, the clock's tick was like a bird chirping, every now and then a log settled in the grate; Lily looked sleepily round the little room, so rich and peaceful, and thought, I wish we were staying here. I wish we needn't go back to that horrible pub ... She leaned against Tom's comforting arm.

'Look at the sky,' she whispered to him. 'Out there between the geraniums. Blue!'

'And ee'll come up and see my spare bedroom, won't ee now?' Mrs Hatching said, breaking off the thread of her questions – which indeed was not a thread, but merely a savouring of her pleasure and astonishment at this unlooked-for visit – 'Bide here, why don't ee? Mid as well. The lil un's fair wore out. Us'll do for ee better'n rangy old Noakes, proper old scoundrel 'e be. Won't us, William?'

'Ah,' William said appreciatively. 'I'll sing ee some o' my songs.'

A sight of the spare room settled any doubts. The great white bed, huge as a prairie, built up with layer upon solid layer of mattress, blanket, and quilt, almost filled the little shadowy room in which it stood. Brass rails shone in the green dimness. 'Isn't it quiet,' Lily whispered. Mrs Hatching, silent for the moment, stood looking at them proudly, her bright eyes slowly moving from face to face. Once her hand fondled, as if it might have been a baby's downy head, the yellow brass knob.

And so, almost without any words, the matter was decided.

Three days later they remembered that they must go to the village and collect the scooter which must, surely, be mended by now.

They had been helping old William pick a basketful of beans. Tom had taken his shirt off, and the sun gleamed on his brown back; Lily was wearing an old cotton print which Mrs Hatching, with much chuckling, had shortened to fit her.

It was amazing how deftly, in spite of his blindness, William moved among the beans, feeling through the rough, rustling leaves for the stiffness of concealed pods. He found twice as many as Tom and Lily, but then they, even on the third day, were still stopping every other minute to exclaim over the blueness of the sky. At night they sat on the back doorstep while Mrs Hatching clucked inside as she dished the supper, 'Star-struck ee'll be! Come along in, do-ee, before soup's cold, stars niver run away yet as I do know.'

'Can we get anything for you in the village?' Lily asked, but Mrs Hatching shook her head.

'Baker's bread and suchlike's no use but to cripple thee's innardses wi' colic. I been living here these eighty year wi'out troubling doctors and I'm not faring to begin now.' She waved to them and stood watching as they walked into the wood, thin and frail beyond belief, but wiry, indomitable, her black eyes full of zest. Then she turned to scream menacingly at a couple of pullets who had strayed and were scratching among the potatoes.

Almost at once they noticed, as they followed the path, that the sky was clouded over.

'It *is* only there on that one spot,' Lily said in wonder. 'All the time. And they've never even noticed that the sun doesn't shine in other places.'

'That's how it must have been all over the world, once,' Tom said.

At the garage they found their scooter ready and waiting. They were about to start back when they ran into Mr Noakes.

'Well, well, well, well, *well*!' he shouted, glaring at them with ferocious good humour. 'How many wells make a river, eh? And where did you slip off to? Here's me and the missus was just going to tell the police to have the rivers dragged. But hullo, hul*lo*, what's this? Brown, eh? Sun-tan? Scrumptious,' he said, looking meltingly at Lily and giving her another tremendous pinch. 'Where'd you get it, eh? That wasn't all got in half an hour. *I* know. Come on this means money to you and me, tell us the big secret. Remember what I said, and round these parts is dirt cheap.'

Tom and Lily looked at each other in horror. They thought of the cottage, the bees humming among the runner-beans, the sunlight glinting in the red-and-gold teacups. At night, when they had lain in the huge sagging bed, stars had shone through the window and the whole wood was as quiet as the inside of a shell.

'Oh, we've been miles from here,' Tom lied hurriedly. 'We ran into a friend, and he took us right away beyond Brinsley.' And as Mr Noakes still looked suspicious and un-satisfied, he did the only thing possible. 'We're going back there now,' he said, 'the sun-bathing's grand.' And opening the throttle he let the scooter go. They waved at Mr Noakes and chugged off towards the grey hills that lay to the north.

'My wedding dress,' Lily said sadly. 'It's on our bed.'

They wondered how long Mrs Hatching would keep tea hot for them, who would eat all the pasties.

'Never mind, you won't need it again,' Tom comforted her.

At least, he thought, they had left the golden place un-disturbed. Mr Noakes never went into the wood. And they had done what they intended, they had found the sun. Now they, too, would be able to tell their grand-children, when beginning a story, 'Long, long ago, when we were young, in the days when the sky was blue . . .'

Dead Language Master

Mr Fletcher taught us Latin. He was the shape of a domino. No, that's wrong, because he wasn't square; he looked as if he had been cut out of a domino. He had shape but no depth, you felt he could have slipped through the crack at the hinge of a door if he'd gone sideways. Though I daresay if he'd really been able to do that he would have made more use of the faculty; he was great on stealing quietly along a passage and then opening the door very fast to see what we were all up to; he used to drift about silently like an old ghost, but if you had a keen sense of smell you always had advance warning of his arrival because of the capsule of stale cigarette smoke that he moved about in. He smoked nonstop; he used a holder, but even so his fingers were yellow up to the knuckles and so were his teeth when he bared them in a horse-grin. He had dusty black hair that hung in a lank flop over his big square forehead, and his feet were enormous; they curved as he put them down like a duck's flippers, which, I suppose, was why he could move so quietly. Even his car was quiet; it was a huge old German thing, we used to call it his Strudel, gunmetal grey, and he kept it polished and serviced to the last degree. He loved that car. The way it whispered in and out of the school yard, it was a wonder he hadn't run anyone down yet, and everyone thought he would sooner or later, as he was very short-sighted and wouldn't wear glasses. If someone kicked up a disturbance at the back of the classroom he'd first screw up his eyes and stick his head out, so that he looked like a snake, weaving his head about to try and focus on the guy who was making the row; then he'd start slowly down the aisle, thrusting his face between each line of desks; I can tell you it was quite an unnerving performance.

He seemed ageless; I suppose he might have been in his sixties but you couldn't be sure. He used to go to Germany every holidays and he had this dog Heinkel, a Dachshund. Heinkel looked older than his master, he was wheezy and rheumaticky, blind in one eye and had a wooden leg; I'm not kidding, he'd had to have a front foot amputated for some reason, and had this little sort of stilt strapped on so that he could hobble slowly about, very dot and carry. He didn't bother much, though; sat in the car most of the time, dozing and waiting for the day's lessons to finish.

None of our lot cared greatly for Latin, we didn't see the point of it, so we didn't have much in common with old Fletcher. We thought he was a funny old coot, a total square – he used words like 'topping' and 'ripping' which he must have picked out of the *Boys' Own Paper* in the nineteentens. He was dead keen on his subject and would have taught it quite well if anyone had been interested; the only time you saw a wintry smile light up his yellow face was when he was pointing out the beauties of some construction in Livy or Horace. Personally I don't mind, if you've got to do a thing you might as well do it decently, but a lot of the guys thought he was a dead bore. That was as far as it went until Pridd arrived, and till Fletcher became our form master.

Pridd's father was the new manager of the new supermarket; the family had just come to live in the town. Pridd was a big lumping boy, pobby, with a small head perched on no neck, and small knowing Chinese eyes. He liked maths, but every other subject bored him; he used to sit at the back of the room reading Hotcha inside his exercise book or filing down a bit of brass curtain-rod to shoot peas through. He detested Latin; couldn't see the point of it.

'I'm going to help my dad in the shop as soon as I get out of here,' he said, 'so what the hell's the use of a lot of crummy Caesar and Virgil? Latin's a dead language, who cares about its flipping principal parts? Principal parts! I'll bet old Fletcher hasn't even –' and he added something obscene; Pridd was very foul-mouthed and thought himself highly witty, but personally I considered him an utter thick; he used to barge straight into girls on purpose with his ten stone of misdirected energy, specially if they were trying to carry home a bowl of custard or jelly they'd made in Dom. Sci. His favourite idea of a joke was flicking glue on to girls' hair or pouring a bottleful of ink into somebody's desk when they weren't looking.

It was Pridd who christened Fletcher the Dead Language Master. 'Look out, here's the D.L.M.' he'd call in a piercing whisper, just loud enough to be heard, as Fletcher creaked in. Somehow the name stuck; it seemed gloomily appropriate to the poor old boy.

When Fletcher became our form master we suddenly realized that, instead of seeing him three times a week in Latin periods, we were stuck with him nearly all the time. He used to drift round like a moth between periods to see what we were up to, and there was nearly always trouble.

'Nyaaah,' he always began his sentences. 'Nyaaah, Pridd, what are you doing up on that windowsill?' He had a nasal, croaking voice like some rusty old bird.

'Nothing, sir,' Pridd would answer innocently, dropping the paper waterbomb he'd just constructed on to some girl's head and sliding back into the room all in one movement.

'Nyaaah I don't really think that's so, Pridd, I'm afraid that means another visit to the headmaster.'

Pridd scowled. We don't have beating at our school, the main punishment is Saturday detention, and after Fletcher had been with us for three weeks Pridd had piled up enough Saturdays to last him right through the term. This riled him, because on Saturdays he always put on a white overall and helped his dad in the shop, earning three or four quid a time.

'I'll get my own back on the old scouse, you wait and see if I don't,' he muttered.

He needn't have bothered. His mere presence in the class was revenge enough. From the day of his arrival our form began to go to pieces. Sometimes only the four guys in the front row were making any pretence of following the lesson; everyone else would be watching Pridd and snickering at his crazy antics.

'Fat woman going upstairs,' he'd say, puffing out each cheek alternately, squinting at us out of his mud-coloured slit eyes. He'd buy plastic balloons and blow them up into rude shapes, or pass round pictures, or tell stories, of which he had an endless supply; most of them were just stupid but a few were funny. If he couldn't think of anything else to do he'd pretend to accidentally knock all the books off his desk, or let fall the lid with an almighty crash, anything to create a distraction.

Most of the masters tolerated him to some degree, slapping him down when he really got them riled, but Fletcher frankly loathed him; the loathing was mutual, you could feel it between them, cold as liquid air. He really made Fletcher's life hell. The Latin lessons soon deteriorated into utter chaos; no one even tried to learn. You could hear the whistling and stamping and talk and laughter all the way along the passage. Fletcher began to look more and more wizened and yellow: scooped out and sunk in like some old vegetable marrow that's thrown out on the compost heap because it's past eating.

Funnily enough I forget what act of Pridd's it was that started the final build-up to crisis; maybe it was tying a black thread round Fletcher's inkwell and twitching it off his desk when he was translating; or it might have been the time when Pridd sawed half through the blackboard pegs so that the board crashed down on Fletcher's toe as soon as he started writing. Whatever the deed, it made Fletcher so mad that Saturday detention wasn't enough; he also cancelled Pridd's permission to see the Fenner-Giugliani fight, and sent back the money to Pridd's father, and gave the ticket to another boy.

Pridd was absolutely savage with rage and disappointment; he'd been dead set on going to that fight. The school had had early privilege tickets and it was now too late to get another for love or money; nobody liked Pridd enough to give up a ticket, though he went round offering huge sums.

He began to plot revenge.

It was a tradition that Fletcher always took his form for a picnic to Butt Lake on the last Monday of the summer term, and at first Pridd had it planned that he'd somehow contrive to trip Fletcher and push him into the lake.

'I bet the old twat can't swim,' he said. 'Wouldn't it be a laugh to see him flapping about in the water, silly old goat? "Nyaaah, save me, save me, oh, won't somebody please save me?"'

In the end, however, fate gave Pridd a different opportunity.

We were fooling about in the school yard early on Monday morning when we noticed a gaggle of boys round Fletcher's car, all staring in.

'Perhaps the old fool's left his wallet in the car,' Pridd said hopefully. 'Let's go and see.'

It wasn't a wallet, though. It was the dog, Heinkel, stretched out limp and dead on the seat; he must have died of heart failure or old age almost as soon as his master had gone off and left him; not before it was time either, poor thing. Whenever my father saw him he used to say, 'That dog ought to be put to sleep.'

Pridd joined the group and stood staring at Heinkel with his hands in his pockets. Then he began to snigger.

'We can do something with this,' he said. 'This is luscious!' He tried the door handle.

Usually Fletcher locked his car doors but today he hadn't. Pridd leaned in and picked up the dog.

'Keep round me, you lot,' he said, 'we don't want anyone to see us. Oh, won't the old D.L.M. be surprised!'

'Wotcher going to do, Priddy?' someone said.

'Wait and see,' he said. I think he wasn't sure yet himself, as a matter of fact.

Suddenly I felt fed-up with the whole business. I waited by the door as they went nudging and giggling up the stairs to our classroom. I was still hanging about, reading the notices in the hall, which I'd read hundreds of times before, when the school secretary came out. Her name's Miss Figgins, we call her Fig, of course; she's not a bad old thing, grey-haired and dumpy and motherly.

She looked in the car window and said, 'Where's Heinkel? I promised to have him while Mr Fletcher's in hospital.'

'Hospital?' I said. ''Is he going to hospital?'

'Oh dear,' she said. 'Slipped out. Shouldn't have mentioned it – he doesn't want it talked about. Don't pass it on, Gant, there's a good boy. I know you can be sensible if you choose.'

'Okay,' I said. 'But you needn't bother about Heinkel, anyway. He's just died – the boys went to tell Mr Fletcher.'

'Oh dear,' she said, 'poor little thing. Mr Fletcher will be upset. Not but what it was time, I must say. Well I suppose I needn't trouble, then.'

When I got up to the classroom Fletcher had already arrived. He looked at me tiredly as I slid into my desk but didn't say anything. There was no sign of Heinkel, but the atmosphere in the room was electric; I looked about cautiously, wondering what Pridd had done with him. Then I noticed that everyone's attention was focused on the cupboard where Fletcher kept the books like Cicero and Ovid and Horace that weren't used every day; whenever Fletcher moved that way the tension in the class shot up a couple of degrees.

Fletcher wasn't getting out any books yet, though; he was returning homework, making sharp remarks as he passed each exercise book back to its owner.

When he'd returned the last one he cleared his throat and addressed the whole form.

'Nyaaah! Attention, please. Attention!'

Pridd muttered something to his neighbour and a line of giggles shot along the back row like fire through dry grass. Someone spluttered, someone else coughed, and in a moment half the class were rocking about in hysterics, paying no attention to what Fletcher was trying to say.

I noticed Fletcher's hands were trembling. He looked about him two or three times, hurriedly, as if he hardly knew what he wanted, then snatched up the poker from the stove and banged on his table twice.

'Attention! I *will* have attention when I speak!'

A sort of silence fell. Only at the back Pridd was heard to mutter, 'Dopey old nana,' and someone let out a suppressed titter.

'Pridd!' Fletcher shouted. His chest heaved. He clutched the poker and started to step forward. We all waited breathlessly, wondering if Pridd had really gone too far this time and if Fletcher was going to bash him. But he didn't. He wiped his forehead with the back of his other hand and said, 'I'm not going to give you a lesson today. I'm not going to teach you any more. I'm leaving.'

'Hooray,' somebody muttered, just audibly.

'I'm leaving,' Fletcher said, raising his voice. 'And if you want to know why, it's because of you. It's because you've made my life an utter misery these last few terms with your stupid, senseless insubordination and your idiocy and your *malevolence*. You used to be a decent enough lot of boys. I don't know what's come over you. I really don't. All I can say is, I'm sorry for the next man who tries to teach you Latin. You've finished me, and I hope you're proud of yourselves.'

He stared at us trembling, and we stared back at him. There were beads of sweat on his yellow forehead. He noticed he was still holding the poker and threw it down.

'I shan't be taking you on the usual picnic,' he said. 'Frankly, I've no wish to. Mr Whitney will take you instead. Gant, you're head boy; here's ten pounds, you can buy some food with it.'

'Oh, gosh, thank you, sir,' I said. I didn't want to take it but he pushed it at me and went on speaking.

'I only hope that some day you'll come to understand the amount of suffering you caused. Maybe then you'll learn to behave like civilized human beings. That's all.'

He turned and walked out of the door. Thunderstruck, we gaped after him. Then Pridd exclaimed,

'Christ, we've got to get the dog back into the car somehow!'

'Why?' someone said.

'Why, you nut? We don't want the dog in the cupboard for the next term, do we? Come on, pretend to take the old goat's Latin books down.'

Fletcher was just getting into his car when half the class hurtled into the yard. He didn't seem worried about Heinkel – evidently assumed Miss Figgins had taken him. He gave us a short unsmiling look.

'What is it?'

'We just came down to say good-bye, sir, and thanks for the money,' Pridd said unctuously. 'You forgot your books, sir. Shall we put them in the boot?

'You needn't have bothered – I shan't want them again.' But Fletcher pressed the button that opened the luggage compartment. The flap swung back and down. Two or three boys clustered by the driving window and two or three more stood round Pridd as he took Heinkel from under his blazer. He sat his fat bottom on the lid and leaned far in, to stow the dog's body right at the back of the compartment. He was grinning again, his Chinese eyes were like slits, and it was plain that he was relishing the thought of Fletcher's actions when he opened up to get out the books.

Fletcher started the engine and glanced into his rear-view mirror.

I'm not sure how it happened; evidently Fletcher couldn't see Pridd's head in the mirror, for he pressed the button to shut the boot. The flap swung up, Pridd hastily and instinctively pulled his legs in, and, hey presto! the boot was shut and he was inside it. Fletcher released the handbrake and the car shot silently forward, across the yard and out of the gate.

Somebody shouted, somebody waved frantically. But Fletcher took no notice – I suppose he thought we were just waving a ribald good-bye. Or did he *know* he had Pridd with him?

We shall never learn the answer to that, because Fletcher wasn't seen again. He didn't go to hospital. His car was found five days later, on a lonely stretch of coast, with Fletcher's clothes in a neat, folded pile on the driver's seat. Otherwise the car was empty, except for the contents of the boot.

Some other books you might enjoy

THE FIRST OF MIDNIGHT
Marjorie Darke

Eighteenth-century Bristol, where the slave trade continues to flourish in defiance of the law, and from the shores of Africa, bearing a sense of his own humanity which triumphs over the evil scheming slave masters, Midnight battles for his freedom.

LET THE CIRCLE BE UNBROKEN
Mildred D. Taylor

The story of the Logan family's attempt to lead a decent life in racist Mississippi in the 1930s. A long, sophisticated book, but one which offers great rewards.

MARTINI-ON-THE-ROCKS
Susan Gregory

Eight short stories about teenage life in a multi-racial urban setting. From battles with teachers to a young Hindu wedding to the problems of being with the in-crowd; an extremely absorbing and contemporary collection.

THE DISAPPEARANCE
Rosa Guy

A powerful story about a young boy on probation who tries to make a success out of living with his new wealthy foster family.

EDITH JACKSON
Rosa Guy

The story of a young black orphan, struggling against poverty and prejudice to keep together the remains of her family. (Sequel to *The Friends.*)

GANESH
Malcolm J. Bosse

Jeffrey has lived in India and America, but where does he belong? The fascinating story of a young boy growing up and finding his way in two different places.

IF IT WEREN'T FOR SEBASTIAN

Jean Ure

Maggie's decision to break the family tradition of studying science at university in favour of a course in shorthand and typing causes a major row. But the rift with her parents is nothing to the difficulties she meets when unpredictable Sebastian enters her life.

BROTHER IN THE LAND

Robert Swindells

Which is worse? To perish in a nuclear attack? Or to survive? Danny has no choice. He and his young brother Ben have come through the holocaust alive, only to discover that the world has gone sour in more ways than one. And when the authorities finally arrive, help is the last thing they bring.

AN OPEN MIND

Susan Sallis

David had had enough of people being nice to him just because his parents were divorced. He'd got used to living with Mum and only seeing Dad on Saturdays. But then it dawned on him that his father might remarry and he was determined to do all he could to prevent this. Then Bruce, a spastic boy, appears on the scene and his life begins to look rather more complicated.

FUTURETRACK 5
Robert Westall

Henry Kitson lives in the twenty-first century, where success is determined by being good – not too good – and by a willingness to conform. Those who don't make it are consigned through the Wire, lobotomized or, in Kitson's case, allocated to Tech – a small body of people who maintain the computers. It's not much of a life. But meeting bike champion Keri is a turning point for Kitson and the two form an uneasy friendship to find out what makes the system tick.

THE HAUNTING OF CHAS McGILL AND OTHER STORIES
Robert Westall

Eight supernatural tales to send shivers down your spine! Some are weird and mysterious, where Chas McGill comes face to face with a soldier from the past. Others are more sinister, and some are disturbingly *possible* – all very different but with one thing in common: the ability to make your skin crawl!

THE GHOST ON THE HILL
John Gordon

Ralph didn't realize what effect he and his mother would have on the quiet East Anglian village of her childhood, or that they would act as the catalyst that eases the slumbering tensions and finally releases the ghost on the hill.

ROLL OF THUNDER, HEAR MY CRY
Mildred D. Taylor

The Mississippi of the 1930s was a hard place for a black child to grow up in, but still Cassie didn't understand why farming his own land meant so much to her father. During that year though, when the night riders were carrying hatred and destruction among her people, she learned about the great differences that divided them, and when it was worth fighting for a principle even if it brought terrible hardships.

EMPTY WORLD
John Christopher

Neil is alone after the death of his family in an accident. So when a virulent plague sweeps across the world, dealing death to all it touches, Neil has a double battle for survival: not just for the physical necessities of life, but with the subtle pressures of fear and loneliness.

HOSTAGES TO FORTUNE
Joan Lingard

The fifth book in the series of novels about modern Belfast which highlight the problems of the troubles there, in the story of Protestant Sadie and Catholic Kevin. Even an 'escape' to England fails to solve their difficulties.